THE
OPHIUCHI
HOTLINE

THE OPHIUCHI HOTLINE

by

JOHN VARLEY

QUANTUM SCIENCE FICTION

The Dial Press / James Wade

New York

Published by
The Dial Press/JAMES WADE
1 Dag Hammarskjold Plaza
New York, New York 10017

A Quantum Science Fiction Novel

AUTHOR'S NOTE

To answer your first question . . . it's
pronounced *off-e-YOO-ki,* from Ophiu-
chus, the serpent-holder or doctor, a con-
stellation that just missed fame by being
a few degrees away from the zodiac.

To My Mother

THE
OPHIUCHI
HOTLINE

1

Daily Legal Bulletin, published by the Intersystem Office of Criminal Control Research. Aquarius 14, 568 O.E.

Case of *Lilo-Alexandr-Calypso* vs. *The People of Luna.*

(Legal Summary—For immediate release)

The State charges that Lilo-Alexandr-Calypso, during the period of time 1/3/556 to 12/18/567, did willfully and knowingly conduct experiments upon human genetic material with the intent of artificially inducing mutations in said material. The State further alleges that defendant did produce human blastocysts and embryos reflecting potential structures atypical of the permitted spectrum of Humanity, in violation of the Unified Code of the Eight Worlds Confederation, Article Three (Crimes Against Humanity) Section Seven (Genetic Crimes). The State asks the penalty of permanent death.

(Class I read-rating)

The file was started on Lilo when CCR computers noticed she had been dealing with Ophiuchi Hotline data tagged by analysis as probably related to human DNA. Crimcon agents obtained a warrant to investigate her subscription records and use-charts with Star-Line, Inc., principal broker for processed Hotline data. The grand jury data bank authorized further surveillance both by computer model projection and human operatives. A warrant was granted 11/10/567 pertaining to her home, places of work, and personal property, including her body.

(Class II read-rating)

Crimcon G-cops will tell you, "Lilo was tough. Crafty. Thought we'd struck ice when we broke down the door at Biosystems Research. No joy. We were punching holos. Tapes, notes, all wiped clean when we touched them. Code crackers at CCR chewed and spit: Zip. Phi. Nothing. Rerun that for her house; we were chewing vac. But she had money. Ten years back, gene patents on Bananameat Trees ©. Made a bundle. Checked her travel records. Access! Five trips to Janus. Hopped a 3gee tank-tripper and busted down the door, lasers ready. Nobody home, but one of her booby traps fritzed. Came home with two grams of mutated meat. Her ass was in the recycler now. X rays were pure no-go, but we opened her anyway and what do you think we found? A billion and one bits of data wrapped around her spinal cord! Eat death, gene trasher! The Hole waits!" Crimcon G-cops will tell you, crime does not pay.

(Illiterate read-rating)

Photocomics and holotapes attached.

Prisons are not what they used to be. I did a little reading on the subject when it occurred to me that my work might cause me to see the inside of one. Some of the prisons of Old Earth were pretty barbaric.

My cell was nothing like that. It was better than the average run of workers' warren apartments. There were three rooms, well furnished. I had a vidphone, if I didn't mind the warden listening in. I didn't use it.

What the cell had in common with old prisons was the most basic thing of all: The door would not open to my command. Beyond that door were dozens of others, all closed to me. There was a camera in each room that followed my movements.

I was in the Terminal Institute for Enemies of Humanity, three kilometers beneath Ptolemaeus, on the Nearside. I had been there just over a year. Six months of that was consumed in the gathering of evi-

dence against me. The trial was held in a few milliseconds of computer time one morning while I was still asleep. I was told of the results—no surprises—and scheduled for execution the following morning. Then my lawyer got a six-month stay.

I had no illusions. The stay had been granted, most likely, because my execution was to come before the end of the semester. The Institute was running short on Enemies of Humanity, and there were theses to be completed. Twice a day one of the walls of my cell changed color and began to glow. On the other side of the wall a professor was lecturing a psych class. If I put my face up close I could see ranks of students sitting in the lecture hall. But I quickly tired of looking.

About once a week I was visited by teams of graduate students. They would sit on my sofa and fidget, a series of girls and boys with earnest faces, brows furrowed in concentration. They would interview me for an hour, plainly not knowing what to think of me. At first, I thought up bizarre answers to their questions, but I tired of that, too. Sometimes I just sat there for the whole hour.

My life crawled toward its termination.

Lilo-Alexandr-Calypso sat in her cell and waited for morning. She still had not decided if she could bear to mount those lonely stairs. A year ago, when it hadn't been so goddam *imminent*, it had been easy to be brave. Now she could see that her bravado had come from the deep inner conviction that no one would actually kill her. But she had had plenty of time to think.

Gas chamber, gallows. Electric chair, stake, firing squad. Hang by the neck till you're dead, dead, dead, and may God recycle your soul.

Imaginative as those devices had been, they had an extremely simple purpose. They were intended to stop a human heart from beating. Later, the criterion for determining death was brain activity.

That was no longer enough. The sad fact was that it was no longer possible to kill someone and be absolutely sure the person would not show up again. Lilo's execution in the morning was therefore largely symbolic, from the viewpoint of society.

From Lilo's viewpoint, it was much more than that. She was toying with an idea she had entertained only once before in her life: six months earlier, just before her stay of execution. She was thinking of committing suicide.

"And why not?" she asked herself, a little startled when she realized she had said it aloud.

Why not, indeed? A few years earlier she could have given a thousand reasons why not. She had been in her early fifties, still young, with her life stretching endlessly in front of her. But now she was fifty-seven, and suddenly ancient. Soon she would be dead. *Dead*. You can't get any more ancient than that.

Physically, Lilo was twenty-five. It was a popular age to be, and though Lilo did not like to ape popular trends, she had never felt good looking any older than that. Her body was largely her own, with a few surgical modifications. Her hair was light brown, her eyes were set far apart to accommodate a wide, slightly flat nose. She was tall and slim, and it suited her.

Her one vanity was her legs. She had added ten centimeters to her leg bones, making her two point two meters tall, slightly above average height. She wore fine brown hair, like chinchilla, from midway down her calves to the tops of her feet.

She got up and restlessly paced the room. What amazed her was that, once she had accepted that she was going to die, suicide began to seem like an attractive possibility. The State of Luna did not care if she killed herself; she was going to The Hole in the morning, dead or alive. No attempt had been made to clear her cell of harmful tools.

The tool she was examining now was a knife. It was a lovely thing. Stainless steel, mirror-bright—it had a symmetry of line she found appealing. Cross-hatched grooves wound around the handle, giving a sure grip on cool metal. She drew it across her throat, keeping her mind blank. Her hand shook as she brought her fingers up to her neck. No blood.

She thought about the two alternatives facing her.

Tomorrow would be an emotional moment. She was sure nothing could possibly match the anticipation of mounting the stairs over The Hole. She had a horror of breaking down completely, of having to be restrained and thrown over the brink rather than stepping off by her own volition.

On the other hand, she felt reasonably calm now. All hope was gone. Could she meet her death now, by her own hand, in private? Was it better to go that way?

It seemed to her that it was. She told herself that three times in succession and reached for the knife. She drew it over her wrist. Shuddered, and felt her heart pound. She opened her eyes and looked down and there wasn't even a red line. She was *sure* she had been bearing down. Something trickled over her cheek. Alarmed, she brushed it away.

She sat in her chair beside the small table and gritted her teeth. She leaned over the table and rested her forearm on the surface. She put the knife blade to the soft part, looked at it, looked away, dragged her eyes back and felt them drying out as she refused to blink.

There was a red trickle of blood.

"Put the knife down, Lilo."

She jumped, and dithered with the bloody knife in her hand, blushing furiously. Trying to hide it in the cushions of the chair, she turned to see who had entered the room behind her.

"Is it serious?" he asked, walking toward her.

She looked at it. Just a small cut, the bleeding almost stopped already. He tossed her a cloth, which she used to dab at the blood on her hands. Taking a seat a few meters from her, he waited until she had cleaned herself.

"There's someone I'd like you to meet," he said, and gestured toward the cell door. It opened, and her blue-uniformed male guard entered, followed by a nude woman. She was tall, staggered slightly as she walked, and looked drugged. Her brown hair was plastered over her shoulders in ropes and nets; she dripped a thick, syrupy liquid from her hands and nose and chin. Her eyes met Lilo's for a moment, without comprehension, then she bumped into a chair and fell over. The guard helped her to her feet and half-carried her to the bathroom. A woman, also dressed in blue, entered the cell, and closed the door. She followed the other two. There was the sound of water running.

Lilo managed to look away. The woman's face had been terribly familiar. It was her own face.

Gold. Everything was yellow-gold. I opened my eyes underwater and knew that I was not breathing. For some reason, it didn't bother me. I sat up and felt thick liquid roll sluggishly from my body.

I choked, tried to cough, and a great amount of fluid came out of my throat. For a moment I couldn't cope with it. I was drowning. But someone was slapping me on the back and then I was gasping.

Being born is not easy.

Her eyes wouldn't focus. Someone was holding something out to her and all she could see was the end of an arm holding the object. It was a cup. She recoiled, but it followed her. She took it, and drank deeply.

She was sitting in a glass tank, wheat-colored liquid up to her waist. Wires trailed from her body, which still twitched from time to time under the influence of the muscle-tone program, winding down now after three months of enforced exercise.

Disorientation. She couldn't string two thoughts together. The tank should have meant something to her, but it didn't.

"Come on, let's get up," someone said. It was a woman in blue, who reached over and helped the naked woman out of the tank, to stand dripping, swaying, leaning on a strong shoulder with a hand holding her firmly around the waist. She wanted to go back to sleep.

"Is she ready?"

"I think so." There was a second person, a man, also dressed in blue. "This won't take long."

She knew they were talking about her. She tried to shake the hand off, but she was too weak. It annoyed her, hearing them talk. She wanted them to stop.

"Leave me alone," she said.

"What did she say?"

They were leading her down the hall, helping her step up through the doorways, dogging them behind her. She couldn't hold her head up; it kept falling to the side. All she could see was her bare feet, her legs, and wetness dripping from her body onto the carpet. It struck her as funny; she laughed, nearly slipping from the woman's arms.

"What's the matter with her?"

She didn't hear the reply, she was laughing so hard. There was another door. They stopped in front of it and she became aware of someone slapping her face. She tried to make him stop but he wouldn't and she started to cry. Then a harder slap that rocked her back against the far wall. She recoiled, realized that she was standing on her own and looking into the man's face.

"Are you awake now?" He peered into her eyes.

"Yes . . . I . . ." She coughed, and tried to look around her, but he kept pulling her head back until she thought she would cry again. "I . . . that is . . ."

"She's all right. Take her in."

The man again. "You follow me, you hear? Just follow me."

She nodded. He seemed to think it was very important and she was willing to do anything if he'd let go of her head. But she was all wet, her hair was all over the place, and she felt clammy. She tried to tell him that, but he had already gone into the room. She felt a shove on her shoulder, and staggered over the lip of the door.

She got a glimpse of the people sitting in the room. There was a man in a funny coat who tickled her memory. She knew him, but couldn't remember the name. And there was a woman in a chair. She knew that one. It was herself.

I never thought I'd meet ex-President Tweed face to face. You can't avoid him on the cube; he's there all the time on one program or another, pushing his crazy schemes. He'd been a fixture on the telepolitical scene since the time I was born.

Tweed dressed like a political cartoon from the turn of the twentieth century. He had allowed himself to develop a paunch, always wore striped pants and a claw-hammer coat, top hat, and spats. He smoked a cigar, and when elected, called the Presidential Warren "Tammany Hall." And he won elections. Though I never followed it closely, I knew he had been elected to three consecutive terms.

He paved the way for the current Lunar clown show we call government. Recognition is all, and the public had shown a perhaps understandable confusion between political rhetoric and the fantasies that surround it on the cube. So now we have our Tweeds, our Churchills, and our Kennedys. There is a Hitler, a Bonforte, a Lewiston, and a Trajan. Put them all in the same place and you might as well call it a circus.

Luckily, elected officials don't do that much any more; the posts are largely ceremonial or supervisory over the computers who do the actual governing. I've never been sure if that's such a good thing, but Tweed made me thankful for it. Not that my opinions mattered at the moment.

I put political ruminations aside and prepared to listen to whatever pitch he was about to make. It had to be better than what I was facing.

"Don't get any ideas," he said, in that famous bass rumble. "I'm protected against anything you might try to do."

Lilo realized he was talking about attempts on his life. Nothing could have been further from her mind. He was here, where he had no legal right to be, he had just shown her what had to be an illegal clone; she could think of no reason he would have done these things unless he had something to offer her, and she was very interested in hearing it.

"You will find in our future dealings that I am invariably protected."

"I don't see how that information can be of any use to me unless I'm going to be dealing with you in the future. As you know, my future is limited at this moment." She tried to keep it light, to keep the hope out of her voice, but it was impossible. The guilty weight of the knife pressing against her thigh and the trickle of blood on her arm testified to how much bargaining leverage she could bring to the conversation.

"Yes, you will be dealing with me in the future. You—" he gestured toward the bathroom "—or that . . . other woman. The choice will be yours."

She could hear voices from the bathroom; the sound of water running and an angry voice that she barely recognized as her own. Her twin was waking up, and she dreaded it.

"What's the choice?"

"First, understand your position. I—"

"I *know* my position, damn it. Get on with it."

"Be patient. I want you to know a few things first." He paused, then took out a cigar and went through the process of trimming and lighting it. He was an extraordinarily ugly person, Lilo thought, with the ugliness that only caricature can achieve. As repulsive as a twisted, stunted ghost from the past on Old Earth.

"The clone was grown illegally, obviously," Tweed resumed. "But you are no longer a useful witness to anything. You will never have a chance to tell anyone what you have seen here today, should you refuse me. Your only contact from now on will be with Vaffa and Hygeia, the two guards you just saw. Both are loyal to me."

"What else can you tell me that I'm so goddamn anxious to know? You didn't do all this to taunt me. You're a . . . never mind. I don't like you much. Never did."

"And I don't like you. But I can use you. I want you to work for me."

"Fine. When do we get started? As you pointed out, we'd better hurry, because I don't have that long to live." But the sarcasm fell flat, even in her own ears, because her throat hurt so badly when she said it. He laughed, politely, and she was so receptive to him that she nearly laughed herself. She stifled it when it threatened to turn into a sob.

"There is that little problem," he agreed. "I'm offering you a chance to bow out of your execution. I'm offering you a stand-in."

He looked at the bathroom door—there were sounds of a struggle—and back to her. He raised his eyebrows.

The cold water made me gasp and choke, but some of the grogginess washed away. For the first time in that dizzy few minutes I could think straight. More than anything in the world I wanted to sleep, but things were happening too fast, and seemed to be out of my control.

Tweed! That was his name. What was he doing out there in the other room, talking to someone who looked exactly like me, in my own cell? And the tank. Had I died? I woke up in a vat, which had to mean that I had died. But I was under a death sentence; I shouldn't be waking up ever again.

I pushed my face under the cold stream. Stay awake, stay awake. Something important is happening and you're being left out. I sputtered and gasped, slapping my face and legs and shoulders. I thought I saw it now, and it was dirty, rotten; so bad I couldn't believe it. But I had to.

I stumbled and fell against the wall of the shower. The woman guard took my arm and pulled me to my feet. My eyes wouldn't focus. I struck out at her, but she was big and alert and the blow didn't land. Then I was screaming, lashing out.

She came running out of the bathroom, pursued by the man and woman. The man grabbed her, but she was slippery and powerful with hysterical strength. She got away, kicking at him with her bare heels as they grappled on the floor, then scrambling on her hands toward the woman in the chair. She screamed again.

Banging hard into a table as she tried to get to her feet, she toppled and fell loosely in front of the couch where Tweed sat. The man reached her and started to haul her away, but Tweed held up his hand.

"Let her alone," he said. "I think this is her room, after all." He looked at Lilo, sitting in frozen fascination. She couldn't seem to drag her eyes away from the woman on the floor. "That is, unless you want it."

Lilo tore her eyes from the clone. She opened her mouth to speak, but the words caught in her throat. The clone was looking at her again. The fear on her face was almost too much for Lilo to bear. To accept Tweed's offer would be to condemn this woman to death. She didn't want to think about that.

But the clone was looking at Tweed now, and Lilo could almost hear her mind working. She gripped the edge of the couch and got to her knees.

"I don't know what you were talking about," she said, "but I think you should tell me. I know I'm not up to date; I just woke up. Things have been happening, I can see that. I got the stay of execution, right? She's who I think I am, but six months later, right?"

"That's right," Tweed said, and smiled at her.

Lilo felt a chill pass through her, and realized she was afraid of the clone. She did not want Tweed smiling at her. There was no reason to think Tweed had a preference; the clone might do as well for his purposes as the original. Nothing said she had to be the one saved just because she was older.

"Whatever the deal is," the clone was saying, "I can be just as good at—"

"I'll take the job," Lilo said, as loudly as she could. Tweed looked at her.

"Are you sure?"

The clone was looking dully from one to the other.

"Yes." She swallowed, hard. "Yes. Kill her. Let me live."

I felt as though I had suddenly disappeared.

Tweed and the other woman were talking right through me, right over my head as I knelt there on the floor. I couldn't believe it. I couldn't follow what they were saying; there was a roaring in my ears and I was dizzy again. I think I hit my head when I fell.

I had to make them notice me. My life depended on it. I got up, shakily, and stood between them, but still they took no notice. It was a nightmare. I screamed at them, but it was no use. They were getting up and leaving the room, the female guard imposing herself between me and the door. Her face was hard.

I lunged, struggled with the woman, but she held me tightly. They were gone.

I went in and out of consciousness, sitting in my chair, alone. Hygeia, the guard, had given me a double-dose of painkiller a few hours ago and I had been sitting there, waiting for it to take effect. My dreams were black and formless, except for the familiar forest I had always run through in my dreams: a forest beneath a blue sun.

When I could no longer feel much in my hands and feet I got up. Everything went black, and I found myself in the bathroom without remembering how I got there. I turned on the shower.

I stared down at my wrist for a moment. There was a deep cut, the blood was pumping sluggishly through my fingers and splattering on my bare legs and feet. How had that happened? My head was thick as soup, but I thought I remembered . . . I had put the knife down . . . hadn't I? That woman—what was her name?—had been in my room. Had she tried to kill me, and make it look like suicide?

Warm water was flowing over me. Pink rivers wound between my

toes. I staggered, and hit my head on the wall. I knew it was too late.
I was dying. It was so cold. I would be dead soon.
The spray was in my face. My feet were freezing. I looked at my
wrist again and saw that the blood had stopped flowing. I got up,
slipped and fell on my face in a puddle of red.
*   In the main room again. Unable to stand up. I was looking for*
something. What? There was another blank in my mind. The knife. I
was going to finish the job the woman had started. Or was it me? I
left the knife . . . where? In my hand. Hacking, my fingers losing
their grip. The knife was gone again. I crawled.
*   I saw booted feet in front of me, tried to stand up.*
*   "You passed out again." It was Hygeia.*
*   "There's no pain," I told her. "Don't be afraid."*

Circum-Luna 6 was a metal shell, five hundred meters in radius.
The gravity on the outer surface was five meters per second squared,
but a visitor descending through one of the three entrances would experience a perceptible rise in weight for each step downward. CL-6
had few visitors.

All orbital power stations were "holes," but only CL-6 was known
as The Hole. Five or six times a year it was shut down for a few
hours so people could descend into what had recently been a hell of
radioactivity.

It was shut down now. At the one-gee level a terrace hung beneath
the gargantuan field generators which held the black hole suspended
in the center of the station. Arcing away from the terrace was a span
of unsupported metal with rails on each side and low steps built into
it. The thirteen steps were traditional, just a few centimeters high.
The stretcher rolled over them easily, the body strapped to it bounc-
ing as the black-clad man and woman pushed it out to the end of the
arc.

One of the executioners removed the drape from Lilo's body while
the other attached the stretcher to an ejection mechanism. Finished,
they stood for a moment under the eye of the camera, then walked
down the span and climbed to the surface.

The stretcher tilted, hung suspended for an instant, and then fell.
It picked up speed asymptotically, and the interior of CL-6 blazed in
hard light. Far down the slope of the hole, halfway to infinity, a tiny
mass of neutronium that had been Lilo was orbiting at almost the
speed of light, releasing energy as it was stressed to the limits of matter before it finally decayed into oblivion.

2

Living Together: A Child's Introduction to the Law, by
Ariadna-Clel-Joule. Tycho-Under Educational, 552.
Read-rating I.

There are three kinds of lawbreakers. From bad to
worst, they are violators, misdemeanants, and felons.

Violations are crimes like jostling, creating a nui-
sance, verbal abuse, and body odor: crimes of bad be-
havior. If you are accused of a violation, you may de-
fend yourself in court. You may demand a human jury.
If you are found guilty, violations are punished by fine,
either to the offended party or the State.

Misdemeanors are crimes like robbery, burglary, assault, rape, and murder: crimes of property. The more
serious misdemeanors are those where the property involved is a citizen's body. All misdemeanors are
punished by fines of 90% of the criminal's possessions.
In cases of violence to a citizen's body there is a man-
datory death penalty with automatic reprieve. The
criminal's right to life remains in force, so after execution the criminal is revived at a subjective lifeline point
before the first conception of the crime and is required
to undergo preventive rehabilitation.

The worst crimes are felonies. These are crimes like
arson, sabotage, possession of fissionables, vectoring,
blowouting, and tampering with human DNA. Felonies
involve a threat to the whole human race, or a large
part of it, and are known as Crimes Against Humanity.
The punishment for convicted felons is revocation of
the right to life. The State will search out and destroy
every memory recording and tissue sample of the exe-

cuted criminal. The criminal's genotype is published
and declared outlaw, and if detected again will be put
to death, as many times as is necessary.

(Read-rating II, see companion volume: *Crime
Does Not Pay*. Comics and tapes accessible to verbal
request.)

Vaffa took me from my cell. He hustled me through deserted corridors and into an elevator. I had been curious to see how they were going to get me out of there; thinking about doing it on my own had occupied a great deal of my time over the last year. I had made a study of escapes. Most of them involved bribery, help from the outside, or perseverance, in that order. I had nothing to bribe with, and no one on the outside I could appeal to. As for perseverance, the Count of Monte Cristo would have been stymied by the Terminal Institute. It was three kilometers below the surface. Worse, it was fifty kilometers from the nearest tube station. The only way to get out of it was to walk, or ride the unpressurized induction-rail. For that, a suit was helpful. Naturally, keeping track of suits was the major security precaution.

On the way up, I suddenly remembered what Tweed had been doing in the years since his last term of office. He had been appointed Commissioner of Corrections.

The elevator stopped and Vaffa motioned for Lilo to get out. She had gone about ten steps when he grabbed her arm and directed her through a door. The corridor on the other side was dim and narrow. Vaffa didn't seem worried. Obviously Tweed had many people he trusted at the institute. It looked as though it was going to be easy.

She stopped thinking that when Vaffa directed her to a door marked EMERGENCY AIRLOCK. She stepped inside, and noted with more than casual interest that there was no suit in the small chamber. She stared at the red light on the second door. Beyond it was vacuum.

"Wait a minute," she said, abruptly. "What are you doing?"

"There was no way we could get an unauthorized suit into the institute," he said. "Suits are monitored by a section we don't control."

"Yeah, but—"

"The sensor on this airlock has been disconnected. The computer won't know it's in use. Take these, and put them on." He handed her a pair of thick, flexible boots.

"Wait a minute. I can't."

"You must."

"I *can't!* You're trying to kill me, that's it! I should never have listened to you people. Let me *out* of here!" She was on the edge of panic. Like all Lunarians, Lilo had a powerful fear of vacuum. It was the enemy they fought from the day they were born, as fearful as Hell had been to earlier humans. She felt physically ill.

"Put them on," Vaffa said, reasonably. "You need them to protect your feet."

"What's . . . what is it I have to do?"

"If you hurry, you'll be in vacuum for five seconds. A crawler will be near the door, two meters away, at the most."

"What time of day is it out there?"

"The lock is in shadow."

She felt the panic rising again. "No. No, it's impossible." She was going to say more, but he touched her shoulder and held it tightly for a moment.

"If I have to knock you out and carry you, it will be much slower."

She saw that he meant it. He smiled slightly as he saw her realize he was too big for her to fight. So there was only one way out of the lock for her. She put the boots on and faced the door. Vaffa released the latches. The door was still tightly shut, held in place by fourteen thousand kilograms of pressure.

"When?" she asked.

"The crawler must not stop. The guard in the tower must be distracted at the right moment, because we don't trust him. The car will be in range for ten seconds, and it should arrive in one minute." He looked up from his watch, and smiled. "If everything is still going according to plan." For the first time, she thought he had said something he had not been told to say. He stepped out of the lock and closed the inner door.

Suddenly, it was time. She heard a scream that was very familiar, but she had always been in a suit when she heard it before. It was the quick-release valve. Strangely, she didn't feel anything. She belched continually. The sound died away in a few seconds. She yanked the door open, and was running in silence. There was a dark moving shape, a hand reaching out for her, and she was pulled into the crawler. The door shut, and a shriek took form in the air that rushed in to fill the sealed cabin. Lilo was suddenly shivering.

"I made it," she cried hoarsely, and passed out.

* * *

A woman was leaning over her.

"Don't move, please." Lilo's left arm felt numb. She glanced down. It had been severed at the elbow.

"This will only take a moment," the woman said. There was a caduceus tattoo between her breasts: a medico. Lilo propped her head up on her other arm and watched.

"What's this for?" she asked.

"We'll be leaving the crawler at a station about a hundred kilometers from here. This is to get you through customs." She took a forearm from a metal lifetank and attached it to her black bag. The white chunk of meat began to color, and the fingers twitched. She popped Lilo's own arm into the tank.

"I'm Mari," she said, with a slight rising inflection on the end. There was the hint of a smile on her face.

"Lilo," she responded, and they touched palms, Lilo's right to Mari's left since Lilo was not equipped at the moment to do it properly.

"That'll be ready in a minute," she said, gesturing to the arm. She was reaching into a bag on the shelf behind her. There were two deep purple robes in it. She stood up to pull one over her head. "You can put that on when I'm done with you."

"Where am I being taken?"

"To see the Boss." There was a tone in her voice that said Mari respected the Boss a great deal. So she was a Free Earther. Well, it wasn't exactly a disease. Lilo could tolerate them, except when it came to a fanatic like Tweed who wanted to lead the whole race into oblivion.

Mari got to work again, fitting the elbow joint together, attaching tendons, splicing nerves and vessels. In five minutes the skin sealed up and there was nothing but a faint red line to show where the arm had been grafted. She pulled a plug from the socket at the back of Lilo's head and the arm became more than dead weight. It was full of pins and needles, and cold.

"Sorry about the job," Mari said, packing things away. "You'll only need it for an hour or so, so there's no sense, is there? You won't have to use it much."

"That's okay. I'm right-handed." She made a fist. The arm was about five centimeters too short.

"Oh, really? So is my mother."

"Whose is this?"

"It was grown from somebody who is supposed to be in Luna. We put the genotype through customs every so often so the computer has a record of her . . . but I don't think I should be telling you this."

"Suit yourself." Lilo had figured it was something like that.

"You don't look very happy for a woman who's just busted out of an escape-proof jail," Mari said. Her smile had grown by stages; now it was wide and friendly. Lilo felt herself smile back.

"I guess I haven't had time to react. I've lived with a death sentence for so long."

Mari shifted a little closer. "Would you like to cop?"

"No, thanks. I guess I'd like to start with a man, after such a long time."

"Sure." The medico turned her attention to the flat, pitted landscape and angular shadows out the window.

Lilo tried to come to terms with the fact that she now had a chance to survive. It still didn't mean anything to her. She kept thinking of that other woman, the clone, who would die in her place. She began to cry, surrendering herself to the confused emotions that had to get out. It was not until Mari decided she had gone through enough and touched her on the shoulder that Lilo realized how hungry she had been for a friendly face, for the touch of another human being. She calmed down almost at once. Mari started to withdraw her arm, but Lilo stopped her with a touch.

"How long till we get there?"

Mari glanced at the chronometer on her thumbnail. "About two hours. Would you like to cop now? It might be the best thing for you. I know a little of what you're going through."

"Oh, what the hell." So they did. Mari had been right; it did untie some of the knots in her gut. Mari was skilled and considerate, a good player except for a tendency to talk shop. She would kiss something—nose, navel, knee, labia—and want to know who had done the work. Usually the answer was "it just grew that way."

Mari scored most of the points. Lilo was too distracted to pay much attention to what her mouth and fingers were doing. She knew she had been a poor partner, but Mari said it was all right, and seemed to mean it. It was a nice gesture, but didn't seem to merit the second upwelling of tears that it caused in Lilo. When it subsided she knew the medico had brought her out of the emotional pit she had occupied for the past year in a way the intellectual knowledge of her reprieve could not have done.

She was going to live!

The crawler stopped at Herschel, one of the smaller warrens on the outskirts of the Central Highlands. Mari drove into a lock and parked, and they went straight into town to catch the local tube to Panavision. Lilo kept her eyes open for a chance to run, but they were quickly joined by a man and woman. They laughed and joked with Mari, but it was clear they were watchful. The chance would come, she was sure of it. It would be best to wait until she knew a little more of the situation.

She put her hand into the customs machine and felt the sampler scrape along the dry skin of her palm. It clucked to itself, and was satisfied she was someone else. Too bad she wouldn't be able to keep the new hand, she reflected. It would be invaluable. But tissue rejection made that impossible. In less than a week it would die.

Panavision was an artists' town, full of performers and directors. Many of them had been altered into a part; it was an outlandish place. They joined the line for the gravity train to Archimedes. The four of them boarded, the car was sealed, and Lilo's weight dropped away as the car fell down the inclined tunnel for almost four hundred kilometers. Somewhere under the Apennines the tunnel began to slope up again, gradually slowing their speed to a crawl as the car nosed into the elevator which took them back up to inhabited levels. The trip was over by the time Lilo felt settled in her seat.

The Grand Concourse at Archimedes was frightening. She had forgotten there were that many people or that much noise. There was no time to worry about it; she was hustled through the crowds to a private tube station. When she got her wits back, she saw she was alone again with Mari in an eight-seat capsule.

"Where now?"

"I'm not supposed to say," Mari said, with a shrug.

It didn't take Lilo long to figure it out. Most Lunarians know little selenography. They might not get out on the surface more than once or twice in several years, most likely for a trip like that Lilo and Mari were taking: enclosed in a capsule riding an induction rail while landscape whizzed past the windows. But Lilo knew the surface map pretty well. They were going north into the Imbrium flats, and when peaks began to loom up over the horizon she knew it was the Spitzbergen Mountains. So that was where the Boss lived. That kind of information was not exactly a state secret; but it was not advertised, because of the constant danger of assassination.

Tweed's home was on the surface—as it logically would be, Lilo realized, so he could see Earth at all times. Tweed was obsessed by Earth, and by the Invaders. There was one massive geodesic, surrounded by clusters of smaller ones. A spidery telescope with a twenty-meter mirror stood in the shadow of a cupola. It was trained on Earth.

Mari cut away the arm and replaced it with the original, then said Tweed was waiting for Lilo in the main dome. She pointed the way. Lilo took her time, looking into open doorways she passed. There would be just the one tube station, and the suits would be carefully watched. She fully realized this was as much a prison as the institute had been, but the time to start planning was right now.

Water was flowing down the hall. She splashed through it until the hall became a brook running through trees, in an artful mix of holos and real plants. She hadn't detected the transition. The creek bed was lined with polished stones of varicolored crystal and the deeper pools were full of fish. A panther studied her from the shore, joined her as she reached dry land, and stropped himself against her after smelling the fur on her calves. She fussed with him for a while, then sent him away with a cuff on the head.

The trail led to a clearing, and in the clearing was Tweed, sitting in a chair with a nude woman standing beside him. She spotted a man, also nude, in the trees at the edge of the clearing.

Lilo had been trying not to be impressed, but it was useless. She had no idea how much money it took to maintain a pocket disneyland like this, but she knew it was a great deal.

"Sit down, Lilo," Tweed said, and a chair unfolded from the high grass. She did, putting one foot up on the seat. She searched the pockets of the robe, found a brush, and began to comb the burrs from the wet hair on her legs.

"You've already met Vaffa," Tweed said, gesturing to the standing woman. Lilo glanced at her, noted the stance and the attitude of the hands. This woman could kill her in a second, and would. She had *thought* there was something familiar in the eyes.

"How many of them do you keep?" she said. There was a boa constrictor, fully twenty meters long, coiled in the grass at the woman's feet. "That's a hell of a pet."

"You don't like snakes?"

"I wasn't talking about the snake."

Tweed chuckled. "Vaffa is very useful, loyal, smart as can be, and totally ruthless. Aren't you, Vaffa?"

"If you say so, sir." Her eyes never left Lilo.

"In answer to your question, there are many Vaffas. One here, the other who helped you escape a few hours ago. Others in other places." Lilo did not need to ask why Vaffa was so useful. Though the faces and bodies were entirely different in the two she had seen, the feeling was the same. This was a killer. Quite possibly a soldier, though Lilo was not expert in mental diseases.

"Tell me about the Rings," Tweed said, unexpectedly.

"It was brought out at the trial," Lilo stammered. "I thought you knew."

"I knew, but I'm not convinced you were telling the whole truth. Where is the life capsule?"

"I don't know."

"We have ways of making you talk."

"Don't give me that crap." Tweed had a habit of talking that way, like an actor reading his lines in a third-rate thriller. "It's not a question of telling you," she elaborated. "I admitted setting it up. If I knew where it was, it wouldn't be much good to me, would it?"

At that moment, Lilo could see it might do her some harm instead of good. Tweed seemed unhappy, and that was disturbing. Keeping him happy had become very important.

Five years earlier, when her research began taking her into areas where she might expect to have trouble with the law, she had decided to build the capsule. She had contacts among the Ringers, and the money to get the project going. The idea, which had looked good at the time, was that if she got caught and convicted her work could go on without interruption. Now she was not sure her motives had been that selfless. The urge to live is a strong one, as she had just learned.

"They questioned me with drugs," she said. "I have a friend out there. When I left the capsule, she moved it. I can't lead anyone to it. I don't know where it is."

"This accomplice," he said. "Did you have any way of getting in touch with her?"

"Have you ever been out there?"

"No, there's never time." He shrugged expressively. Lilo had seen it before, on the cube. Tweed was adept at the self-effacement routine, playing the part of one who's always busy with the People's work.

"Well, the Rings are *big*. If you haven't been there, you can't know just how big. I might get in touch with her by radio, but we couldn't think of a way she could be protected, too. I mean, anything could be drugged out of me, and she'd have no way of knowing if she was being lured into something. It was hard enough to get her involved in this, anyway. Ringers tend to be solitary. They don't worry much about other people's problems."

"But you have a way of getting in touch with her?"

"If you mean finding her, no. I can leave a message at the Janus switchboard. She calls every twenty years, like clockwork."

He spread his hands. "Not very efficient."

"That was sort of the idea. If it was easy for *me* to stop this project, it would be easy for someone who knew what I knew."

Tweed got up and walked slowly a few paces away, looking at the sky. The snake stirred, and coiled around Vaffa's leg. She bent over to stroke it, never looking away from Lilo.

"What was the name of this accomplice?"

"Parameter. Parameter/Solstice."

3

Song of the Rings, by Clancy-Daniel-Mitre. A collection of early human-symb collaborative poetry. Circa 240–300 O.E. Open read-rating.

Of all the things received over the Ophiuchi Hotline, none is more wonderful than the symb. In the early part of the third century, symbs were seen as the salvation of the human race. Futurists saw the day when each human would be paired with a symb partner and forever free of reliance on airlocks, hydroponic farming, and recycled water. Each human would be a tiny model of lost Earth, free to roam the solar system at will.

It's easy to see what inspired the optimism. The symmetry of the concept is overwhelming. Each human-symb pair is a closed ecology, requiring only sunlight and a small amount of solid matter to function. The vegetable symb gathers sunlight in space, using it to convert human waste and carbon dioxide into food and oxygen. At the same time it protects the fragile human from vacuum and the extremes of heat and cold. The symb's body extends into the lungs and through the alimentary canal. Each side feeds the other.

What we didn't bargain for is the mind of the symb. Since it has no brain, a symb is nothing but a lump of artificial organic matter until it comes in contact with a human. But upon permeating the nervous system of its host it is born as a thinking being. It shares the human brain. The early experimenters learned that, once in, the symb was there to stay. Since that time relatively few have opted to surrender their mental privacy in exchange for utopia in the Rings.

But out of the disappointment we have been given a precious gift. Ring society is not human society. We live in rooms and corridors; they have all of space. We each have the right to be the mother of one child in our lifetimes; they breed like bacteria. We are islands; they are paired minds. It is a relationship that is difficult to imagine.

Somewhere in that magical junction of two dissimilar minds a tension is created. Sparks are struck, sparks of dazzling creativity. All Ringers are poets. Poetry is a normal by-product of living. To those of us without the courage to pair, who wait for the infrequent contacts of Ringers with human society, their songs are beyond price.

Parameter floated over a golden desert that no horizon could contain. She faced the sun, which was a small but very bright disc just to anti-spinward of Saturn. Saturn itself was a dark hole in space, edged by a razored crescent with the sun set in it like a precious stone.

She saw none of this. She perceived the sun as a pressure and a wind, and Saturn as a cold, deep well that pulled.

The sunrise had been delicious. She could still taste the flavors of it flowing through the wafer-thin part of her body that had opened to receive it. She was a sunflower.

Sunflower mode was a lazy, vegetable time. Parameter had Solstice, her symb, disconnect the visual centers of her brain so she could savor the simple pleasures of being a plant. Her arms were spread wide to the light and her feet were planted firmly in the fertile soil that was her symb. It was a good time.

Seen from the outside, Parameter was the center of a hundred-meter filmy parasol, slightly parabolic. She was a spider sitting in the middle of a frozen section of soap bubble, but the section was shot through with veins, like the inner surface of an eyeball. Fluids pumped through the veins, some milky, some deep red, others purplish-brown. From a point near Parameter's navel a thin stalk extended, with a fist-sized nodule at the end of it. The nodule was at the focus of the parabola and received the small percentage of sunlight that was reflected from the sunflower. It was hot there, a steamy center for Parameter to revolve around. In the nodule and in the capillaries of the sunflower, chemical reactions were going on.

Activity in her brain was damped down to almost nothing, interrupted only by the passing peaks of Solstice, who never went completely to sleep.

"Parameter." It was not a voice, even when Parameter was more fully conscious. It was words forming in her head, like thoughts, but they were not her own thoughts.

"(Recognition; slight reproach; receptivity)"

"Come on. Wake up."

"What is it?" Coming awake was effortless.

"Are you ready for vision now?"

"Sure. Why not?"

Solstice, functioning as a switchboard in the back of the cerebrum, closed the contacts that would allow Parameter's visual cortex to communicate with her forebrain: She saw.

"What a lovely morning."

"Yeah. Very nice. Wait till you see the morning papers. You won't be so happy."

"Can it wait? Why ruin it?" Parameter felt no sense of urgency. It had been a century since she felt rushed.

"Sure. Let me know when you're up to it."

Parameter communicated wry amusement to her symb. (Picture of herself buckling on sword, dagger, donning brass helmet and picking up embossed shield.) Solstice responded. (Picture of Parameter climbing a staircase, gazing at the stars, failing to see she was reaching for a top step that wasn't there.)

Parameter stretched, causing the filmy parasol to undulate slowly. She made tight fists of all four hands—she had no feet, having surgically replaced them with oversized hands at the time of her pairing—then spread twenty fingers. One hand caught her attention. It was pale, but was turning pinker as she watched. She had the coloring of an albino; the skin under her nails was amber, turning quickly to orange. Solstice was packing up, pumping liquids around, getting ready to move.

Nothing she saw was real. Her eyes were protected behind the opaque substance of Solstice; no light had fallen on her retinas in over seven years. Had she looked at the sun with her eyes, as she seemed to be doing, cells would have been destroyed. What she saw was the product of nerve impulses sent to different areas of her brain by Solstice's sensory receptors. But it looked to her as though she were floating naked in space, feeling the raw sunlight on her body. The illusion was complete.

"Okay. What's up?"

"This is up. I monitored this broadcast two minutes ago. It came from the Janus transmitter, channel nineteen. Where do you want it?"

"I don't care. Anywhere."

A three-dimensional image built up between Parameter and the dark semicircle of Saturn. It looked as real as anything else she could see. The view was the interior of a room. It could have been any room, but the woman sitting in it was someone Parameter knew. The voice-over explained that Lilo, the convicted Enemy of Humanity, had been put to death. It gave the time, the place, and a brief summary of her crimes. As the commentary moved on to a lecture about the evils of genetic experimentation, Solstice tuned it out without Parameter needing to ask for it.

"We knew it would happen," Parameter pointed out, wondering why the news did not affect her more.

"So did she."

"Okay. Where is she now?"

Her view shifted. Saturn appeared to rotate beneath her until she saw the Rings from the top. She seemed to be hovering over the north polar region.

At the bottom of the Ring, near where the shadow of Saturn cut across it, a small green arrow blinked on and off.

"That's us," Solstice said. Further around the curve of the Ring, about sixty degrees to spinward, a dark red arrow appeared. Its color told her the mass of the rock in question. It was on the edge of Ring Alpha, the outermost of the rings, where perturbations would not have been severe over five years.

Solstice caused the picture to zoom in. There was Lilo's life capsule as Parameter had last seen it, retrieved by Solstice from areas in their common brain that Parameter could never reach without hypnosis.

It was a rock—slightly larger than average, but in all a quite ordinary rock. Inside it was a nuclear generator, a computer, a modest rocket engine, a life-support system—and Lilo. Or someone who could become Lilo; a clone who, when Lilo's recorded memories were played into her, would become the Lilo of five years ago.

"Has it really been five years?"

"And sixty days and three hours, Old Earth Corrected Time."

"Doesn't seem like that." She studied the two arrows again. It was a long distance.

"One hundred forty-one thousand eight hundred and ninety-five kilometers, as the rock rolls," Solstice supplied.

"Well, we made a promise, didn't we?"

"I was waiting for you to say it."

It was six years ago they had first met her. Lilo had set up her private research station on Janus, hoping that the status of that satellite as the interface between human and pair society would mean less vigilance, looser enforcement of the genetic statutes. Parameter/Solstice had met her there on one of their infrequent visits, and they had immediately liked her. That was rare for them. Humans and pairs do not generally mix.

They had hung around her small lab while they were on Janus, and when they were ready to leave they had suggested she move her entire operation into the Rings. Lilo had not been willing to go that far, but had approached them with the idea of setting up a robot station on the edge of the Rings. She was worried about getting caught. They had agreed to supervise the awakening of the clone if she ever needed it.

Now the long journey was ahead of them. It was impossible to hurry. Though they could reach speeds of fifty kilometers per hour in their travels, they had to stop to feed each day. It would take them nearly a year to reach Lilo.

"Well, every trip starts with one push," Solstice said. "Let's go."

4

I'm not a frequent visitor to any of the disneylands. To me, a desire to work in the dirt with your bare hands and eat dirt-grown food is harmless, but silly. It makes us yearn for something we can never have, something that's always up there in the Lunar sky. It leads to lunatic fantasies like the one that had obsessed Tweed for so long: the retaking of Earth, the liberation of our home planet from the Invaders.

I grew up surrounded by metal, and have never felt deprived because of it. Stories of Old Earth glories leave me unmoved. Our frontiers will be found not by trying to recapture the past, but by looking within ourselves. I had tried to do that, and ended up in jail.

Tweed must have set the thermostat on his private paradise at around forty degrees. I was sweltering. Maybe the plants needed a summer, but I definitely didn't. And some unspeakable little vermin had found their way into my leg hair. Nature. I stripped off the bulky robe and tried to cool myself while Tweed pondered my fate.

Lilo saw Tweed make a signal to the man on the edge of the woods. She tensed. Was this it? He could decide she wasn't worth the trouble—she *still* didn't know what he had in mind for her—and things could start to happen fast. She watched Vaffa carefully. If they came at her, she vowed to do some damage on the way out.

But Tweed was hurrying through the thick grass. Vaffa relaxed a little when Tweed had gone out of sight. She sat in the grass and stroked the snake. This female Vaffa was two and a half meters tall, had no breasts and very little fat anywhere, and was completely hairless. She was bone-white all over. A death's-head: spare, economical of movement, powerful and lethal.

Someone came running through the field toward them. Lilo wondered why anyone would run in this heat. Was she in trouble? But it was sheer high spirits. She saw the tattoo first, then the face.

"Hello, Mari."

"Hi," she gasped. "Isn't it *wonderful?* Being here, I mean."

"Uh-huh." Lilo slapped at something that buzzed; her hand came away red. Bloodsucker!

"Hi, Vaffa." The woman nodded to Mari. The medico was covered in sweat, and seemed to love it. She stood for a moment, getting her breath back. "You're supposed to come with me," she said.

"What for?"

"I have to make a recording of you. Boss's orders. Come on, it won't take a minute."

Lilo knew it took a bit longer than that, but followed her along a path leading into the woods. Turning, she saw that Vaffa was following, giving more attention to the snake than to Lilo. It wasn't very flattering. It would have been nice to think of herself as dangerous, but Vaffa did not seem impressed. Well, that was probably best. Maybe she'd get a surprise one day.

She had thought she would be taken back to the more conventional part of Tweed's residence. Instead they went to a glade in the middle of a dense forest. There was a waterfall nearby. Mari had carried her bag with her; now she set it on the ground and gestured to Lilo. A thin plastic sheet had been spread on the ground.

"Right here?" Lilo said. "Don't you need . . ." But Mari was opening what looked like a tree stump. Inside was metal.

"Why not? Don't worry, you'll love it."

Lilo had to admit the setting was more restful than the standard medico's operating room. Maybe it would help her over her nervousness.

Lilo's fear of memory recording was a common one. She could tell herself as often as she wished that what she feared simply could *not* happen; she could not be awakened after the recording process to be told she had died and it was now several years later. A *clone* could wake up and learn that, but not her. Human consciousness is linear, and her mind was stuck in the body she lived in, for all time. What memory recording did was to make it possible for a second personality, exactly like her own, to be implanted into a second body, also exactly like her own. But Lilo could never participate in the life that clone would lead, though it had her memories to the time of the recording.

She tried to relax as Mari plugged her in. She felt herself go limp and numb all over as Mari turned the dials on her black bag. From then on, it was impossible to see what the medico was doing, but she knew the process well enough. The top of her head was opened—she could see the blood on Mari's hands as they came into her range of vision.

There were tiny metal channels implanted in Lilo's brain, put there when she was three years old. They enabled her to interface with a computer, and also served as conduits for the recording medium: single-molecule chains of ferrophoto-nucleic acid. Mari strapped a recording band around Lilo's forehead. In operation, the recorder would render Lilo unconscious for three minutes.

It was simple enough in operation, impossibly complex in theory. Lilo often wondered if the human race would ever have perfected it without the information from the Ophiuchi Hotline.

Memory is a holographic process. A memory is stored not in one place, but all over the brain. It cannot be recorded or deciphered by any linear process, such as magnetic tape running past a playback head. It must be grasped all at once, whole, like a snapshot or a hologram. The FPNA made that possible. Each strand, containing billions of bits, was interfered with by every other strand when the process took place. Unlike a visual hologram, where each segment of the photographic plate contains all the information of the whole picture, one strand of FPNA was useless by itself. Only in combination with the sheaf of other strands—forty-six in all—could the picture have meaning. The recording band would cause magnetic fields to be set up all through the brain, producing a code of nearly infinite permutations.

Lilo had never worried about whether the process was actually capable of holding everything. She was not too impressed with notions of a soul, a *karass,* a *karma,* or an *atman. S*he knew people who had died and been brought back to life by memory recording and cloning, and there was no way to tell the difference.

Mari flicked the switch, and the last thing Lilo recalled was her smiling face.

The face was still there when she woke up, still smiling. Lilo smiled back, glad that it was over. She started to get up.

"Hold on, not so fast," Mari said, lightly. "I have to unhook you first, and close you up."

Something was different. She looked again, and realized it was the background. Something *behind* Mari's face had changed.

It was the leaves on the trees. They had been green, and now they were a riot of red and gold and purple.

"O God, no. No, I . . . I don't like this. I don't want—"

Mari touched her forehead lightly. "I don't want to have to turn you off."

Lilo sagged. Gradually she became aware of a circle of faces at the edge of her vision, between Mari and the canopy of trees, looking down at her. There was Tweed, and Vaffa, and . . . the other Vaffa. Male and female, looking down at her.

Mari finished her work. "Let me give you a hand up," she said. "You're going to need it." Lilo let herself be pulled into a sitting position, then helped to her feet. She stood, dizzy for a moment but rapidly regaining her balance. She let herself feel, not daring to think: the grass under her feet, hair brushing her face, the cool skin and underlying warmth of Mari's naked back under her arm, the play of muscles in her legs and feet. Mari put her arm around Lilo's waist and walked her in a circle, like a drunk.

"You'll get your legs back in no time," she said, soothingly. "I exercised you all through the growth process, while you were in the tank. You're strong, you're just not used to it yet. Feel ready to stand on your own?"

Lilo nodded, not trusting herself to speak. Mari let her go, and she stood facing Tweed. He had some papers in his hand.

"So I died," she said. He glanced at his papers and made a check mark.

"Doesn't anyone have anything to say to me?"

Tweed said nothing, just looked at his papers again and made another check. The male Vaffa was looking into the treetops, smiling. It was the first time Lilo had seen him smile. The female had her hand in front of her mouth, and Lilo realized she was trying not to laugh. Were they amused at *her?* What kind of people *were* they?

"What the hell is going on, would someone please tell me that?"

Tweed tore a sheet of paper and handed it to Lilo. She glanced down at it, looked back at Tweed, then had to look down again at what she was afraid she had seen.

"So I died."

"Doesn't anyone have anything to say to me?"

"What the hell is going on, would someone please tell me?"

The words were machine-printed, and each sentence had a fat check beside it. She felt dizziness again. There was an apparition: at the edge of the clearing, a huge elk, with crystal antlers refracting blue sunlight. Hallucination? She looked away from it. She wanted out of this crazy place.

"You'd better sit down and rest," Mari said, putting an arm

around her again as Lilo's knees buckled. "Maybe you should cry it out."

"*No!* I'll cry later. Right now I want to know what's going on."

"And you shall," Tweed said. He gestured, and the male Vaffa unfolded a chair for him. He settled into it. "Mari, I told you not to interfere."

"I'm sorry, Boss," Mari said, helplessly. "I just can't seem to . . . when someone's in trouble, I just—"

"Never mind. I shouldn't have had you here for this. It's not that important, though. Lilo, as you already saw, you are not what you thought you were. You are a clone. Perhaps you know what happened to the original Lilo. I have reason to believe that she was hatching her plans even before I had her recorded. If not, she at least entered our partnership with a . . . a state of mind that was not the best. Do you know what I'm talking about?"

"You're saying I tried to escape. And I didn't make it." She glanced at the two Vaffas. Their expressions were unreadable.

"That's it exactly. You were planning it from the moment you realized you were not going to be executed."

"I guess there's no sense not admitting it, is there?"

"No, there isn't."

I'm afraid, she thought, but didn't care to say it. He might have it written down somewhere. She felt something building in her, something that had to find release. She welcomed it, even if it meant her death. She was going to rip the skin from his face, expose the flayed bone, and crack it with her teeth. She was going to kill him. She looked at the ground while the bloodlust built in her. She was about to spring . . .

She was looking at two bare feet. Her eyes went up a pair of legs, past hairless genitals and a flat chest to a bald head. The knees were bent, the arms slightly away from the sides. Her lips were pulled away from fashionably stained teeth. She *wanted* Lilo to attack. One of the Vaffas had moved between Lilo and Tweed before the thought even began to form in Lilo's head. The anger drained away to a hard knot in her stomach. Vaffa relaxed a little.

"She knew where to be," Tweed was saying. "Do you see that?"

"Yes. I see."

"You are predictable, Lilo."

"I see that, too."

"Would you like to hear what has happened to you? You're four months out of date, you know."

"I guess I'd better."

* * *

I had been foolish. I saw it now, how ridiculously easy the escape had been.

They had taken me on survival training in the Amazon disneyland, three hundred square kilometers of climate-controlled tropical rain forest twenty kilometers below Aristillus. It was in the back country, the part the public never sees, where the rain falls all day and the clothes rot off your back in the suffocating humidity.

We were on our way home through the public corridors. There was only one guard this time; Vaffa had been called away at the last minute. I had stolen the skin sample I needed from Mari's workshop. I was watching for an opening. The guard looked away—

I bolted through the crowd. In two seconds I was invisible. In thirty seconds I was two levels down and a thousand meters east on a crosstown slidewalk, doubling back. I passed customs with the skin sample in my palm, boarded a train to Clavius.

The car stopped for an override signal. Thirty minutes later the door sighed open at a familiar station. I wondered what they would do to me.

Vaffa stood there, the woman, the face I had come to know so well. I looked down at the dark metal thing in her hand, then back at her bared teeth. I still didn't understand.

Lilo retched helplessly. She had long since emptied her stomach, but she continued to be sick. Mari held her as she knelt on the grass above the mess of bile and vat fluid she had brought up, while Tweed put the pictures away.

"Vaffa is rather direct," Tweed said. "As I told you a long time ago, they are useful." He glanced at the two. Lilo saw the look, and wondered for a moment if he might be a little afraid of them, too. "Are you able to go on?"

She sat back on her heels. There was Vaffa, the woman who had shot someone who looked just like Lilo and then held up the bloody body with the face and chest caved in for someone to take a picture. Her face moved only when she blinked.

"There's more?"

"I'm afraid so. You don't give up easily. If you did, you wouldn't be the kind of person I'm looking for."

"And more pictures?"

"Yes. You must see them."

"Let's get it over with."

* * *

I had been foolish.

I saw it now, and prayed forgiveness from my two earlier incarnations. I had thrown away their deaths by my failure. It didn't seem likely that I would be given another chance.

And the cost: Mari, Mari . . .

Perhaps Tweed would not bring me back again. Or if he did, maybe he wouldn't tell me about Mari and my shame.

Vaffa appeared at the door to my room. I welcomed him.

Tweed had lit another of his cigars. He blew a cloud of smoke, and Lilo saw the female Vaffa edge a step away from him. Her nose twitched.

"The first time, you bolted," he said. "You saw the chance I had arranged for you to see, and you took it." The elk, which turned out not to have been a hallucination, had entered the clearing and was cropping the grass behind Tweed. Lilo watched the light refract from the antlers as Tweed talked. She did not want to think.

"The second time you had learned, but not the lesson I want you to learn. You had decided to be more careful. I presented you with the same opportunity, and you wisely turned it down. You were going to make your own escape this time."

"What did I do?"

"Now we come to the point of this whole distasteful exercise. I will not tell you how you tried to escape. Can you see why?"

Lilo tried to think about it, but it did her no good. All she knew was that she felt trapped. Nothing made sense.

"All right. I don't expect you to absorb all this at once. It will take some getting used to. What I want you to try to understand is that you did your very best to get away from me. You had no help this time. You planned for two months, and to all appearances you were cooperating with me. You came up with a plan. What you must understand is that *it was the best plan you will ever come up with.*" He thundered the words. Everyone looked at him; they could not help it. He could be a powerful speaker when he wished to be.

"That's what the demonstration with the script was meant to point out to you. I have seen you revived twice now. You reacted exactly the same each time. You had no choice; you can only be what you are. You started off each time with memories identical to the day you were last recorded, right here in this clearing. You became a slightly different person each time. The original Lilo was foolish, she didn't think it out far enough, and she paid for it. The second was very crafty. She killed Mari, and came as close as you will ever—"

"*She what?*"

"You heard me."

Mari was at her side. "Lilo, don't get—"

Lilo recoiled from the woman in horror. "No! I couldn't have. I could have killed . . . *that*," she pointed to the paired Vaffas. "I could have killed either of those things. But not Mari."

"I didn't say there was no remorse," Tweed said. "Vaffa says you seemed relieved when he killed you."

"Lilo, I don't hold it against you," Mari said. "I know it sounds strange, but I got to know you . . . I got to know you twice now. I like you. You did what you thought you had to, and you waited until I'd had a recording taken. I only lost a few days. The Boss told me it was painless, you didn't make me suffer."

"That's true," Tweed said. He was studying Lilo.

"But I just can't *believe* . . ."

"You must. And know this, too. I *know* you now. There are signs I can look for, things you will not be able to hide from me. If I see them, I will know you are following the script. You, on the other hand, will never be sure." His fat fingers, ticking off the arguments, were like the bars of a cage closing around her.

"I'll leave you to think about what I've said. When you've decided if you'll cooperate, come and tell me. It's your choice, and I want a firm decision from you this time, not the lies you told me at the institute. I've spent enough time and energy on you already."

He left, trailing the male Vaffa behind him like a faithful dog. Lilo and Mari were left virtually alone, as the other Vaffa seemed to have forgotten about them. Lilo watched her as she tried to coax her snake down from a tree, then scrambled up a vertical trunk to join it.

The silence grew uncomfortable.

"I wish I knew what to say," Lilo whispered. "I really wish I knew."

"Say you'll do what he says. You don't have any choice."

"No, I . . . I wasn't talking about that. I don't . . . don't have much choice about that, I guess. That's how it looks, anyway. I just don't know what to say to *you*."

"There's nothing you need to say. *You* didn't do anything. I have nothing but good memories of you. So who was hurt? Someone who used to be me, and someone else who was you."

Lilo wished she could look at it that way. She knew she would be eternally shamed by what that person had done. But the only way to cope with it was to see it as Mari suggested.

"I fixed your legs the way you like them," Mari said. Lilo looked down. It hadn't occurred to her that her legs would be different, but of course they would have been. The design in her genes did not include the hair.

"Thank you. I appreciate that."

"I knew you would."

Lilo gritted her teeth. She knew Mari meant no harm by it, but she would never be able to hear those words again without emotion. She did not relish being predictable. Not at all.

Wondering if it was what she had said the last time around, she said, "I guess I'd better go talk to the Boss."

Consider the shape of my life:

I had lived fifty-seven years rather normally. Like everyone, I got a memory recording every few years. Then I was arrested.

The recording I owned had been confiscated and held pending the outcome of my trial. When I was condemned, it was destroyed, along with the tissue sample that would have been used to grow a clone body if I were to die.

At the time of my stay of execution Mari must have made another recording of me. I had probably been drugged; it would have been easy enough.

I had been confronted with the clone Tweed had grown, who had then gone to The Hole in my place. (In whose place? After all, she was as much me as I am. It gets confusing.)

That person—the original me; though it's hard to accept, I'm now living in a clone body—had managed to survive only a few weeks beyond the next recording, taken in the forest at Tweed's. Return to square one, in the first step of a depressingly repetitive process. A new "me" was awakened, missing those weeks from the original recording until the death of the original "me." This second clone was started on the same course as the original. She played it safe for two or three months, made her break, was caught and killed. Number four—me, me dammit—wakes up in the forest and sees Mari smiling down on her. But this time Mari is a clone, too. Number three had killed her while escaping.

Think of it in four dimensions. Think of the long worm with arms and legs that's used in school to illustrate the idea. Picture an infant as one end of the worm, emerging from mother's vagina or the placentory, depending on how mother likes to do it. On the other end is death. Make marks on the worm each time a person's memories are recorded. Each mark is a potential branch.

Eight or nine months ago, at the time of my reprieve, my four-dimensional cross-section had diverged into four branches. (Or could it be five, or six? Tweed had grown several clones of me while I was in jail, since as soon as I died each time he was able to revive me in a new body the next day. He must keep clones of Mari, too, or else she could not have been there the day after number three killed her.) Each had started with the same memories, ending on the day Mari recorded me. Three of those branches were terminated, dead. I was traveling, second by second, down the fourth branch.

Five years before that, when I made my own recording in the capsule orbiting Saturn, there was the potential for another branch. I had no way of knowing if that one had produced another Lilo, but it was possible. I hoped I would never meet her. I had met myself once, and learned something about myself I would have been happier not knowing.

But since I did know it, since I had seen what lengths I would go to stay alive, I intended to live.

I intended to live forever.

Survival training took Lilo three months to complete. At that, she gathered she was getting the short course.

She never complained, but it seemed a lot of foolishness to her, and highly uncomfortable foolishness. Unless Tweed was seriously preparing to establish a beachhead on Old Earth, it seemed pointless.

But she went along with it, from the Amazon to Egypt. She spent a week in each of the major disneylands. The Free Earth Party spent a lot of money to be allowed in the wilderness areas of the environmental parks. In return they had the pleasure of dehydrating under desert suns and getting frostbite in Siberia.

Lilo was in a class of twenty. All the others were initiates into the cult-party, with the exception of Vaffa-female, who accompanied Lilo and made everything look easy. She got to know the Free Earthers.

She suspected many of them were not as fanatic as Tweed about the actual liberation of Earth. Many were there for the interesting experiences.

She grew to have a great deal of respect for Tweed's profile of her. He was sticking his neck out every time he allowed her to come in contact with someone who was not a member of the tight inner circle of Free Earthers. Presumably she could tell someone who she was. Tweed could not be sure that any of her classmates were sufficiently committed to the cause not to report her to the government. If anyone did, if the State found out Tweed had abducted her from the institute, his ass was in the recycler.

The catch was that Lilo would be condemning herself to death along with him. He knew she would not do that.

Actually, though she would never have admitted it, she came to like living in the bush. Slogging through a snowstorm was no fun, but huddling in your igloo with five other people under a polar-bearskin blanket was. There were many good moments.

There was also loneliness. It was much harder to take than the physical hardships. She had learned to live alone during her year at the institute. Now she ached to have friends again, to find a lover. But she could not be friends with anyone in the survival class. It was unthinkable to love someone and not be able to open up, to tell everything, and she could not do that. There were secrets she must guard. The people at Tweed's residence were even worse. They knew all her secrets, but they knew she was not one of them. She was treated with civility, but would never be trusted. Only with Mari could she begin to get close. Lilo knew Mari liked her, but it was the broad, uncritical affection that was a part of her personality. Mari thought genetic experimentation of human DNA was wrong, and Lilo thought the dream of the Free Earthers was crazy. There was little for them to talk about.

So she was alone in a crowd. In some ways, it was worse than the confinement of prison. She began to hang back during the nights around the campfire when everyone got together for singing and telling stories and copping. She told herself it was because she didn't care for sex in the Great Outdoors. "Cop on the beach," she told Mari, "and spend the next day digging sand out of yourself." Only when the yearning became unbearable would she find a partner, but increasingly, her most trusted lovers had been the fingers of her right hand.

She was lonely, her sex life was terrible, and she began to suffer anxieties of recapture by the authorities. It would be awful to face ex-

ecution at this point, after all she had been though and the shameful
things she had done. If she died now, somehow, all the previous
deaths would have been for nothing.

Lilo had not seen Tweed since the day of her awakening. She assumed he had been present at that so her responses would be as they
had been before. He was teaching her a lesson, and connecting it with
his own person. It was good psychology, and it worked. She found
that she did fear him.

From that day on he seemed to take no further interest in her. She
tried to get in to see him, but was brushed off by aides. The Boss was
always too busy.

It had been oddly comforting to see herself as very important to
Tweed, someone he must have even at the risk of abducting her from
the institute. She gradually had to change that picture. When she realized she was going through an established curriculum for clandes-
tine agents—which implied there were others, perhaps hundreds of
others, like her—she became depressed. Maybe she was no more important to Tweed than Mari, whose skills he could hire at any labor
exchange in Luna.

The more she looked at it, the more it became apparent that she
was being put through machinery that had been in place long before
the need to abduct her ever arose. The Free Earthers' control of the
institute was such that Mari could grow a full-term clone—a six-
month undertaking—inside the walls with no fear of detection. In the
light of that, Lilo began to wonder if her sprint across vacuum had
been necessary. Had it been some sort of test? Free Earthers seemed
to like tests; her training, if it had a purpose at all, consisted of an
endless series of them, putting her up against environments she would
never see, since they were all Earth environments.

It seemed certain that Tweed was not after Lilo personally, but
people *like* her. Looking at it impartially, there were only three things
she could see in herself that set her apart from anyone else. She was a
scientist, but surely he could hire all the scientists he needed. She was
a condemned criminal, but she could not even venture a guess as to
why he might value that quality. So it had to be the nature of her
researches, the work that had resulted in her arrest.

No one could have been more surprised than Lilo when she had
found herself drifting gradually but persistently into proscribed areas.
She had had time to reflect on that while in prison, and more time
now, during her training, to review again the steps that had made her
an Enemy of Humanity. That still amazed her.

Lilo had wanted to be a medico. As early as she could remember she had been good with her hands, and while she was growing up her most cherished toy was her junior surgery kit. She would operate on herself and her friends, always keeping abreast of the latest fashions in face and figure.

But her mother and her teachers knew she was cut out for better things and steered her into a skilled profession. She did not object; she was a reader—all her ancestors had been, all the way back to pre-Invasion times—and devoured any book that was left in her reach. Her teachers knew their business; eventually it seemed that she had always wanted to be a genetic engineer.

She was good at what she did. Her services were in demand with all the big companies, and she worked for several before going into business for herself. Her specialty was foodstuffs, an area that had been neglected for a long time but was then undergoing a new surge of interest.

While most of her colleagues concentrated on hydroponic fad foods—exotic blends of existing flavors that made a splash for a few months and then were forgotten—Lilo took a new look at staples. She refined rather than invented, and it paid off. The production companies knew that with a big advertising budget and promotion they could create a transitory demand for almost anything. In the long run, however, they made their money licensing gene patents for improved beef trees and egg plants.

Lilo concentrated on pork trees. She succeeded in improving the yield and sweetness of the pink inner meat, while at the same time decreasing the fat-to-lean ratio of the bacon. It made her enough money to improve her facilities, and she turned to new horizons.

Her work on pork trees had brought her to realize that there were many base organisms which had long been neglected because of inability to compete with the artificially created strains people now thought of as staple crops. There had been a time when wheat, soybeans, potatoes, corn, and rice had been the major foods of the human race. Now there was no one alive who had ever seen them.

But they existed in the Life Bank, as did virtually every plant and animal that had lived on Old Earth. It dawned on her that the foods she had eaten all her life were all created plants, and that all of them were over four hundred years old. It seemed that the age of invention in plant genetics was behind her, that no totally *new* staple food had been invented since human civilization had established itself in the Eight Worlds. She did not bother wondering why that was; she set about to invent a new staple.

The result was the bananameat tree, and it was an instant and steady success. As its name indicated, she derived it from tropical fruit stock, but the flavor was not derivative of anything. It was something new, and the attempts to describe it as tasting "like chicken" or "like venison" always fell short.

Lilo did not advertise the fact, but the meat that came closest to the taste of bananameat was human flesh. Her first questionable act, done innocently and in the spirit of investigation, had been to include a tissue culture from her own body in the samples she was analyzing while making a study of human taste parameters. Her first illegal act had been to introduce changes into the culture and transplant sections of DNA into banana genes.

Bananameat made her rich. Not fabulously so, but with the time and resources to tempt her back to her first love: the human body.

She remembered the happy days spent tinkering with the external structure of her own body and the bodies of others. While she still saw it as a phase she had been going through—and by now was contemptuous of most cosmetic body changes—it continued to fascinate her.

She thought about the tremendous genetic accidents that had shaped her life, and that shaped the lives of all humans. She was a reader; there were many citizens who were not. The prevailing social explanation for illiteracy was that there were people who were temperamentally unsuited for reading—and indeed there were few callings in a computerized, video-saturated world that required literacy. Lilo accepted that, but had always had a feeling that most people never learned to read because they simply were not smart enough.

This did not make her feel superior. It was an *accident,* and it offended her. Her intelligence was not of her own doing, but had been predetermined when two gametes blundered into each other in a placentory.

As she chafed under the restraints of the genetic laws, she researched into their origins and was appalled to discover that the five-hundred-year ban on human experimentation had been intended only as a moratorium. It had made a lot of sense at the time, with the human race in a state of flux, facing an uncertain future. But how long is enough? The present scope of humanity represented all the changes that could be rung on a small gene pool of survivors of the Invasion. All the actual genetic diseases and defects had been weeded out early, before the ban on research. The human race was healthy enough, but was it going anywhere?

Her shock increased as she learned about the reproductive aspect of genetics. Lilo was *not* a geneticist or a breeder. In the same sense that the builder of a machine might know little of the metallurgy that had produced its parts, Lilo was only vaguely aware of the laws of inheritance. Her job was to take something that was already there and bend it to her will with the direct manipulation techniques learned from the Ophiuchi Hotline. Now she delved into the world of recessives and inbreeding. She began to wonder if the human race might be turning into idiots, with no baseline to indicate the change.

She tried to stir up some interest among other genetic engineers, but had no luck. There seemed to be no political current she could tap in an effort to have the genetic laws rescinded. If there was a taboo in human society which had taken the place of sex, it was human genetics. No one wanted to look at the problem, simply because no one saw it as a problem. It was accepted as a fact of life, the way things were; human DNA was inviolable.

Lilo thought for a year about the courses open to her.

She could forget it. That was a real possibility, and even now she was unsure of why she had gone on. Some days the inertia of society had felt like an actual drug in her veins, soothing her and telling her to leave things alone. If it was good enough for your grandmother, why isn't it good enough for you?

Or she could explore it, cautiously. In the end, that's what she did. But not cautiously enough.

Her guide was the Ophiuchi Hotline. Of the huge volume of encoded transmissions that came down the Line, fully ninety-five percent had always been untranslatable. But she had heard rumors that a part of that, maybe a lot of it, had been found to relate in some way to human DNA. She set her computer to scan portions of the data which were in the public record. It was blind work; she had little idea of what she was looking for. The field was so unexplored that she had to go back to pre-Invasion records to find any meaningful work on the subject. She knew it was a job for hundreds of researchers, for the type of scientists who had existed in the days of basic research and who she suspected were no longer to be found. She had come to the realization that she had not been trained to be a scientist; she was an engineer, or at best, a tinkerer.

The indications were good. She did not bother herself with the question of how the Ophiuchites were able to know so much about human genetics; they seemed to know just about everything, and the human race had been relying on that stream of new knowledge for centuries. She set up a base on Janus and began her first halting experiments on her own egg cells. She had no intention of producing

living human beings. What she did was introduce changes and grow
the result to a fetal stage of development, then use what she had
learned to guide her next step.

She was not sure what she was seeking. She was not sure why she
was doing it. At her worst times, she suspected she was merely act-
ing out the desires of a little girl who had loved to play medico.

But at other times she was sustained by a vision. She did not know
where it came from, but at times it felt as though it were not really a
part of herself, not a product of her own mind. It was a vaguely
defined but compelling vision of a human race scattered to the stars,
redefined, transformed.

There was one vivid picture that went along with the vision. She
saw it every night as she fell asleep. She was running through tall
grass and trees under a blue sun. It was a lovely blue that washed
into her skin and the flowers that waved beneath a gentle breeze.
There was someone running with her.

Lilo was staying at Earthhome, Tweed's pocket disneyland, sleeping in a grass shack she had been forced to build herself.

Her first visitor every morning was Mari. Lilo could not leave
Earthhome without someone to escort her. She had tried several
times, but had been unable to find the stream-bed entrance to get out.
It was a trick of the holos which made the entrance effectively one-
way. So each morning Mari came and blindfolded her, then led her
splashing through the water.

But this time the two of them reached the embankment leading
down to the stream and Mari did not reach for the scrap of cloth.

"Himalaya this week, right?" Lilo said, casually.

"No," Mari said. "You're shipping out today."

"Today?" But it made sense. If she had known when she would
leave, she might have made an escape deadline.

"That's right. Take my hand, and hold on to your gut. This is not
too pleasant until you get used to it." She led Lilo to a tree that grew
from the opposite bank. Lilo was sure she had explored it. They
started to go around the tree. . . .

Lilo had an attack of vertigo as everything seemed to tilt down in
front of her. She held back. The scene was distorted, like looking
through a bottle. Mari pulled on her hand.

"Step *up*," she said. "Three steps. You won't fall." Lilo gulped,
and stepped into the empty air. She felt concrete under her bare feet.
She was rising, but it looked as though she were going down a vertical hillside. "Turn left, then left again. Close your eyes, it'll be

easier." But Lilo kept them open. She had seen trick holos like this at funhouses, but none so perfect. They emerged into the water-filled corridor.

"Can you tell me where I'm going?" Lilo asked. "So I'll know what to pack?"

Mari laughed. "No. Truthfully, I don't know where it is."

They stopped off at Mari's lab. An hour later, Lilo emerged minus her left lung. In its place was a null-suit generator, something she had never used before. It seemed to indicate that she was going to Mercury or Venus, since those were the only places where null-suits were necessary to get by. She curiously fingered the small metal flower below her collarbone, which was the air exhaust valve and control unit of the suit, as Mari explained how to operate it. She had a slight soreness in her neck where Mari had installed the binaural radio and voder that went with the suit.

Lilo was sure she was going off Luna when she was introduced to Iphis. He was certainly a spacer, since he had no legs. He was obviously on a layover too short to justify the expense of getting legs grafted on. He sat strapped in a padded basket on top of a spidery walker.

The female Vaffa appeared, as she had a habit of doing, right beside Lilo's elbow.

"Where's Tweed?" Lilo asked.

"He said to tell you he can't come," Mari said. "Vaffa will be coming with you. I asked to go, but the Boss needs me because there's another prisoner who . . . oh, I'm not supposed to tell you that. But it doesn't matter." She kissed Lilo. "I hate good-byes," she said, looking away. "You be careful. Maybe we'll meet again."

"I hope so."

Lilo did not see the ship. She followed Iphis and Vaffa through a collapsible tube into the living quarters. They were quite small. Iphis heaved himself out of his walker and into his couch, and Vaffa put the contraption out of the lock.

"Grab seats," Iphis said. "We lift in two minutes."

Lilo tried again. "To where?"

"Titan."

They had planned a tacking maneuver on Jupiter. Lilo didn't like it, but was not about to mention the fact. She had not bought a ticket, and couldn't complain about the service.

But a few days before the insertion Vaffa had a surprise for her.

"We're not really going to Titan. I am, eventually, but you're not."

"Where am I going?"

"Little place called Poseidon."

"Where the hell is that?"

Vaffa and Iphis exchanged glances. Lilo had the uncomfortable feeling that the name should mean something to her.

"Try Jay-eight. Jay dash vee eye eye eye. Roman numerals."

"One of Jupiter's retrograde moons," Iphis explained. "A chunk of rock about twenty kilometers through, twenty million kilometers out."

"But that's . . ."

"Illegal?" Vaffa laughed, and was joined by Iphis. "Tell it to the Invaders."

"Invaders," Lilo mumbled.

Why We Can't Go Home. The Mach 5 Oral Creative Co-op. (Illit. level transcribed tape)

They came in the year 2050, old style. (Two as-teroid-sized objects entering the solar system from in-terstellar space. Palomar scope pans upward. Astrono-mer bends over eyepiece.) They were decelerating, heading for Jupiter.

Two astronauts, Purunkita and Mizinchikov, were diverted from a regular supply mission to the Mars base. (Stock footage of P & M boarding spaceship *U Thant.* Cut to actors in ship: watching instruments, getting radio message, firing engines, eating meals, cop-ping.) They were to swing out to Jupiter in six months and arrive with empty tanks. Their orders: Sit tight, observe, and await the arrival of a robot tanker. (Proc-ess shot of P & M at port of *U Thant,* Jupiter outside.

P is as black as space. Her arm is around M. She is pregnant.)

One of the objects did orbit Jupiter. The other changed course at the last moment and headed for Earth. It landed in the Pacific Ocean, near the equator. That was the Year One of the Occupation of Earth. (Flat newsreel footage of Invader ship, twenty-kilometer sphere sitting half-submerged in water, dull-surfaced, pocked with holes.)

What little we know of Invaders comes from Purunkita and Mizinchikov, the only people known to have entered one of the ships and returned. This is what happened to them. (The alien ship matches with the *U Thant*, swallows it. Camera follows P, M, and infant daughter through water-filled stone tunnels.) They met Doctor Ellen Bronson and her two companions, who had entered the ship that landed in the Pacific. They had been in the ship no more than a day, but had entered on the day of landing. On that day, the astronauts had still been three months from Jupiter.

If the story the astronauts told is true, space and time exist in a different manner inside the ships. There is little reason to doubt the story.

Doctor Bronson is thought to be the only human ever to have seen the aliens themselves and survived. (B alone, entering large chamber, as big as the interior of an engineered asteroid. It is half-full of water. In the distance, special-effect distortions represent Invaders. Tight shot of B's face, indicating shock and fear. She turns and runs.)

Bronson claimed to have had a strange experience. Things were told to her in a mysterious way, and she could never account for it when she told Purunkita and Mizinchikov. (Five figures gathered around a fire on a beach within the ship, whispering.) No one knows whether to believe her story, but it's the only one we've got. This is what she said.

The Invaders come from a gas giant planet like Jupiter. Their purpose in coming to the solar system was not the invasion of Earth, but unknown motives concerned with the inhabitants of Jupiter. Bronson said there are intelligent Jovians who are much like the Invaders. (Animation sequence in the Jovian atmosphere. Huge shadowy shapes swim by.)

The invasion of Earth was secondary. It was done for the benefit of the three intelligent species of Earth: sperm whales, "killer" whales, and bottle-nosed dolphins. (Stock footage of aquatic mammals.)

Bronson said there are levels of intelligence in the universe. On top are the Jovians and Invaders. One step below are the dolphins and whales. Humans, birds, bees, beavers, ants, and corals are not considered intelligent.

No one knows if any of this is right. But it's all we have.

There were no explanations given to humanity. No ambassadors appeared, no ultimatums were offered. Humans resisted the Invasion, but the resistance was ignored. H-bombs would not go off, tanks would not move, guns would not fire. (Panic in the streets, helicopter shots of jammed highways.) No one ever saw an Invader. Pictures show distortions in the sky that no observer noticed at the time, like blind spots in the human eye. Perhaps these things were the Invaders. (Still, flat photos of building toppling, streets being uprooted, with colorful whirlpools in the sky.)

As far as anyone knows from information sent up before the transmitters went dead, the Invaders never killed a human. What they did was destroy utterly every artifact of human civilization. In their wake they left plowed ground, sprouting seedlings, and grass.

In the next two years, ten billion humans starved to death.

Poseidon is an irregular chunk of rock. It is the most distant object of any size that Jupiter can be said to claim. Being retrograde and inclined one hundred and fifty degrees from Jupiter's equator, it is one of the more difficult bodies in the solar system to rendezvous with.

The *Earthhome II* was a free-faller, a cargo ship designed to carry bulky, nonpriority freight. It traveled by hyperbolic orbits, not the straight lines of a high-booster.

"Congratulations, Captain," Lilo said. "That was a neat bit of work."

"Huh? Oh, you mean the approach?" He shrugged, but she saw he was pleased. She had gotten to know him pretty well on the twenty-nine-day trip to Jupiter.

"Really," she said. "Most ship pilots are like slideway operators nowadays. They make travel pretty dull."

"Yeah, I won't argue with you on that."

"You make me think of the days when people just set out. Nothing on the other end, no refueling stations, no air, nothing at all. And I think you like it."

He smiled at her. "I guess I wouldn't be doing this if I didn't. I always felt born in the wrong age, though. No adventure. This run is about the most dangerous thing you can do, and it's illegal. You must have wondered how we get away with this, going to Jupiter." Iphis explained Tweed's system.

It was illegal to assume a closed orbit around Jupiter, or to land on any of the moons. The loophole was that it was legal to use Jupiter to alter an orbit on the way to somewhere else. Passenger ships never did it—too many people were afraid to approach Jupiter at all. But there were plenty of independent operators who were willing if it would save them time and fuel.

The trick was to have two ships. Tweed had obtained one at Pluto, listed as missing and presumed lost. An identical ship had been purchased openly. Now both ships bore the same registration numbers. More important, they had the same captain. Lilo went to Jupiter in the *Earthhome II,* captained by Iphis II. But there was an *Earthhome I,* and an Iphis I, a clone, whom number two had never met and probably never would.

"Customs, by its nature," Iphis explained, "is only interested in *incoming* ships. I take off for Titan, listing only Vaffa as a passenger. I come to Jupiter, and meanwhile my clone and another Vaffa are on their way down from Poseidon. He takes my place on the course I was traveling. Everything's airtight at Titan, because he'll get there carrying only what I declared at Luna. If anyone's ever noticed my exhaust out here in the moons, no one's ever said anything about it. They probably think it's Invaders up to something."

Lilo sobered at the mention of Invaders. It had been twenty hours since they had swung around Jupiter. It was not something she liked to recall.

She looked out the port again. "Isn't it about time you thought about landing us?" The moon was getting uncomfortably large; she could no longer see the edges. Something moved on the surface. With a shock, she realized it was a person. They were that close.

"Don't worry. You don't land a ship like this on a pebble like that.

You could fart your way right into orbit." He glanced out the port, and his hands went to the controls. With a few pops from the attitude jets, they seemed stationary. "Now they'll pull us in with ropes and tie us down. You can get out now, if you want to." He vaulted from his couch. It astounded Lilo how graceful he was. She knew that legs were encumbrances in weightlessness, too overpowered for any job they might be called on to do. She had not realized they were actually dangerous. She had nearly split her head three times on the first day of the flight. All her traveling had been done on one-gee ships.

She found herself looking around for something. Her suit. A deeply ingrained reflex was trying to keep her from stepping into the lock in only her vest and kilt. Those horrible seconds escaping from the Institute came back to her. She repressed the memory. It annoyed her to be prey to unreasoning fears. She knew the null-suit worked; it had come to life a few hours from Jupiter, when the radiation level in the ship had become dangerous.

Sealing herself into the lock as soon as Iphis and Vaffa had gone out, she pressed the cycle button. Goose pimples broke out on her bare skin; then the suit came on and she was fighting for breath. She suppressed the reflex to gasp.

A null-suit was not easy to get used to. Some of it was merely disconcerting, such as finding yourself wrapped in a mirror that followed every curve of your body at a distance of one to one and a half millimeters. When she looked at herself, what she saw was a distorted picture of the things around her, twisted like a funhouse mirror. But some of it was downright alarming. Lilo had been breathing air for fifty-seven years, and suddenly to stop was not easy.

The suit contained a neural link that suppressed the part of the autonomic nervous system that controlled her diaphragm. When the suit was on, the breathing reflex was turned off. But it was not quite that simple. Below even the level where digestion, heartbeat, and breathing are controlled was a primitive ape that was just smart enough to realize she was not breathing, but not smart enough to understand the suit was taking care of it. The result was a jittery near-panic reaction.

Lilo knew she could cope with it. Others had done so; on Mercury and Venus people grew up in null-suits. But for the first five minutes she just held the side of the lock and tried to stop shaking. She found it helpful to think of the process that was keeping her alive. She visualized the irregular metal implant Mari had put in place of her left lung. It contained the nullfield generator, a thirty-hour supply of oxygen, and artificial alveoli that connected with her pulmonary circulation system. The null-suit exchanged oxygen for carbon dioxide, but much more efficiently than her lungs could. The oscillation of her suit's field created a bellows action that forced nearly pure carbon dioxide from the exhaust valve under her collarbone. There were ancillary systems, such as the binaural radio which she could work by subvocalizing in her throat.

She began to feel better. Below her, about five meters down, was the surface, which was a dirty gray color. Some attempt had been made to level it in places, especially the area around the *Earthhome's* berth. But beyond that it was a shattered, frozen landscape. A network of silver ropes stretched between metal supports. It was Poseidon's equivalent of a road system.

Stepping out of the lock had seemed like a good idea, but after a few seconds Lilo saw her mistake. On the way down she had time to calculate the acceleration of gravity, which she found to be almost one centimeter per second squared, or six thousandths of a Lunar gravity. She landed—too hard, with too much reaction—and had time for more calculations as she drifted down again, a little frightened this time. But the escape velocity was quite a bit higher than her legs could deliver. The gravity well was three hundred thirty meters deep, under standard Lunar conditions.

When she approached the surface again she was more careful. She grabbed a rope and pulled herself down. The rope had the same mirror brightness as her body. She watched her silver hands wrap around it, and saw that her suit joined the rope seamlessly as she touched it.

She pulled herself toward the mirror the others had entered. It was another nullfield, protecting the entrance to an underground warren. She tried to go through it, but only got as far as her neck. Vaffa was inside, floating in a bare rock corridor, and she was smiling slightly. Lilo backed out and took off her vest and kilt, which had not been enclosed in her suit when it came on. There had to be a way to get them in, but she couldn't see what it might be. She entered, leaving her clothes behind.

Vaffa was still there, and now she was holding something out to Lilo. It was a pressurized suitcase.

"You'll have to learn about nullfields," Vaffa said. "Nothing gets through them but something that's encased in another nullfield. Except some of them are tuned to let in certain frequencies of light. That's how you can see through your suit."

Lilo was angry, but wasn't going to say anything. She took the box from Vaffa and turned around. The mirror surface was invisible from the inside. She seemed to be looking out the end of an open shaft. As she stepped through, her suit formed around her again.

"Is this some sort of initiation?" she snapped, as she returned with her clothes. Vacuum had not done them any good. The kilt contained volatile plastics which had begun to boil off.

"No," Vaffa said. "Not really. Though it never hurts to get it through your head that things are different here." She paused, and looked at the ruined clothes as Lilo took them out again. "I hope those weren't your favorites or anything."

Lilo said nothing.

"I'll give you a few useful tips," Vaffa said. Lilo looked up, vaguely surprised. Vaffa had never been the type to volunteer anything.

"For free?"

"Sure," she laughed. "One is when you go outside, hold your hair back out of your eyes. The field will compress your hair to your head, tightly, as the air spaces in it are squashed out. If your hair is in your face, you won't be able to see."

"Thanks. I'll remember that."

"The second thing is to be careful when you're talking. That thing in your throat will broadcast whenever you subvocalize. If you think too hard, you might find everyone listening in."

"I'll remember it."

The corridor was round and looked unfinished. Someone had simply bored it out, not bothering about leveling the floor. Sprayed stripes of yellow and green indicated the top and bottom, and arrows directed traffic. Lilo knew it would make sense eventually, but her disorientation was nearly total after three turns. Had she gone up or down, left or right? Was the yellow stripe the floor or ceiling? Looking into the rooms that branched off the tunnel every fifty meters was no help; furniture was attached to any convenient surface.

Vaffa took her to a medico's shop. An unsmiling woman sat in a chair behind a desk attached to the rear wall.

"Mari!" Lilo started forward before she recalled. Then she felt the blood rush to her face. Her ears were burning.

"Yes, I understand you knew my clone on Luna," Mari was saying, drifting toward them. "I also know what you did to her."

"I'm . . . sorry. I—"

"Don't tell me. You didn't do anything. Number three did, I know that, and you're number four. And you didn't do it to me. Nevertheless I think you'll understand if I tell you I don't have much to say to you. Let's get on to business."

Business turned out to be mostly medical. Mari tested her and began a course of treatment that would continue as long as she remained on Poseidon, designed to overcome the effects of weightlessness. Her goal was to keep all the inmates at the standard point nine-gee muscle-tone level. Mari believed—along with Lilo—that allowing human muscles to adapt to lower gravity states was dangerous in the long run.

Lilo was given a tranquilizer to help her through the disorientation she was feeling, taken to a small cubicle, and told to sleep eight hours, after which she would be briefed on her duties at the station.

7

Poseidon base was a maze of catacombs more than forty years old. It rambled through the rock like termite trails in rotten wood, and eighty percent of it was abandoned.

Lilo had discovered the empty sections on her first full day at the station, after having been told to look around and familiarize herself with the place. Some corridors ended in mirrors. When she passed through them, her suit formed around her to give protection from the vacuum on the other side.

Poseidon had been a much larger operation when Tweed had been President, and able secretly to funnel taxpayers' money into the project. Now that he was out of office and had to rely on his own funds and those of the party, it had been cut back. Still, it was a large undertaking for one man, involving eighty adult prisoners, their children, and an indeterminate number of guards, all of them clones of the ubiquitous Vaffa.

There was no way to tell how many Vaffas there were simply because they were never all in the same place at the same time. They had their own section of the station, walled off by a nullfield that was tuned to allow them to pass, but to bar everyone else. They came in the two standard models—male and female—and they were all completely hairless. There were at least six of them, but there could have been twice that many. It was impossible to tell how they worked the watch periods and how many remained behind the impenetrable wall at any given time.

Security was unobtrusive. Everyone was free to go anywhere on the base, with the exception of the guard room, and interference was minimal as long as the assigned projects got done. Each Vaffa carried a laser sidearm. It had been learned at great cost that the guns were effective for shooting prisoners, but useless for shooting Vaffas. They would shoot through a nullfield as long as a Vaffa wasn't behind it. Some had tried to adjust their suit generators to screen out the laser frequency. That worked fine, but only outside when the field was in operation. And the air in your lung would only last thirty hours. When the rebels had to come back in, they were shot.

Lilo learned all this quickly. No one seemed reticent about discussing past escape attempts, and they were all willing to listen to what might be new ideas. But there was an answer for everything she proposed. The general opinion was that Poseidon was escape-proof. Lilo reserved judgment, but admitted to herself that it didn't look good.

"But anything's better than being in a death cell," she said.

"I suppose so. I wouldn't know."

Her companion of the moment was a man named Cathay. She had met him in the mess hall a few minutes earlier when he came to sit with her at breakfast. They were the only people in the room; it was early, and Lilo's schedule was not yet synchronized with the rest of the station.

The mess hall was one of the areas that was centrifuged, spinning slowly in a hollow in the rock. There was a larger wheel that was used as a gymnasium for running and weight lifting, and a third which held bunk rooms for those who did not like sleeping in free-fall.

Cathay was a tall, thin man. He had a lot of untidy brown hair, long legs, and a boyish face with incongruous muttonchop sideburns. He was handsome without overdoing it and Lilo liked that, felt a definite physical attraction without having actually touched or smelled him, and that was rare for her. Physical beauty was cheap and universal with cosmetic surgery, but it tended toward about a dozen standard types. Lilo was bored with them all. Any visual stimulation she got from a man was in proportion to the degree he departed from the current, stultifying fashion.

"Then you weren't kidnapped from the Institute?" she asked, mopping up the last of her maple syrup with a piece of pancake.

"I was kidnapped, but not from the Institute. I was *gene*napped."

"You mean you didn't do anything . . . well, to deserve being here? Would you like some more coffee?"

"Yes, please. What I did to end up here was to trust Tweed. I should have known better, but then who could have expected *this?*"

Lilo placed a white plastic mug in front of Cathay, then leaned back in her chair. She hooked her shoulder blades over the chair back, stretched out her legs, and held the warm mug on her belly.

"Okay," Cathay went on. "I was in trouble, admitted. But I wasn't in jail. Tweed came to me with a good offer. He said he'd . . ." Cathay stopped, then looked away from her. He glanced back once, sighed, and went on, not meeting her eyes.

"I'm a teacher," he said. *"Was* a teacher. There's no sense in trying to hide it from you. I was kicked out of the Education Association. Unjustly, I believe, but there's no way I could prove that to you." He looked up at her again. Lilo shrugged, decided that wasn't enough, and smiled at him.

"It makes no difference to me," she said. "I'm an Enemy of Humanity, remember?"

"Well, that's mostly crap, too," he said, easily. "You're not the only one here. A couple of them are really nuts, but most of them are just like anyone else. They went a little too far, but it was usually from some sort of principle." He raised his eyebrows, but Lilo was not yet ready to talk about that. Not yet; not to someone she'd just met.

"Go on."

"Well, Tweed said he could get me work again, teaching kids. I was really desperate. It had been five years. I *need* kids, I really do. Anyway, the deal was that I do two jobs for him. One was teaching the kids at some remote, unspecified place. The other—I *thought* the other was after I'd finished the *first,* you see—was to work for him on Pluto. He didn't say what kind of work, and I didn't care. After a few years, he'd let me go and see to it that I was reinstated under another name."

"So what happened?" Lilo reached over to stir another spoonful of sugar into her coffee, hoping to mask the taste. "This stuff's terrible."

"Yeah, isn't it? See, I should have been suspicious when he said he could reinstate me. That means he has access, illegally, to some pretty high-powered government computers. He can *get* things. You know what I mean?"

"Yeah. I'm afraid I do. What did he get? Your recording?"

Cathay smiled. "Uh-huh. Turns out that all along he meant for me to do both jobs simultaneously. He sent me out to Pluto, I assume. He took my recording and played it into a clone. Me."

"Shanghaied."

"Exactly. There's about ten others like me here. People who made a deal with Tweed and found themselves being awakened in a clone body."

Lilo sipped at her coffee. "That's really rotten. Doesn't he have any . . . what? Shame? Principles?"

"I don't know. When something is important to him, though, it gets done. One way or the other."

"Then the rest of the people here are like me? Condemned prisoners?"

"No. There're about fifteen. He seems to like them. The rest of the people here were stolen, as simple as that. They're scientists, most of them. Tweed decided he needed them. Apparently it's easier for him to steal their recordings and a tissue sample and grow his own scientist than to abduct the original."

"I can see the logic. This makes no waves at all. No one even knows a crime's been committed."

Cathay got up to refill their cups, and they sat in silence for a while as people drifted in for breakfast. No one joined them, but Cathay waved to many of the people.

"What no one's told me so far," Lilo said, "is why Tweed needed a genetic engineer. What will I be doing here?"

Cathay made a face. "For starters, you could breed us a better coffee plant. Can you do that?"

"Maybe," Lilo laughed. "I'm a pretty good cook, too, and it looks like you could use one. Is that why Tweed sent me here?"

"He didn't tell me why, actually. But if you can cook, he's not as ruthless as I thought."

"All genetic engineers learn to cook," she said, forcing herself to finish the coffee. "I got my start developing a thick-shelled egg plant with a double yolk for a company on Mercury. I learned a thousand ways to cook eggs so I could save on food bills and not get sick of eating them. But you really don't have any idea of why he wanted me here?"

"Maybe an idea. Most of the people here are planetary specialists, physicists, inorganic chemists, mechanical engineers, and so forth. Once every couple of months we've been running a skimmer through the atmosphere of Jupiter. We've been picking up some living organisms. They probably want you to work on that."

Lilo was fascinated, but still puzzled. It had long been known that Jovian life existed, but no one had ever studied it.

"Why me? My field isn't so much analysis as restructuring."

Cathay shrugged. "I'm not the one to ask. But don't get the idea there's anything like pure research up here. Whatever they have you doing, it'll be aimed at defeating the Invaders."

"It still doesn't sound like they would want my skills."

Cathay stood up. "What can I tell you? Tweed is sometimes more interested in the person than in the skills. That's why he robs prisons, I'm told. He wants the oddball, not the committee mind. In a way, it's like picking a gear for a machine because of its pretty color instead of because it has the right number of teeth."

"Which sounds like a hell of a way to run an army. Where are you going?"

"Out to play." He grinned. "Making my rounds. I have seventy-three pupils up here—now don't look so surprised, things are different here—and one of them is my very own second child. Ah ha! Now I've scandalized you."

"No, I . . . I'm surprised. It'll take some getting used to. Do you mind if I tag along?" Lilo had been telling the truth; she was not scandalized, but it was a shock to hear that the most basic rule of human civilization—One Person, One Child—was being violated: that an entire community of people was breeding as it wished.

They took the elevator to the hub of the cylindrical room, then entered the corridors and moved along with easy pushes of feet and hands against the walls. Lilo was getting good at it.

She had not seen that many children. The reason, she soon found out, was that they spent most of their time in the dead areas. Cathay grabbed a lamp and she followed him through one of the nullfield barriers. Soon they began to hear voices over their radios. Then they started to encounter them, in groups of two or three, intent on their own business. They seemed to like Cathay, enough so they would tolerate being introduced to a strange woman. But she had a growing sense that they had their own society down here in the abandoned caverns. Elaborate fantasies were being played out, drawn from television broadcasts and educational comics, having little to do with reality.

They were strange children. But then, she thought, they would have to be different. Many of them were growing up with brothers or sisters. How different that could make a child Lilo could barely imagine. And she finally did get a real shock when she saw one child strike a smaller one. Cathay did nothing, so she started to move in.

"Leave them alone," Cathay warned. "There's nothing you can do about that."

"But . . ."

"I know. It was very hard for me at first. But look. It's settled, isn't it?"

The fight had not gone very far, she was glad to see. But she felt strongly that the smaller one had been wronged, and said so.

"Of course he was. And he had to demean himself, back away from the fight, because he's little. You've got to understand that I'm the *only* teacher for this entire group. I can do just so much, and I've found I should concentrate on teaching them to resolve their own conflicts. It's rough justice, but so far no one's been killed."

Lilo began to understand just how different these children were.

Cathay had been a victory of sorts for the people of Poseidon. It did not show too much on the surface, but Poseidon had an extremely brutal social order. Its inhabitants had come there through abduction, or as the only alternative to death. Once there, they quickly understood that they were expected to work, and that little else mattered. The only rules were to do what you were told, and not attempt to escape. The only punishment for infractions was death.

Other than that, Tweed did not care what they did. The Vaffas conducted a constant patrol for evidence of someone trying to build a rocket drive or a radio. The first was so difficult and would take so much time and stealth that it had only been attempted once. The second was suicide, though Tweed did not rule it out. It was true that if the Eight Worlds ever heard about Poseidon, Tweed would be ruined. But it would also mean the death of everyone living there. Even the abductees were illegal clones. The confederation would have to dispose of them, regretfully, because only one person could legally exist with any given set of genes. Vaffa had never found a transmitter.

The pace of research was slow. Tweed had no intention of advertising his presence to the Invaders and the Jovians. Jupiter was watched constantly with every instrument known to science, and from time to time a probe was sent into the atmosphere. The scientists on Poseidon knew more about the giant planet than anyone in the system, but it was still not much.

The second aspect of the work on Poseidon was the search for new weapons that might be effective in the future war with the Invaders.

There was a lot of free time. The inmates were free to spend it as they wished. Eventually they began to have children, as it became clear they were there for the rest of their lives. And in time, someone had the radical notion that she didn't need to stop with one child.

Tweed had been delighted. He even sent a sociologist to study the only unlimited-breeding society outside the Rings. He hoped to use what he learned as a template for the society to come, on Earth, after the defeat of the Invaders.

But the children had caused the only organized resistance that ever had any effect. The parents got together and told Tweed they wanted teachers, or there would be no more work. The first and only strike was organized. They asked for twenty teachers. What they got was Cathay, and a promise that if they ever went on strike again they would all be killed. Tweed could do it and replace them all with a second set of clones exactly like them, but he was reluctant to do so. It would mean the loss of knowledge and skills acquired by the inmates since their last recordings.

"They tried to persuade me to be cloned, like Vaffa," Cathay said. "I'm sure it's the practical solution, but I couldn't do it. The whole idea made me sick. I don't want to be a dozen people."

"You don't have to explain it to me," Lilo said, with a shiver. "It gives me the creeps, too."

A group of five silvery children came rocketing down the corridor. They stopped long enough for Cathay to introduce them.

". . . Olympica, Cypris, and the tiny one over there is Iseult. The handsome one standing over there is my child, Cass."

Cass was a tall child. Lilo guessed his age at about twelve, then had to look closely to be sure if he was a boy, while wondering if it would ever be easy to see people whose bodies were curved mirrors. She was getting anxious to be inside again, in the air. She had not seen the faces of any of the children, only twisted reflections.

Cathay noticed her discomfort and led her back through the maze to the inhabited corridors. Lilo took a deep breath—her first in over an hour.

There was a male Vaffa waiting for them. He was idly patting his holstered weapon, and seemed to know who he was looking for.

"You're to start work this shift," he said. "Follow me, and I'll show you what I want done."

8

Tweed must have chosen me as some sort of wild card. I couldn't see what possible use I might be to his plans. Not that I was upset about it; I had no burning urge to help him defeat the Invaders. I suppose I sympathized with the goal, on an abstract level, but I just did not think it was possible. Fighting Invaders is like repealing the law of gravity.

There were workers who had much more meaningful work than I did, however. If you call that meaningful. I was shown drawings and small demonstration models of some new weapons systems that were ready to go into production, awaiting only Tweed's reelection and access to the government blank checks he had once controlled. There were some frightening new applications of nullfield theory, for instance, including one device which could project a spherical field at great distances. The idea was to enclose an Invader in one, then contract the field down to about one atomic diameter. It was hard to imagine a creature that could survive that. Then you turn off the field. Presto: a pocket H-bomb.

I saw blueprints for ships of war, the kind that hadn't been built since pre-Invasion days. And all the other bric-a-brac of warfare, from servo-powered fighting suits, to rifles and tanks and grenades, to fusion bombs and neutronium bombs. On paper, Poseidon could have outgunned any member planet of the Eight Worlds.

But what would we be shooting at?

Lilo was able to get her real work out of the way in about an hour each day. At that, she often stayed in her lab more for appearances than anything.

The first month had been interesting, from an academic standpoint. There was a backlog of atmospheric samples awaiting analysis. Lilo knew a little about the types of organic materials to be found in the Jovian atmosphere from reading about ancient research conducted before the Invasion. The chemists and plantologists on Poseidon had added to that body of information, and had picked up some spores and microorganisms. Then, about a year ago, something had impacted the scoop of the robot probe. It wasn't very big; it had massed about as much as an adult mouse. Anything larger would have wrecked the probe.

There was not much left of it on a structural level. It was a glob of jelly frozen in methane and ammonia. But on a cellular level there was much to be learned. Lilo got that out of the way in the first week, working twelve- and fourteen-hour days. She mapped the chromosomal structure present in the undamaged cells. The organism was similar in many ways to the upper-atmosphere animals that had been collected by probes on Uranus.

She worked with Chea, the inorganic specialist, to learn the chemical properties to be expected from the organism. In common with certain higher Martian life forms, upper-layer gas giant creatures had been found to utilize catalysts and polymers in ways that had been accomplished on Earth only in refineries. Her specimen was no exception. She managed to clone one of the cells at the end of her third week, when she found remnants of a reproductive system. The cell grew into a gauzy sphere filled with hydrogen that lived for a few hours in her jury-rigged Jove Chamber, then collapsed. The balloon was made of a vinyl plastic. On the underside was a thin cross-shaped swelling, which contained a bony structure.

Having done that, the rest of her work was routine. She established a tissue culture from the remains of the specimen and set about finding ways of killing it. It was completely hit-or-miss. If she had been working with a creature using a water-oxygen economy she could have found a dozen ways to attack it merely by studying its genes and synthesizing a virus. But no work had been done on genetic structures of Jovian organisms. Almost all her work on terrestrial life was done with computer calculations, and there were no programs for nonterrestrial genes. To attack them, she had to make changes almost at random at different points on the gene, then sit back to see what happened.

"But Tweed wants some kind of bug that will kill Jovians," Chea pointed out one day. "Is this going to find one?"

Lilo shrugged. "It's as likely to as anything else. But no, it's not very likely. I might come up with something that would kill *these* things. But not Jovians, if you mean the intelligent creatures down there."

She was in the farm tank with Chea, Cathay, and Jasmine, who was the chief planetologist. They were all getting their hands dirty with the new strain of pork trees Lilo had made which yielded bacon superior to what they had been eating. They knelt on the warm, black dirt and talked as they transplanted the tiny seedlings. Overhead was the brilliant central core of the farm, while beyond that was the far side of the spinning cylinder. They all wore dark goggles and their bodies were coated with UV-screening lotion and sweat. It was a happy time for all of them.

Lilo was spending most of her time farming—in the hydroponic nursery and outside on a plot of ground she had prepared to take the vacuum-resistant plants she was making. The food was already better, and she had become something of a hero with the inmates. Lilo loved working with plants, but was not so fond of cooking. She was teaching Cass and three other children how to do that. They were coming along fine, but in the meantime there were hardly enough hours in a standard day.

"You mean you don't think the Jovians are like this creature?" Cathay asked.

"I have no reason to think so," Lilo said. "And Jasmine could probably give you plenty of reasons why we shouldn't expect it."

Jasmine got another plant from the bucket and started digging a hole. She was a small woman with wide eyes and large, capable hands. She wore her blond hair in thick braids and had a collar of fur around her neck—her only surgical alteration. Cathay had been sharing a room with Jasmine for two years before Lilo arrived, and the two of them had expressed an interest in inviting Lilo to join them. Lilo wasn't sure. She had been doing well rooming with Chea, who was as capable a co-worker as she had ever found. But that phase of their relationship had ended when they finished their work on the Jovian organism. Chea was doing other work now, work that didn't involve Lilo. Since then he had not been around as much as she could have wished.

"There's no way to know for sure yet," Jasmine said, patting the dirt around the roots of her plant. "I mean if what Lilo's learning about the upper organisms will have any bearing on the ones who live deeper. But it's unlikely."

"How come?" Cathay was the perpetual straight man when the discussions got into science, but he didn't mind. He cheerfully admitted that he knew next to nothing about it. He was not a teacher of skills or knowledge, but a primary teacher: one who led children into exploring themselves, discovering and developing their aptitudes.

"We know a lot about the nature of the Jovian atmosphere," Jasmine said. "It's stratified. Hydrogen on top, then under that ammonia, ammonium hydrosulfide, water, and liquid hydrogen, all of them in various crystalline states, or melted, or diffused through each other. There's no reason to think the creature Lilo has could survive if it dropped a few hundred kilometers."

"And plenty of reason to think it couldn't," Lilo added.

"You say this thing had a hydrogen gasbag," Cathay said. "How could that keep it up if it floated in hydrogen?"

Lilo laughed. "Good question. I wondered about that myself, and I'm really not sure. I think I might have seen it in an early stage. Maybe it's born in a lower layer, makes hydrogen to fill its balloon, and rises to the sunlight. After that, it would need a new method of staying in the air. There's plenty of energy it could tap. It's a violent place."

"It's possible that Jupiter has several biospheres," Jasmine said. "They might mix a little, like Lilo's suggestion that her critter might be born at a lower level and rise to the top. But it's going to be tough to study it, especially down at the lowest levels where the Jovians probably are."

"Why do you think they're down there?"

"Well, I . . . you're right. They might live in the upper layers. But it's unlikely, I think, if only on straight probability. There are so many strata they could occupy. The probes I've sent in have identified thirty-seven distinct environments, like layers of an onion. Some of them mix in different weather conditions, which makes even more possibilities. But it's hard to imagine anything that could live in all of them. Down there at the bottom, just before my probes stop sending, is a core of hot metallic hydrogen. I don't know if anything could live in *that,* but I wouldn't take any bets that it's impossible to live in the layer just above."

"And what's in that layer?"

"It's a layer of liquid hydrogen, but it's hot. About twelve thousand degrees. Three million atmospheres pressure. And don't ask me what *kind* of life might be there. It wouldn't be like anything Lilo's ever studied. But if the Invaders and Jovians live in that stuff, all bets are off. We may never touch them."

The conversation was disturbing Lilo. She was new to the concept of weapons research; it was not something she had ever thought of before. It was not pleasant to think that your research is aimed at only one result: to kill anything you could discover.

6

After finishing her work in the lab and spending some time in the farm, Lilo would often go exploring with Cathay and Cass and Jasmine, or sometimes just with one of them. After about a month, however, Jasmine gradually lost interest. At one hundred and fifty, she was the oldest of the group. Jasmine had borne her child over a century ago, found that she wasn't really interested in children, and had not had another on Poseidon.

The situation with the three of them grew awkward. Lilo had moved in with them and things had gone well for a while. But it gradually became clear that Jasmine was more drawn to Lilo than to Cathay. Cathay was unhappy about it, and a little resentful of Lilo. Jasmine was talking about having a sex change, which further alienated Cathay since he was a confirmed male with no interest in other men. Lilo, on the other hand, liked them both. She was a female-stable personality—though not to the degree that Cathay was male-stable —and had spent only three of her fifty-seven years as a male. Jasmine was a member of the no-preference majority.

The months went by. Jasmine got her sex change from Mari. For a short while it seemed that it might work with the three of them, but eventually Jasmine drifted out of their lives. Lilo and Cathay got along well, in all but one area.

"You're crazy. We'll never get out of here until Tweed is ready to let us go."

"Which will be never." She didn't want to get into an argument with him about it, but could not help feeling aggravated at his acceptance of imprisonment. She looked at him and saw herself after ten years.

"You're right," he said. "Never. That is, unless you think there's a chance we'll find a way to defeat the Invaders—"

"And I do not, not for a—"

"—in which case we'll be welcomed all over the system as heroes. Otherwise, one of these days he's going to run out of money or get tired of the project."

"And we'll all be eliminated."

"Exactly. Surely you don't think I *like* that idea? But what the hell can we *do* about it?"

"We can devote *all our energy* to trying to do something!"

"Fine, fine. I'm all for that. What did you have in mind?"

Lilo swallowed her anger and tried to discuss it calmly with him. This is what it always came to: Give me a concrete proposal, tell me your plan. And every time she mentioned one, half-formed and highly tentative, someone would pick a million holes in it.

"I don't have anything specific," she admitted, again.

"Okay. Why don't you think about it some more and—"

"But I'll *never* get one without some *help!* Can't you see that giving up is the surest way to stay here forever? I know all my plans have been bad ones. *So far!* But I keep meeting with this fatalistic attitude. And from you! That continues to amaze me." She stopped, and calmed herself again. She had not meant to yell at him, and now he seemed hurt. She put her arms around him. He was unresponsive for a time, but gradually softened.

It was good with Cathay. He was a considerate lover, a good man, and a person she could trust.

"There are some who are working on getting away," he said. "But they're pretty much stuck, too, the last I heard. You might want to talk to them. There was one plan to move the whole damn moon. But it's crazy."

"Who? That's all I want to do; talk to people who want to get away."

"You're talking to one. We all want out. But the only ones who are still working on it that I know of are Vejay and Niobe."

Vejay hovered near the ceiling of his room, hanging by one foot, rummaging in a box of papers. The room was cluttered, all six walls holding furniture and boxes stuffed with paper.

"It's a simple principle, really," he said. "It's even been done a couple of times, in the asteroid belt. But it's not economical." He found what he was looking for—a ragged sheet of blue paper, much folded—and began to spread it in the air. Lilo twisted and came up beside him. She wrinkled her nose as she got close to him. Vejay was not very popular; on a civilized planet he would always be in trouble with the law for forgetting to bathe.

Vejay often forgot to eat, and never exercised at all. He neglected taking his booster pills to the point that he was all skin and bones, with just enough muscle to move him around in a weightless state. Mari had told Lilo he was healthy enough, as long as he never had to cope with gravity. Vejay believed in operating at an optimum state, and on Poseidon, that meant massing thirty kilos soaking wet.

There could not have been a greater contrast between Vejay and the third occupant of the room. Niobe the Dancer was a flawless physical specimen. Every muscle in her body was perfectly defined, standing out in a graceful pattern of swells and hollows all over her arms, legs, belly, and back.

"It's a good space drive," Vejay was saying. "But it only works well for something massive. The hole itself would outweigh any ship I ever heard of. The hole is on the other side, directly opposite us. Have you been over there to see it?"

"No. I've been meaning to, but I didn't think it was really important. I think I will now, though."

"You should. It's rather remarkable, being on the surface of the moon. You put one down on Luna and if something goes wrong it would just sink right through the surface and start orbiting underground. Pretty soon, no Luna."

Lilo shivered. No one really liked black holes.

It would have been easy to dismiss them as just another scientific abstraction if they had stayed decently distant from human affairs. When black holes were first postulated, it was thought that only a huge star which had burned itself out could ever form one. When the nuclear fires in the core of a star could no longer support the star's mass, gravity would take over; it would begin to collapse. Eventually it would reach a size and density that meant its escape velocity exceeded the speed of light.

But it was determined that at the creation of the universe, during the Big Bang, there were forces powerful enough to form tiny black holes, some of them being smaller than an atomic nucleus. Shortly afterward, that theory was modified. Though the holes might have been formed, they would have quickly evaporated, and would no longer be around to give human scientists headaches.

That theory had held until shortly after the Invasion, when tiny "quantum" black holes were discovered in the cometary zone, beyond the orbit of Pluto. These mysterious objects were tiny; the largest in use was only a fraction of a millimeter across. But their gravity was tremendous. If they came in close proximity to a material object, they would destroy it, and energy would be released. That energy could be captured and broadcast from the orbital power stations to receivers on the ground.

One of them had gotten away, two hundred years ago, as it was being warped into orbit around Pluto. It had drilled a ten-meter hole straight through the center of the planet. The area of destruction was much more extensive than that, with tidal disruptions and quakes as pressure forced rock to flow like warm butter and fill in behind the hole's passage.

"What keeps that from happening here?" she asked.

"It could happen," Vejay said. "But it's not a huge hole, and Poseidon's a small rock. It'd fall through slowly, and what with the irregularities we'd be able to catch it on the other side. See, look here, this is how it works."

Lilo studied the diagram as Vejay explained it to her. She had thought it an extravagance to use a black hole for the station's power supply, and her opinion was confirmed by the figures. The hole was capable of putting out enough power to run a small city; Poseidon was able to utilize only a fraction of the output, even after much of it was siphoned off to maintain the hole against the pull of gravity.

"It's just sitting out there right now," Vejay said. "It's got a nullfield under it, bowl-shaped, like this." He pointed out a hemisphere which hovered over the surface of Poseidon, open end pointed outward. "The field protects the equipment under it from overheating, or the rock from melting. Also it means you can go right up close under the thing to service the support facilities." He indicated three massive domes on the ground.

"The hole has a charge on it, and it's held up by these electromagnets. Big ones, supercooled."

"So how does this help us escape?"

Vejay cocked his head, studying the drawing as if seeing it for the first time. He looked up, baffled.

"Doesn't that nullfield hemisphere shape suggest anything to you? It's not the most efficient design—we could tune it to whatever shape we want when we take control—but it would work as it is now."

Lilo looked again. Of course, why hadn't she seen it?

"A rocket exhaust nozzle."

"You got it. The hole is just sitting down there in that bowl, which points up from the surface of Poseidon. When we dump matter in there—anything at all, but not too much of it—the hole's gravity compresses it. It compresses it so hard that any nuclear reaction you want to think of can take place. A lot of matter gets destroyed, and that means energy, which we can tap for our power needs here.

"Even at the rate we put matter into it right now, there's a slight thrust generated, since the bowl is open at the top. It's almost too small to measure when you realize the whole mass of Poseidon *and* the hole is resisting the acceleration. So what we'd do is drop rocks into the hole just like we're doing now. Only instead of using dust particles and measuring them out with an eyedropper, we'd need a conveyor belt. We'd need a steady fuel supply.

"So we've solved the *second* problem. Now all we have to do is solve the first."

Lilo frowned. "Maybe I'm slow."

Niobe laughed. "Don't worry. I thought we were on our way when I saw this, too. Vejay, you go too fast. She just got here."

"Sorry," he said. "Okay. The second problem is where do we go when we eliminate all the Vaffas. Any of the Eight Worlds would execute the lot of us as illegal clones. With this, we can go anywhere. I suggest we go *far* away."

"You're talking about interstellar travel?"

"What else? This drive would get us up close to the speed of light. We probably couldn't push it much faster than a twentieth of a gee, but we'd get there. Alpha Centauri in maybe twenty years."

"But what about the mass . . . ah. I think I see."

"We'd have enough. We use the mass of Poseidon itself, of course, just like we do now."

Lilo thought about that for a while. It was awfully damn frustrating, because, while Vejay had not mentioned the first problem, she saw what it was. It would take construction, utilization of the heavy equipment that had been used to hollow out the corridors—a myriad of details. A space drive cannot be designed and slapped together overnight.

"How long do you think it would take to get it ready?"

He shrugged. "Working hard, with no unplanned complications, I might have it working in two weeks."

And Vaffa inspected the site every day. It always came back to Vaffa.

I began to sleep badly. Meeting Vejay and Niobe had fired up my hopes, whetted my appetite for actually doing something about getting away. I was still as far from escaping as ever, but I didn't feel

like it. We had solved the easy end of the equation of freedom. The
problems all still lay ahead. At least six of them, possibly as many as
ten, all of them named Vaffa.

A Vaffa could be killed. It was difficult, but it had been done twice
over the years by desperate people. I heard both stories told a hun-
dred times. They could be ambushed and overpowered indoors. Out-
side, they were as invulnerable as their suits. Bury them alive under a
ton of rock; their suit fields would protect them and they would last
as long as their air held out—plenty of time to be rescued.

Bury them all at once? You could blow up the whole rock, but
where would that leave you?

"What are they?"

"Sugar babies. Are you kidding? How could you not know what
sugar babies are?"

But Lilo did not. They were in a large glass jar with a narrow neck
that she had discovered in Cass's hideout. Apparently he had tired of
them, but they seemed to have done well.

The bottom of the jar was covered with dark soil, and growing
from it were five dwarf elm trees, three Douglas firs, and a lot of
moss. There was a cave formed from piled rocks, and standing in the
entrance to the cave were three bipedal figures, one millimeter tall.
Their bodies were white, and the tops of their tiny heads were black.
They looked just like little people.

"It looks like they have faces," she said, leaning closer.

"You aren't kidding. You've really never seen them before."

"Never." But as she said it, she had a funny feeling that it was not
true. She shook her head, but the feeling persisted.

"Well, they do have faces. But take a closer look."

There was a magnifier embedded in the side of the jar. Lilo looked
through it, and the illusion fell apart. What looked to be hair on the
heads was just coloring of the exoskeleton, concealing multifaceted
eyes. The faces were three dots and a line. The things were seg-
mented at the joints and waist like marionettes, or like . . .

"Ants. These are ants. "

"That's what they started off with," Cass confirmed. "They
changed them. You can see the fifth and sixth legs at the waist.
They're real small."

Lilo felt sick, but could not take her eyes from the creatures. More
came from the cave, walking crazily on their hind legs, the jointed
arms waving about.

"It's repulsive," she said. She wondered if she was going to throw up.

Cass grimaced. "Yeah. I know what you mean. I got them when I was younger and now I don't know what to do with them. I can't just kill them; it wouldn't feel right."

"Tweed lets you . . ."

"We can order stuff sometimes. The kits to build these were in the supplies from Luna a few years back. All the kids made them. I wish I'd asked for cat eggs instead."

Lilo was feeling dizzy now. There was a sense of disorientation, and a growing feeling of *déjà vu*. She tried to force the memory, but it wouldn't come. Yet it was building inside her, and wouldn't be stopped.

"They can't live outside the jar," Cass was saying. "Special soil, or something, so if they get loose they can't turn into a pest. I don't guess they'll last much . . . hey, are you all right?"

"Just be quiet a minute, please? Don't say anything." She continued to stare at the tiny prisoners. Was it just the fact of their confinement? She didn't see how that could bother her so badly. She never liked to see things caged, had always avoided working with living specimens for that very reason. But that couldn't account for a reaction like this.

She went back in time, several years earlier. She knew she had looked into a bottle just like this one, at a colony of sugar babies. One time . . . no, twice. Wait. She was sure it had happened to her three times. Standing there, staring . . .

Numbers began to tumble through her head. She could see them as if they were solid objects with dimensions and mass. She began to remember.

"I helped make these," she said, softly.

"What?"

"I was on the research team that first developed this strain of ant. It was twenty-five years ago, I was working for Copernicus Biological Labs. There was me, and Thessa, and Zaire and . . . and Yao-kaha. My name's on the patent. They were a big hit for a year, they sold very well, and—" She choked it off. Cass waited silently beside her, looking worried.

Her stomach was feeling better, and the numbers were still there.

"It was a big problem," she said, as if reading from a book. "The base in the Rings was no good to me if I could tell someone where it was under interrogation. And yet I couldn't just leave it there. I had to be able to find it if I was not arrested. I had to know and yet not know."

"What are you talking about?" Cass said. "Lilo, you're giving me the—"

"Deep hypnotic suggestion," she said, as if she had not heard him. "I didn't know what I'd be up against in prison. I had to have it buried so deeply that I could die and never remember it, never know it was even there. I couldn't trust anyone to feed me the hypnotic trigger, and yet the location had to be recoverable if I wasn't arrested. So I set up the trigger stimulus keyed to something that I would encounter more or less at random. But not too often. I couldn't go through this every day, or even every week. It happened three times in five years. Each time I buried the knowledge again."

"The sugar babies made you remember something?"

She looked at the creatures again. The choice had been apt. Pitiful little things. Did they try to get out of their bottle? She could not have known she would survive her own execution when she was making her plans, and it had been sheer luck to encounter the sugar babies on Poseidon. But she knew.

"I know. I know where it is."

10

The rumors had been going around for a month; there was finally going to be a trial run, an actual test of one of the possible weapons in the war with the Invaders. When Lilo heard what it was to be, she could not credit it. Surely Tweed would not do *that*.

But shortly it was official. Everyone was worried, but no one could think of a way to stop it. Tweed was going to remove the black hole from the other side of Poseidon, let it pass *through* Jupiter, then sit back and see if there was any reaction. The general consensus on Poseidon was that if there was a reaction, it would not be necessary to radio the news to Tweed. The whole system would hear about it soon enough.

Lilo talked it over with Niobe and Vejay, then spent hours with Cass and Cathay. They were all frightened. The question Lilo wanted to resolve was what approach to take. Cathay felt that any attempt to stop the project would be suicide, and said the best they could do was hope the Invaders would ignore it. After all, it was a big planet. It might not hit any of them on the way through.

Lilo strongly disagreed, and was backed up by Niobe, Vejay, and Cass.

"You know what I think?" Lilo asked. "I think the time is never going to be better to try and take over Poseidon."

She waited for the reaction to die down. She was breathing hard, determined to get her point across. If only she could convince them, perhaps she could convince herself. She did not wish to die, and what she was proposing looked dangerous, even to her.

"What I'm saying is, what better time is there to go for broke than when it looks like the alternative might be just as bad? I'm willing to take the chance. What about you?"

The discussion went on into the night, and proved inconclusive. The best Lilo could get was an agreement to discuss the situation further, and pledges of support if she could come up with a plan.

She had one, but it was barely formed. It would have to depend on circumstances as they evolved, but it seemed as though the first necessary step in any plan was to be aboard the ship which would position the hole for its drop into Jupiter. If she could do that, there was time to think of a way to steal the ship and return for the others.

So she approached Vaffa about the possibility of using the ship for the launching of another biological probe. She argued that it would make sense to combine the two missions. The electromagnetic tug could first release the hole on a course to pass through the center of Jupiter, then make a slight trajectory change to position an instrument package for an atmosphere-grazing path.

After conferring with her clones and consulting the guidelines Tweed had given them, Vaffa okayed the project. Lilo said that she would need someone to help her, and suggested Vejay. Vaffa quickly vetoed him, on the grounds that he did not have a good reputation. Lilo hastily named Cathay as an alternative. She didn't want Vaffa thinking there was an escape being planned.

She was counting on the fact that, while Tweed might know very well what she would do in terms of planning and preparation, he could not predict how she might react when confronted with an unplanned opportunity. Her policy was to put herself in a place where such an opportunity might occur.

She told Vejay to come up with a means whereby Cathay could kill or disable the pilot of the tug, and, with any luck, take control of the ship. She intentionally made no plans to get rid of Vaffa. Not only did it seem impossible, but she was convinced that planning had to work against her rather than for her. The whole thing would have to be played by ear. She would get onto the ship and remain alert for an opening.

She did her best not to think about it much, because when she did it sounded insane.

Tweed surprised them all, and almost ruined everything. The conspirators assembled hastily when Lilo got the news of what was actually going to happen.

"That's what comes of relying on rumors," Niobe said.

"We should have thought of it," Vejay complained. "We would have been hard up for power here if he'd used our black hole. The standby fusion generator would have carried us, but it would have been tight."

"I just didn't think he cared enough to worry about that," Niobe said.

What Tweed had done was to buy a second hole on the open market at Pluto. It was on its way to Luna to become the ninth orbital power station, but what no one in authority knew was that Tweed planned to pass it through Jupiter before that happened.

It was neat, it was economical; it was typically Tweed. Whenever possible he carried out more than one plan of action with every move he made. The hole, in orbit around Luna, would be enormously profitable to him, so the expense of the project would be justified and absorbed. The huge electromagnetic tug which had accelerated the hole at Pluto would let it go on one side of Jupiter, wait for it to pass through, and pick it up on the other side.

Lilo pointed out to Vaffa that it would still be possible to use the small rocket scooter based on Poseidon to rendezvous with the larger ship as it passed them. Vaffa thought it over, and eventually agreed. The Vaffas might have suspected some sort of plot, but felt secure enough about the scooter. It had the peculiar property of exploding if it passed a certain distance from the gravity well of Jupiter: another of the innumerable precautions against escape.

The scooter was a standard model, little more than an engine with

a framework of seats attached. Three of the four seats were filled
with silvery bodies as Vaffa matched velocity with the mammoth tug.

They had come in laterally from the front, allowing the tug to
catch up with them. None of them wanted to get anywhere near the
aft end of the other ship. Somewhere back there, suspended by invisible lines of magnetic force, was a black hole smaller than a pinhead
but massing as much as a medium-sized asteroid. It would not do to
get too close to it.

Lilo was trying to juggle all the factors in her head, looking for the
chance which, when it came, might last only a fraction of a second.
One crew member in the tug. Vaffa the only one in communication
with him. The homemade gas capsule hidden in the atmosphere
probe, the probe strapped to the outside of the scooter. Vaffa's
weapon strapped to his side. Times and courses: twenty minutes to
castoff, when the tug would let go of the hole and pull away from it;
thirty minutes to the course change that would put the probe on the
right trajectory to graze the Jovian atmosphere.

Cathay was to try to get into the tug first—the lock would take only
one person at a time. After that, it was up to him. If he gassed the
man inside, they were committed to trying to overpower Vaffa. They
might do it, with the help of surprise.

Ten meters away, Vaffa cast a magnetic line to the tug and warped
the scooter in close. The three of them jumped free and began to lash
the scooter. Lilo saw Cathay move toward the compartment where
the gas bomb was hidden, and tried to get between him and Vaffa.

"I know what you're doing," Vaffa said quietly.

"Inspection," Lilo said, desperately. "We have to—"

"Let me see that." He was reaching for his laser.

Lilo put one foot on the scooter and dived at him. Her head hit
him in the stomach, doubling him up. She saw the laser swing by her
face, his grip loosened for a moment. She chopped at his wrist, and
the gun fell away from them, spinning free.

"The lock!" she cried. "Get in the lock! Hurry!" She couldn't see
if Cathay was moving. Vaffa swung at her chin, but the force of his
blow turned his body enough so that he missed her. It had been in-
stinctive, but the wrong thing to do in weightlessness. He saw his mistake and was about to switch tactics when he realized he had moved
out of reach of the ship and scooter. He grabbed for Lilo's foot as it
came by him, just as she reached for a strut on the scooter. He pulled,
she kicked, and her hand lost its grip. The two of them drifted away
from the scooter, not fast, but there was no way back under their
own power. Unless . . .

Lilo kicked again, hitting him in the jaw. He hung on desperately until she had to stop because she was no longer facing the ship. Her idea was to push him from her and get back that way. But he saw it, too, and as soon as she stopped kicking he started to climb her leg. In another second he would be pushing *her* away from the ship.

She kicked again, shaking him back to her ankle, and kept on kicking, this time with both feet. His ribs seemed to crunch under her heel as she connected. Savagely, she aimed for the same spot again. He doubled over in pain, and his hand released her. She was floating free, spinning very slowly.

It didn't look too bad, if Cathay could get control of the ship. She saw Vaffa turning end over end at about one revolution per second, then she spotted the tug. She had drifted about fifty meters away from it. It was impossible to tell yet which way she was moving.

Then she heard Vaffa calling the ship.

"Cathay! He's talking to the pilot. You've got to get him before he can call back to Poseidon and tell them what's happened, or . . ." She stopped, realizing he wouldn't be able to hear her if he was in the ship and in a position to do anything about it. If he wasn't in the ship, it was all over anyway.

Three long minutes dragged by. The only thing Lilo learned for sure was that she was not getting closer to the ship. She was moving away. And she didn't care for the direction, either. Ahead of her, Jupiter was growing, filling the sky with the round circle of the tug exactly centered in it, seen from the stern. Somewhere in the direction she was moving was a black hole.

"You'll get there first," she yelled, feeling lightheaded. "How does it feel, Vaffa?"

There was no reply for a while. The voice that finally came was strained, full of pain.

"Why did you do it?"

"I don't think I could explain it to you. But it almost worked. Still might. I've got my fingers crossed."

There was no answer. Lilo thought she heard a moan. In a few seconds she was sure of it. There was an incoherent noise that stood her hair on end even after she had identified it. It was a subvocalized scream, picked up by the voder in Vaffa's throat and amplified as sheer agony. Then silence. Lilo began to worry. She hadn't hit him *that* hard.

"Lilo? Can you hear me? Are you alive?"

"Yes, I'm here! You got in!"

"It took me a while to get my radio tuned to the suit frequency.

Damn, I wish it was you in here. All these buttons scare me." They had trained him for hours on mock-ups Vejay had built. He could punch in a course, if it came to that, and as long as nothing went wrong he could fly it.

"Never mind about that. You've got to cut the hole loose, and fast. I think Vaffa's dead, and I'm afraid what killed him was the magnetic field interfering with his suit generator. I'm not enough of a physicist to know just what a powerful magnetic field can do, but it didn't sound pleasant. Can you . . . I mean, in a *hurry,* you understand? I don't know how long it will be—" She stopped herself when she realized she was panicking.

"Just a minute. I'll do it." She heard him muttering to himself, then a cry of triumph. "There. They're all reading zero. Did that do it?"

"I'll know in a minute. Now we've got to think fast. Neither of us wants to fall into the thing. You're going to have to move the ship a little farther out. Vejay said the gravity field of a hole is very weak at just a small distance, but it increases sharply the closer you get to it. I'll be all right. But you have to save the ship so we can get back and—"

"It's too late for that. I didn't have time to tell you, but the pilot talked to Poseidon before I gassed him. They know we've taken over. They'll be waiting for us. It's no good, Lilo." She could hear him choking. Oh, God. Vejay and Niobe and Cass, waiting outside on the chance Lilo and Cathay would return in control of the tug . . .

"Cathay, we talked about that. They know what to do. If they're suspected of anything, they'll hole up with Cass and wait it out. We've *got* to get away now, so we can come back with some weapons we can *use.*"

"You're right. We—"

Everything seemed to happened at once. There was a bright flash behind Lilo. She started to turn, thought better of it. It had to be Vaffa impacting the hole, being condensed by the awful gravity into degenerate matter, releasing all the energy stored in the atoms of his body as raw radiation.

That was bad enough, but ahead of her the tug was moving. A thin spear of light shot from it, angled away from her, and the engines continued to burn.

Jupiter had swallowed up the sky. It was beautiful. Even knowing it would be her death, Lilo had to admit that. And she preferred it to the hole, though her death would not be as quick.

From the time two hours earlier when the tug's autopilot had performed its preset maneuver (the details, the endless details; how could she have thought of them all?), Lilo had been overcome with a paralyzing lethargy, a certainty of death. Not that she hadn't struggled against it; she and Cathay had talked over every possible chance of escape. But when the background of stars began to swing around her in a direction she could account for in only one way, she knew her fate was sealed. She had missed the hole, but not by enough.

Vaffa had missed it, too, but by an even smaller margin. His body had come close enough to be compressed into a speck too small to see except for the light of its annihilation. It lasted only a second, then dispersed into space.

Lilo had not come that close. A hole could be a dangerous thing, though not so much from the danger of falling into it. That was very unlikely, since it was so tiny and the space she floated in was so vast. But a near-miss could be fatal. The strength of the gravity field changed sharply as one neared the hole. If Lilo had fallen into a close, hyperbolic orbit around it, the tidal strains induced by the hole's gravity attracting different parts of her body with varying strength would have torn her apart. Or if she came close enough, as Vaffa had done, the gravity could collapse her body to a pinhead-sized mass of neutronium.

She had been lucky, in a way, but not lucky enough. She would remain far enough away from it to stay alive, but she was definitely in a slow orbit around it.

She had discussed it calmly with Cathay. He was going to try getting her with the scooter until she told him what she had seen when the tug boosted. The acceleration had torn the fragile scooter from its moorings and it had come apart. Then he wanted to move the tug in close, but that was out of the question. Even a superbly skilled pilot would not have dared to get that close to the hole.

In a way, Cathay was suffering worse than she was. He still had choices to make, things to do, and none of them was easy. Lilo spelled it out to him with the detached brutality of one whose fate is certain.

"You can't go back to Poseidon; not now. They'll be waiting for you. You have to hope that Cass and the others are okay. You have to go to Saturn. Go to the coordinates I told you, and sit tight. Broadcast on the frequency I gave you. Parameter is not likely to have moved far from the lab, even in a year. I'm out there, somewhere. You have to find me, and Parameter. They'll help you. You have the tug. You can get weapons somehow. Then come back for the children. Come back, Cathay."

"I will. But I don't want to leave. I can't leave you here."

"You have to. I don't want you listening in when . . . when the end comes. I don't want that." She felt the panic just below the surface, and made her voice as hard as possible. "Now *go*. You did everything you could."

It was not until she noticed a faint pressure on her back that she began to wonder *how* she was going to die.

The pressure built with incredible rapidity. She was slicing straight into Jupiter's atmosphere, like a meteor, but the suit was going to protect her. An orange glow built up around her, became so bright that she could see nothing else. Her spinning motion stopped as aerodynamic forces stabilized her with her back to the planet, arms and legs pulled out in front of her by the drag. The deceleration built up steeply, but she knew she could take a tremendous amount with the suit lung feeding oxygen into her blood.

The suit became rigid. Now the tugging sensations at her feet and hands were gone. The only sensation of motion was the feeling that her belly was trying to meet her backbone. The skin on her face was drawn tightly to the sides, and her breasts were trying to find new homes in her armpits.

She had no way of knowing how long it went on. There must have been a blackout in there, though she did not recall going under or waking up. But the pressure had stopped. She had reached terminal velocity for the upper atmosphere, and was now falling under the pull of gravity, almost weightless. She looked around for the hole, which should have been visible as it sucked in the surrounding gases. Then she remembered that the atmosphere would not have slowed the hole at all; it would be halfway through the planet by now. So it would definitely be Jupiter that killed her.

The air was clear, with towering clouds rising around her. From time to time she felt sharp surges of acceleration as the winds caught her and moved her sideways.

It was a timeless thing, the falling. At first she had followed old habits, speculating on how long it would take her to reach the dark clouds below, what the temperature outside her suit field might be, at what point the density of the gases might cause her to float instead of fall. But she became content just to observe. It was a staggering sight. If she had to die, she could do worse than meet death in such surroundings, alone.

That didn't last. She reached the cloud layer and visibility dropped to zero. There was nothing to see but the silvery hand she held in front of her face to assure herself she had not already died. She wondered if it would be possible to die and not know it.

It began to annoy her that her mind would not stop working. With nothing to do and nothing to see, she began speculating again. What would kill her? Would she survive it all, and live until her oxygen supply ran out? That should be an easy death, gradually losing consciousness and never waking up.

She remembered the exhaust valve on her suit, the metal flower below her collarbone through which waste gas and heat was pumped from her body. It was made from a very tough alloy, but it could heat up, jam, melt—any of a number of things. Death would be quicker that way, and possibly more painful. But there was nothing she could do about it. She felt a momentary regret that she would not make it to the layer of hot liquid hydrogen. That would have been something to see.

Later, more soberly, she realized it would probably be as dull as this lousy cloud layer she was passing through.

But now she burst out of the cloud layer. A vast, dim space lay open beneath her. At that, it was still much brighter than she would have expected from the thickness of the cloud layer above.

For some reason, her fear returned then with paralyzing intensity. There was nothing she could do to prevent it. Some part of her mind had taken another look at her situation, concluded she had no hope of surviving, and did not want to accept it.

She suffered another blackout, or an episode of insanity. The clouds were much closer now, a blend of red and violet shapes fringed with bright sparks—(*white, with fluffy gray bottoms*)—tumbling and boiling like a cauldron of electric eels.

There were some yellow shapes just visible, darting from the cloud bank below her—(*above me, floating in a blue sky*)—into the clearer air, then back into obscurity. They were almost certainly alive. She wondered if they were Invaders, or members of the intelligent Jovian race, or simply animals.

(*The ground beneath me was soft, yielding. I grabbed a handful of it; it trickled through my fingers. Sand. I writhed deeper into it, trying to bury myself. A breeze cooled my body, and blew the soft white clouds past me in the blue sky. A yellow shape darted from one of the clouds*)—and back into the cloud bank again. They were getting closer. Her detached calm had returned to her now, and she wondered if they would try to eat her. It made her eyes hurt to try to look at them—

*(Left, right, receding from me, then . . . Ouch! My eyes crossed,
and my head started to hurt. I buried my face in my hands, welcoming
the hurting grit I rubbed over my face. I rolled in the sand, over
and over, hard beneath me, wetness, sliding)*—it was rising, coming directly
at her. Her eyes could not define its shape. In the center of it, if
it could be said to have a center, was a hole, and in the middle of the
hole was a tree—*(a tree)*—and the feeling of sand in her mouth, water
—*(rushing over me, rolling me, pulling, in my mouth and nose)*—salt
and sand and a roaring noise. Disorientation, time running sidewise,
nausea building in the pit of her stomach—

*I stood up in the surf and swayed drunkenly, naked, soaking wet,
dizzy. I took a step and fell over as the ground lurched. On hands
and knees, I vomited into the foamy water. I began to crawl, dazed,
my whole attention focused on the wet strands of hair dangling down
in front of me, swaying back and forth. I saw my hands grip the sand,
and they might have belonged to someone else.*

The sun was setting. It was the most glorious thing Lilo had ever
seen.

She huddled under a clump of windblown shrubbery, hugging her
legs close to her. The wind was coming off the sea, and it was cold.
Her teeth chattered. It was possible that she would freeze to death
before the night was over, and she had no idea of what to do about it.

It was impossible for her to recall when she had decided that she
was not dead, that this was not the afterlife. For many hours she had
sprawled in the sand, insensible, her mind overloaded with too many
impossible things. Rational awareness had returned only gradually,
cautiously, ready to retreat at any moment.

The cold had helped. Awareness of discomfort had forced her to
marshal her wits, to crawl into the thin shelter of the tree, to draw
her body into compactness to combat the chill.

Looking out over the ocean with the sun setting behind her, it had
come to her that she knew where she was. Stars came out one by one
and flickered weakly. So they *did* twinkle, it wasn't a fairy tale for
kids.

Night fell, and after many hours of shivering and growing hunger,
something rose over the water. It was Luna.

She was sitting on the continent of North America, looking out
over the Atlantic Ocean.

The land was flat. Lilo had been walking south along the beach for
several hours. Once she had gone inland a few hundred meters, but

the ground was soft and wet and clouds of insects rose to torment her. Her skin was dotted with welts.

Thus far she had no real plan except to keep moving. She hoped to find some sort of shelter, and possibly plants that she could eat. She had studied some green berries and a type of brown seaweed, tasted both, and moved on. It would take a lot more hunger to drive her to that. The idea of trapping and eating animals was one she was avoiding. All the meats she had ever eaten came from mutated plants. She had not yet considered that she might not be able to catch anything. Part of her mind could not stop thinking that this was a disneyland beneath the Lunar surface. It would be easy to believe that, except for the constant heaviness she felt. Her ankles and calves were throbbing from the gravity and the constant sliding of the sand underfoot.

The beach narrowed to a point; the north arm of a large bay lay to the west. She sank down on the sand and looked across to the land on the other side. It was too far to swim, so she had to decide if she should retrace her steps or strike out along the inside of the bay. There was no way to tell from where she sat if it really was a bay, or if she was on an island.

It was a shock to realize how tired she was. Her head was spinning, and she felt overheated. The sand felt very good as she stretched out on it and rolled over on her side to shield her face from the sun. In minutes, she was asleep.

Lilo woke to pain such as she had never known.

She came to her feet screaming, feeling that she was on fire, frantic to put it out. But touching herself only brought more pain.

Nothing in her life had prepared her for it. The few times she had hurt herself the pain had been easily controllable; help had been as near as the first-aid terminal on every corner. When the pain had gone on for fifteen minutes and gave no sign of abating, she became hysterical and ran blindly down the beach until she fell.

After a while she noticed something. It hurt just as badly as before, but it could be lived with. She sat up, wiped the tears away, and examined herself. She was cherry-red from her ankles to her shoulders. She had received first-degree radiation burns all over her backside.

It had not occurred to her that this could happen on Earth. The atmosphere was supposed to act as a shield against ultraviolet radiation, or else how could life survive? Never had she needed to think about the possible harmful effects of sunlight. The only times she had encountered it, she had been either in a suit or beneath screening plastic in a public solarium.

She could see there were lessons she had better learn.

The land was less marshy now. After following the beach along the inside of the bay for a while, she had decided to go overland when the beach began to curve westward. There had been nothing edible by the water; she hoped for better luck inland.

Lilo noticed that when she moved due north—or as nearly so as she could estimate—she encountered little difficulty. If she went east or west the ground was interrupted with large pits. The trees and underbrush obscured her view of the area, so it was not until she mounted a small hill and could look down that she realized she was moving through the remains of a city. She had been walking down a broad avenue. On either side were regular rows of pits, most of them choked with brambles and half-full of water. Houses had been there, and now nothing was left but the slope-sided basements.

The destruction had been methodical, but not absolutely thorough. There was evidence of subterranean artifacts, half-buried objects of concrete and stainless steel. She found one twisted section of copper pipe sticking two meters out of the ground.

She walked all day, and when there was only an hour of daylight left she came to a place where the bay narrowed and seemed to be more like a river. It astounded her to realize how little she could tell about the land by actually being there and walking on it. The land across the river looked much the same as what she had already seen. Some of it was less than a kilometer away, but there was more in the distance. She couldn't tell if the closer land was an island in the river or a point curving around from the other shore.

But there were two small islands in the middle of the water before her, and she was sure they were artificial. Looking closer at the hill she stood on, she discovered masonry. There had once been a suspension bridge crossing the river; she was sure of it.

She went down the hill and explored its sides, hoping to find the entrance to any hidden room that might be there. Darkness was approaching, and she hoped to find some kind of shelter. But there was nothing.

A large spotted cat looked down at her from the branches of a tree. Aside from sea gulls and crabs, it was the first animal life she had encountered. Lilo knew something about animal species, but was unable to place this one. It seemed to have jaguar blood in it, but was more the size of an African lion. She turned her back on it and started off again.

Something made her turn around.

She saw the cat out of the corner of her eye, then face to face. It was on the ground, running at her with impossible speed. Its head zoomed larger and larger in her vision. It opened its mouth and leaped.

Things happened too fast for Lilo to follow. She remembered hearing the sound of an impact, and the cat hitting her, knocking her over. There was a confused vision of the cat gnawing at its hind leg, and blood spurting out around a long wooden shaft. Then the cat was up and moving, and so was Lilo. The next thing she remembered was being three meters up in a tree with her hands bleeding.

There was a human down there, struggling with the cat. It had him by the arm, and he was hacking at it with a small ax. She saw the cat fall away, and the man straighten. He glanced up at her, then down at his forearm and at the cat, with its head split open, still twitching. Lilo slowly came down from the tree.

"You're only a boy," she said in surprise. He glanced at her again, nervously, but apparently without comprehension. She began to wonder if he really was a child.

He was short, not even two meters tall. He could have stood under Lilo's outstretched arm. His hair was blond and he wore brief leather garments and shoes. She dug through her memory of ancient racial types, and decided he was Scandinavian. His face was long, with a high forehead.

"Thank you for what you did," Lilo said. "But you don't understand, do you?"

He looked up at her and smiled. Three of his front teeth were missing.

"I don't think I've ever seen anything as dirty as you are," Lilo said. "Except possibly me." She kept her voice friendly, and the fact was that she was not afraid of him. Then she wondered if she ought to be, and moved back a step. She had made two mistakes already, with the sun and the cat, and didn't want him to be the third. She tried to remember something about primitive tribes on Old Earth. The few scraps she could recall did nothing to make her think she could trust him.

He said something, and she thought she could recognize a few words. He nodded and grinned at her, made a few gestures that confused her until he pointed at the sun repeatedly.

He was speaking a corruption of American, and probably talking of the approaching night. Lilo was delighted. American was supposed to have come from the same roots as English, or was it the other way around? Lilo was not a student of history. But she did know that her own System Speech was a mix of English and Russian roots. She thought she could learn to talk to him.

She decided to follow him to see if he had food and shelter he would share. He seemed to approve when he looked back and saw her. She had to keep reminding herself that he could be dangerous, especially if he was going back to a tribe of others like him. But the fact was that she had no instincts to make her wary of strangers. The thought of him doing violence to her was so foreign that she soon forgot about it.

He took her to a concealed cavern. It was reached by concrete stairs beneath a thicket of bushes, and was large and flat on the inside. She thought at first that it was a basement that had retained its roof, but when he lit a fire she saw the place for what it was: The design of a train station for short-range rapid transit was still very much the same in Luna.

Lilo was wondering what to expect of the man. Her knowledge of the lives and customs of barbarous peoples was near zero. She did, however, recall some stories of how women had occupied a social position distinctly different from men, back in the days before routine sex changing had obviated the whole question. She wondered if he would want to cop, then, with a shock, wondered if he felt it might be his right to do so. He would get a big surprise in that case, she promised herself.

But he seemed a little in awe of her. He kept glancing at the hair on her lower legs, and when she stood up he gaped as he looked at her. Lilo soon discovered that he was in pain from his wounds. She looked at his injured arm. He didn't protest, and when she smiled encouragingly, he smiled back. It didn't look serious—just four deep punctures and a few ragged cuts.

Once again she had to stop herself. Such a wound on Luna would be of absolutely no consequence once the pain had been stopped. Here, it might take days to heal.

His name was Makel, and five days later he was dead.

The wound never healed. He tended it with water and various leaves and ointments, but each day it grew worse. It began to stink.

Lilo now understood her oversight, and cursed her stupidity. But considerations of sterility were as alien to her as the predatory instincts of the wild cat that had nearly killed her. Luna had been, from the very first, a germ-free environment. Rubber gloves, face masks—even boiled water, which she might have used to treat him—were unknown in Lunar surgery.

He remained vigorous until the last day, ignoring the spreading infection. Every day he hunted, and she went along with him. There was not time to learn a great deal from him, but she picked up some basic survival tactics. She learned to be always alert. It was a different world out there, and it would kill her if she gave it the chance. She learned which berries and fruits to eat, which roots to dig.

Finally he collapsed in a fever. She stayed with him, wiping the sweat from his brow, giving him sips of water when he asked for them. She stripped him and bathed him, and found that her first impression had been correct. He was not an adult, but not a child, either. He must have been in his early teens.

In the middle of the night she discovered that he was cold. She had no way of knowing how long he had been dead.

Lilo cradled his head in her lap and rocked back and forth, crying quietly. She had never seen a human die. She kept trying to tell herself that it wasn't her fault, but she never did believe it.

11

Gold. Everything was yellow gold.

I floated in the dim light, aware, detached from everything but the single color. The liquid began to drain from the tank and still I floated, dry, in midair.

A shock came and made me aware of sixteen needle-tiny sources of agony; my arms and legs jerked convulsively but my heart did not start beating. Then a familiar sensation: I had banged one of my knees.

Another shock, and my heart thumped. I was alive, and about

time, too. I'd rather have died than go through another shock. I took
a breath and was choked by racking coughs. I bumped my head on
the lid of the tank and drew cold hands away from the lump to find
they were streaked with blood. Some had run into my left eye, tinting
the gold with pink.

The cover of the tank popped with a wet hiss of rubber seals.
There was a strap around my middle and I fumbled over it with
hands that felt like inflated rubber gloves. As I sat there massaging
my wrinkled feet, the rest of my senses crept up on me and made me
sick. I wanted to spit out my tongue.

My fingertips and the soles of my feet looked ancient, mummified.
I tried to get my eyes to focus around the room, squinting, wiping
away the blood—

"Who the hell are you?"

The room was small, never meant to hold three people. Luckily,
no one had to sit down in free-fall, not even Lilo, who was so weak
she could not have lifted her arms in a gravity field. She floated,
warming her hands around a tube of broth. She took tiny sips from
the nipple, having found out what disaster she faced if she tried to
drink it faster.

"I think you lost me again," she said, tiredly. More than anything,
she wanted to go back to sleep. Her head was throbbing, and the
voices sounded fuzzy. "What year is it, did you say?"

Cathay sighed, which irked Lilo and made it harder than ever for
her to believe what he had told her. The story was incredible enough
without having to believe her dead clone had loved this man.

But Parameter went on with infinite patience.

"The year is 571, the month of Capricorn. You were arrested in
Sagittarius, 568, and executed one year later. That is, your clone was
executed, according to Cathay. The original Lilo lived for a short
time after that, then she was killed, too. A second clone—apparently
already prepared, if the times are to add up right—"

"That's Tweed's standard procedure," Cathay put in.

"Yes. The second clone was killed escaping, like the original
Lilo. The third clone was sent to Jupiter, where she met Cathay and
was—"

"Yes, yes, I remember that part all right," Lilo said. Actually she
did not want to hear someone say again that she had been killed. The
details of her clone's adventures on Poseidon were murky to her.
That could be straightened out later.

"Now, why the. . . . It seems like I should have been awakened here sooner. What happened?"

Parameter paused, seeming to sense that Lilo was disturbed by the story.

"Maybe we should let you get some rest before we go on."

Lilo looked up. Parameter/Solstice was a comic figure, a human sculpted by a child out of green Silly Putty. The only visible part of Parameter's body was her mouth, from which Solstice had retracted so her partner could speak to the others. The figure had bulging hips, a narrow waist, and no neck; just a huge lump of Solstice's body that covered the head and shoulders. But Lilo was not laughing. Unlike most humans, she was a little in awe of the perfect symmetry they represented.

"No, go on. I'll rest later. But thanks."

"Very well. You're in a clone body; you knew that and you expected it. But it isn't the clone body you left behind seven years ago, when you set up this station. That one died."

"What? Why?"

"Are you sure you want to go on? I can see this is upsetting you."

There was nothing she wanted more than sleep, but she was determined to plow on. It was important to know the extent of the situation, frightening though it might be.

"We don't know why, really. When we arrived, it was dead. You said that might happen, but you didn't say what to do. We went over our discussions with you and concluded we had agreed to awaken you. The trick was in defining what that meant. We decided we had an obligation to produce another clone, and awaken *it*. We weren't very experienced with your machines, so the waking up was a problem, I fear . . ."

"No, don't worry. You did very well, considering. So I'm the second one. Let's see, with the three that were grown on Luna, and my original body, that makes—"

"I'm afraid not," Parameter said. "We studied the problem carefully before we started growing another clone, but I guess we had to learn as we went along. The second clone was a failure. It died when we tried to awaken it. You're the third. Cathay helped. He arrived here three months ago."

"By now," Cathay added, "there's certainly another clone of you on its way to Poseidon."

Lilo crouched over the computer console. Five days had passed since her awakening and she was feeling much better, physically.

Careful exercise had strengthened her muscles, though she knew she was still far from full health.

The capsule was getting too damn small. Not that Parameter/Solstice took up much room; they seemed content to stay in one spot all day; they didn't move just to be in motion. But Cathay was another story.

She took a perverse satisfaction in the fact that she disliked Cathay. It had shaken her to hear him tell of Tweed's methods for ensuring the loyalty of his agents. It was not pleasant to hear that she could be so predictable. But the last Lilo had liked this man, or so he said. Perhaps she had even loved him. Well, goddam it, this Lilo did not.

"Can't we at least talk about it some more?" he said, quietly. "Nothing is solved by your being like this."

"There's nothing to solve, as far as I'm concerned." She was at the computer on the pretext of finding out what had gone wrong with her first two clones raised in the capsule. Actually, she was too angry to concentrate on the figures that flew by on her screen. She was there so she could turn her back on him.

"You're really going through with it." He sounded as tired as she felt. Relenting for a moment, she realized it must be hard for him, too. He remembered her clone. He'd had a relationship with her, before her death. Now Lilo had changed that picture.

"Yes, I am. You haven't given me any alternative, because—"

"It's the chance to save a lot of people who mattered to you . . . I take that back. They would matter to you, if you met them."

"Damn it, you could say that about half the human race! Think what you're asking me to do. Okay, it sounds cold, but the fact is these people are nothing to me."

"Not even your clone? There'll be another there by now."

"Yes," she whispered, angrily. "You've kept reminding me of that, haven't you? *But she is not me.* I have no more obligation to her than to anyone else. I feel sorry for her. But frankly, the thought of meeting her makes my skin crawl." She turned back to her console and sighed. All right, she thought, one more time. Then if he doesn't drop the subject I'm going to kick his ass out the lock.

"I've admitted that the thought of taking that moon and leaving the whole damn system attracts me. It's an insane idea, but it's radical enough to solve all my problems—if it *works.* You've given me no reason to think it will. You're asking me to risk my life—which I have gone to extraordinary lengths to preserve—on the longest gamble I ever heard of. You tell me that isn't so."

Cathay was silent. He would never look at her when she got to this point, and she knew that meant he agreed with her.

"I'm not disputing that the drive would work. I know it has in the past. I'm saying that with the security you've described to me . . . with this . . . this *Vaffa* thing, this obscenity that pretends to be a human being—and a *dozen* of them . . ." She couldn't go on. The situation he had described to her on Poseidon was so utterly repulsive. She took a deep breath to calm her nerves.

"You tell me how we can get around Vaffa and set up the drive. Then I'll consider what you suggest."

"The other Lilo . . ." Cathay trailed off. "Well, she was talking in terms of laser rifles. If we could attack them indoors, when their suits are off—"

"I've never fired one. Have you?"

"No," he admitted miserably. He glanced up at her. His look told her that she was not the Lilo he had known. Well, she had been trying to tell him that for days. After several awkward minutes of silence he got up and went outside to be alone.

"I've fired one," Parameter said, suddenly.

"Have you?" Lilo asked. She wondered what had prompted the statement. Parameter seldom spoke for no reason. "Are you a good shot?"

"The best," Solstice said. When Solstice used Parameter's vocal cords to speak, she used a lower-pitched voice. It was startling until you got used to it. "I never miss. My reflexes and powers of calculation are much better than human."

"I know that. But would that make a difference? Would you be able to kill all the guards before they got you?"

"No."

"I didn't think so. Face it, we're outnumbered. I'll bet each one of those monsters is almost as good as you are. And Cathay and I would be useless."

"Yes." The pair was quiet, but Lilo suspected they were conversing with each other rapidly. It should be interesting when they got through. She was not disappointed.

"It's possible," Parameter said.

"Yeah? You as much as said a fight would be hopeless."

"We never said that. We said we could not win a battle with laser rifles. We've thought of another approach. We won't be going, of course. There's nothing in interstellar space to interest a pair. Not enough sunlight."

"Obviously." Lilo sighed, and rubbed her fingers through her hair.

She winced, and massaged her arm. She was still subject to cramps and spells of weakness. "Well, I'll admit there's no other alternative that attracts me. I had some vague idea of . . . well, of pairing and going out into the Rings. That's what I had in mind when I set up this station. Now that it's actually happened, though . . . I mean, now that I'm actually living in a clone body . . ."

"You're afraid," Parameter finished. "I'm not surprised."

"I'm sorry."

Parameter laughed. "Don't worry about my feelings. I'm quite used to the fact that most humans are afraid of pairing."

"I had *planned* to do it . . ."

". . . but you hadn't thought it out enough. No, it's not for you. That is, it *would* be right for you, but you'll never see it that way. I knew that a long time ago."

Lilo knew Parameter was right. It was a sobering realization. With all the trouble Lilo had gone to, setting up the life-capsule station in the Rings to ensure her survival if she was caught in her illegal experimentation, she had not really thought hard about where she would go when she was revived. She had contented herself with vague thoughts of living in the Rings as a pair. There were no laws in the Rings; never had been and never would be.

But what other place was there for her to go? None of the Eight Worlds would have her; as soon as her genotype was detected she would be arrested and sentenced to the same fate as her original self had met.

She was an outlaw. And out there, circling Jupiter, was a world of outlaws in the same fix she was in.

"You said it's possible," she said, cautiously.

Parameter's exposed mouth grinned.

"You're a groundcrawler at heart, Lilo. You think in terms of hand-to-hand combat, even though you know nothing about it. Get your head out of the tunnels. We're talking about moving a world, taking it right out of the solar system. You have to think *big*."

12

STARLINE LTD.
TOPSECRET; AAA RATINGS ONLY
SUBJECT: OPHIUCHI HOTLINE TRANSMISSION OF 1249
    HOURS 44.3 SECONDS UT, 8/14/570.
TRANSLATION FOLLOWS: (PROBABILITY WEIGHTED)
FOR (A PERIOD OF TIME: CONJECTURE: 400 EARTH
YEARS?) DATA HAS BEEN SENT. NEW SUBSCRIBERS
(43%) ARE GIVEN A (UNTRANSLATABLE) TO ADJUST.
YOUR TIME PERIOD IS EXPIRED (TERMINATED?) (EX-
TENDED?). PLEASE REMIT THE (BALANCE DUE?) (RE-
MAINDER?) OR FACE TERMINATION (45%) OF SERV-
ICE. YOUR ACCOUNT (22%) WILL BE REFERRED (45%)
TO A (UNTRANSLATABLE). SEND PAYMENT (30%) IN
THE FORM OF (UNTRANSLATABLE) IN THE NEXT
(PERIOD OF TIME: CONJECTURE: 10 EARTH YEARS?).
CREDIT (58%) IS AVAILABLE TO (NEW?) (OLD?) STRUG-
GLING LIFE-FORMS. SEVERE PENALTIES, SEVERE PEN-
ALTIES, SEVERE PENALTIES (97%).
ENDS.
MESSAGE REPEATS THIRTY TIMES.
TOTAL BITS: APPROX. 2.3 X 10^8

Gold.
The memory and premonition of yellow gold.
Somewhere was a forest under a blue sun.

The face was still there when she woke up, still smiling. Lilo
smiled back, glad that it was over.

"Not so fast," Mari said, lightly. "I have to unhook you first, and
close you up."

Something was different. She looked again, and realized it was the
background. Something *behind* Mari's face had changed.

It was the trees. They had been green, and now the branches were bare.

They trained her. She had a lot of time to brood about her situation. It was hard to believe that the year was now 571, that it had been two years since Mari had recorded her in the clearing.

Tweed had shown her his frightening script. He had now seen her revived three times in the same place. *Three*. She heard the story of how her original self had tried to escape soon after being set free from the Institute, and how she died. Tweed had pictures. She knew how her first clone, Lilo 2, had died. Then there was Lilo 3, who killed Mari and was herself caught and killed. No one would tell her what had happened to Lilo 4, but she must have been the smartest of the bunch. Or the most intimidated. She had lasted a year.

She was Lilo 5. (And what of the life capsule in the Rings? Was there a number six stirring?)

She intended to be very careful.

They put her on a ship bound for Titan with the female Vaffa and a man called Iphis.

The ship was three days out of Luna when the signal came from Tweed. Lilo wasn't allowed to see it; Iphis and Vaffa took the decoded message and went to the bridge. She could hear angry voices, the loudest belonging to Iphis. Something about schedules, missing the other ship, and reaction mass. But when they came out it was clear who had won. Iphis was glowering, and it seemed like a good time to stay out of his way. Vaffa was her usual imperturbable self, with perhaps a touch more ice around the eyes.

It seemed they were diverting to Mars.

Vaffa wanted to talk to Lilo. She had a rather direct way of letting her know; she grabbed her by the ankle and towed her like a toy balloon.

"We're stopping on Mars long enough to catch the high-gee run to Pluto," Vaffa said, after locking Lilo and herself in the small sleeping area.

"How interesting."

"Yes." She looked thoughtful, relaxed. Then she exploded. Lilo found herself strapped to an acceleration couch with Vaffa's face very close to hers. Her cheek hurt terribly, and she tasted blood in her mouth.

JOHN VARLEY 89

"Yes," Vaffa said, again. "Interesting." She did not look interested. If anything, she was distracted. Lilo had learned that Vaffa was not exceptionally bright, and that she seldom had doubts to resolve. Now she had a problem, and was working it out to her satisfaction. Lilo felt something cool and hard against her throat, and forced herself to swallow.

"The Boss says there's an emergency," Vaffa went on. "I have to go look into it, and he wants you along, too. I know why. There'll be a problem to solve out there, and I'm not so good at that. So you'll be solving it, and I'll be watching you."

"Listen," Lilo said, keeping her voice low. "Surely you can handle it. I'd be happy to stay locked in the ship and out of trouble until you—"

It was only the slightest increase of pressure on her neck, but suddenly she could not breathe.

"No. We'll do it the way the Boss says. I'm supposed to make sure you don't get away. We'll be meeting someone else who's supposed to help me, but I'll have to watch him, too. I want you to know I've studied the character profile the Boss made of you. I know pretty well how you think."

"I believe you—"

She grabbed the straps on each side of Lilo and placed her knee on the hard bone between Lilo's breasts. She pulled, and pressed with her knee.

"I won't say anything against the Boss," she said, pressing a little harder. "But I think he puts too much faith in those profiles. I thought you might be easier to control if you feared me more than you do."

"Vaffa, I fear you already, honestly, I don't know when—" But Vaffa motioned her into silence with a slight movement of her head. For the first time, her brow wrinkled slightly. This was proving to be a tough problem.

"I thought you would fear me if I amputated your arm or leg without turning off your nerve centers. I have the skill to save your life and restore the limb, but it would involve more pain than you've ever imagined. Would that persuade you to behave?"

Lilo was amazed to realized that it was a sincere question, one that Vaffa really wanted her opinion on.

"No. No . . . I, Vaffa, I don't know. Please don't do it. I . . . I think it's more likely I'd just hate you more." She didn't know what else to say. To her extreme relief, Vaffa was nodding.

"I thought of killing you now. I might lie to the Boss, but . . . no, I don't think I could. I'll make a threat, then. I think that if you try to escape from me, I have a good chance of catching you. If you do manage to get free, I'll certainly devote all my time to getting you back. Here's the threat. If I catch you, I'll take a very long time killing you."

"I understand that."

Vaffa was still puzzling over it. She massaged the shiny skin on her scalp, and eased the pressure on Lilo's chest. Lilo breathed a little easier. Finally Vaffa unbuckled her and let her get up. She grabbed Lilo's head, not roughly, and made her look into her eyes.

"I want you to swear to me that you will not try to escape while we're on Pluto. I appeal to your honor."

"What happens if I won't swear? You kill me now, and tell Tweed I was escaping?"

Vaffa looked surprised, and slightly offended. "No. I won't harm you further, no matter what happens, unless you try to escape. I'm not threatening you to make you swear. A promise made under duress is not binding." She stated it like a natural law of the universe.

"All right. I swear I won't try to escape on Pluto."

They sealed the oath in blood, of all things. Making the cut in her own palm without deadening her nerves was one of the most courageous things Lilo had ever done.

It wasn't until later that Lilo realized how childlike the whole thing had been. Was a solemn oath enough to bind her to Vaffa when the stakes were her life and freedom? She didn't see how it could be, but the question troubled her more than she was willing to admit.

Later, Vaffa turned to Lilo in the dim light of the sleeping room. Iphis was snoring.

"We've got to talk." Lilo had been afraid Vaffa wanted to cop again. While Lilo got along well sexually with Iphis, Vaffa frightened her. They moved out into the tiny freefall gym.

"You should read this first." Vaffa handed her a sheet of fax-paper. It was covered with code groups, and under them was a messy translation in Vaffa's seismographic writing. Lilo noted the StarLine name, and the Topsecret, AAA rating.

"I don't know where the Boss got it," Vaffa volunteered. "He has his sources."

Lilo read it through, then again, carefully. She was familiar with the weighting system used in decoding Hotline transmissions. Often the Hotline signal, after traveling seventeen light-years, was considerably garbled. But that couldn't be the case here, not with thirty repeats. So the uncertainty attached to key words was the result of the computer's lack of context for a good translation.

It did not surprise Lilo. She knew most people thought of Hotline transmissions as a sort of substitution code; when cracked, the result would be in good, grammatical System Speech.

But the data received over the Hotline was the result of alien thinking. As long as it stuck to data of a scientific nature, couched in mathematical terms, reasonable translations could be made. Even so, there were huge "gray areas" which were thought to be data but could not be interpreted by any computer programs yet devised. Lilo had her own opinions about the gray areas. Her research into them had put her in jail.

The few times messages had come through which the computers tagged as being something like language, the translations were hedged with uncertainties. The linguists were not surprised at this. Languages embody cultural assumptions, inconsistencies; even contradictions. Given a large body of transmissions, the computers could get closer and closer to the meanings of words. But the Ophiuchites had not shown much interest in talking about themselves, or in doing anything but sending oceans of engineering data. The few verbal messages could have been anything from commercials to religious evangelism, or something that had no human analogue at all.

Lilo read it a third time.

"What's this blowout about accounts, and termination of service? And *payment?* What could they possibly want? What could we give them?"

"Maybe what they're giving us. Information." Vaffa shrugged.

"But we . . . what does it mean?"

"I'm assuming it means just what it says. This is a phone bill for four hundred years of service."

"But . . . that's *crazy.*"

"Is it? Why did we think the Hotline should just go on forever, without us giving anything in return? Why should we expect them to be any less mercenary than we are?"

Lilo calmed down and thought about it before she replied.

"Okay. I can see that. But what would we give them? And *how?* I guess we could build a big laser like they have—I'm not saying it's within our power for sure, but we might—but what do we transmit? Everything we've gotten from the Hotline has been two or three thousand years beyond where our science was at the time. It's like . . .

like asking an Earth primitive for advice on how to fix your fusion motor. What could we have that they want to learn?"

Vaffa grimaced, and took the message back. "I was hoping you'd have some ideas about that. I can't think of anything, and it's got me worried. I guess what I'm really wondering is, what are the 'severe penalties'?"

"I don't see what it could be except a disconnection. I mean, they're seventeen light-years away. What could they do?"

"I don't know." Vaffa brooded for a while as Lilo tried to figure it out. Then she looked up. "Everybody says star travel is impossible, or at least it would take so long it wouldn't be worthwhile. One of the big reasons they give is the Ophiuchites. If they had star travel, they'd *be* here, right? They wouldn't be sitting home beaming messages." She shook her head. "Now I wonder. Maybe we've got them all wrong. Maybe they had another reason for staying away. But I don't think they'd send this unless they meant business."

Lilo wanted to talk about it some more, but Vaffa had withdrawn into a private world. The woman was scared. Lilo wasn't, yet, but she would be.

13

Starline, by the Public Relations Master Program, Main Business Computer, StarLine, Ltd. Read-rating II.

Who'd a thought they'd miss? Nobody figured on it. People were looking for junk from the stars for God knows how long. Way back in old-style time, Project Ozma took a listen. No good. Later on, we turned the big ears on 'em. Centauri, Wolf, Lalande, Procyon, 40 Eridani. Quiet, real quiet. What gives? We listened to 'em all, and no buzz.

Then we started to get *way* far out. Beyond Pluto,

twice that fuggin' far away, and what do you think?
Voices!

Well, not voices, exactly, you readout? Computer
bippety-bips and offedy-ons. Nobody could read 'em
for a long time. (I mean, you should take a *look* at
'em! Press the printout and a zillion acres of fly-
specks.) Even the computers didn't know what the
message was. But a couple things were sure. Somebody
was sittin' on 70 Ophiuchi with one fuggin' big laser,
they wanted to talk, and they couldn't shoot piss into a
pot!

Hold on! Maybe they weren't shootin' at *us*. So they
looked around behind us, you know, but there's nothing but a couple of stars in Orion's armpit. They were
yakkin' at us, all right. But how come they *missed*?
You think they'd build a laser like that if they can't *aim*
it?

No way. Somebody said, "Hey! Maybe they don't
want to talk till we're *ready!* Like, we gotta be smart
enough to get *out* there, or something." Sounds okay,
huh? Sure enough. They've been talking for four hundred years now. They lead us by fifteen billion klicks,
like a skeet shooter. You wanna listen, you gotta go
out there.

Somebody else said, "How come we don't build *us* a
big laser and talk back?" You kiddin'? Who's gonna
pay for it?

Even at the best of economic times, there was little a traveler
would choose to bring to Pluto. The miport duties were the highest
in the system, and the weight penalties charged by the shipping lines
made it more sensible to leave all luggage at home and buy a new
wardrobe on arrival. Normally, the only thing worth bringing to Pluto
was information, and even that was carried as compactly as possible.

But Pluto was in a depression. The government had been on the
losing end of an economic war with Mercury for two years, and the
effects were drastic. Vaffa had used her Intersystem Credit Card on
Mars to get a small amount of cash. Even so, the weight penalty was
steep.

Lilo and Vaffa stepped out of the five-gee express at Florida Port,
groggy and miserable from eight days spent floating in an acceleration tank. Lilo kept coughing up unpleasant substances, and there

was a steady drip of fluid from her nose. She had licked it once, which proved to be a mistake.

Looking for something to wash away the taste, she spotted a drink-vending machine and inserted one of the Martian bills Vaffa had given her.

"I can't change that," said the machine. "Tell you what. If you *deposit* the money, we can do business." The machine explained that it was an authorized branch of the Florida Planetary Bank. A light came on that said INTEREST ACCRUING. It went off in a few seconds. Lilo got her flask of drink, and her bill was returned along with a few Plutonian coins. Vaffa advised her to toss them in the recycler, since they were virtually worthless.

Pluto was in the middle of an inflationary spiral. Money was being dated as it was printed, and it had to be spent quickly before the value dropped. Every Monday one thousand Old Marks became equal to one New Mark. If your money was more than a week old, it would make an economical fire; it would not buy its weight in paper.

Lilo and Vaffa waited in the recovery room of the spaceport lounge until the medicos certified them as being over the effects of high-gee travel. A few steps away was a line of shops which specialized in outfitting naked travelers as they emerged from Inner Planet flights. Lilo wanted to stop.

"Don't shop here," Vaffa advised. "They gouge you."

"What's the difference?" Lilo asked. "We're rich, right?" She entered The Underworld Boutique.

Inside, she was soaped, showered, oiled, and massaged until she felt more human and less like something pickled. She began to lose some of the muscle kinks that plague high-gee passengers for days after a flight. She told the clerks to dress her.

From the things they brought, she selected a red shirt with buckles at the waist and wrists and neck. It had puffed sleeves, but otherwise was quite utilitarian, with plenty of pockets and a built-in chronometer. They wanted to paint her legs, but she refused firmly. She bought a hat, and slippers, mainly because the soles of her feet were wrinkled like prunes. The clerks tried to sell her face paint, a holomist suit, dildopants, and a live mink coat, so she paid and left. She wasn't used to pressure selling, and didn't like it. Vaffa bought nothing.

"Don't you ever wear clothes?" Lilo asked her.

"I don't like them. They can get in your way in a fight. Sometimes I wear a belt with a holster, but not in public."

Vaffa was glancing around nervously. Lilo had observed that the other woman didn't like crowds, even on Luna. Here, she seemed very jumpy. Her movements were quick and jerky as she tried to cover all angles at once.

"Where do we go?"

"I have an address. Maybe we'd better find a map."

Pluto liked to think of itself as the frontier. After three hundred years of steady colonization, the idea was showing signs of wear. In most ways, Pluto was as urban as any of the Eight Worlds. But Plutonian cities tended to be louder and gaudier. There was an air of ostentation, a constant assault of bad taste and commercial and personal display. It was distasteful to both the Lunarian women.

Rough edges of construction were sometimes left unfinished. The carpet in the corridors was thick and soft, but in places it did not fit together right, with raveled edges stopping short of the walls and gobs of light brown pitch in the corners. At one point the slideway carried them past a section of bare rock where workers were installing insulation and plastic facing. The rock was caked with frost; it sucked heat from one side of Lilo's body.

They came to Center, hub of the city's slidewalk network and the main transit nexus where tube capsules departed for outlying suburbs, enclaves, and communes. They got off and looked around. The ceiling was two kilometers above them, but some of the trees in Center Park seemed to scrape it. Eight arcades circled the vast cylindrical area, reached by glass elevators hung from transparent cables. Everything seemed to be in motion or flashing for their attention.

Lilo was feeling oppressed, an outlander. It was dizzying. She was a born Lunarian, conservative in many ways. She dressed for convenience, not decoration. Waste and frivolity offended her. It was the legacy of the Invasion, and in many ways it set Lunar society apart from the rest of human space.

Luna was the planet that was colonized directly from Earth. When the Invaders came, the few thousand humans on Luna dug in for the long struggle for self-sufficiency. They had not been ready; autonomy was supposed to have been thirty years away. But species survival would be decided by what they did.

The first fifty years had been extremely hard. Many had died in selective lotteries or in violent resistance to them when it became clear the population had to be thinned. The survivors had sacrificed all the harder to insure that the martyrs had not died in vain.

The struggle left its mark on Lunarians. They tended to be conservative in politics and morals. They clung to a ghost of representative democracy while the colonies were trying Ordeal-Selectivism. Neuter-sex had never caught on. Current fashions of Mars and Mercury sold poorly on Luna. With the modesty taboo an almost forgotten aberration, the average Lunarian usually wore a vest-of-pockets, carried a shoulder purse, or went nude. It was almost a uniform, and the rest of humanity made endless jokes about it.

A creative surgeon could go broke in Luna. Few were interested in extra legs in odd places, reversed heads, new nose designs, or prehensile tails. They changed their sex an average of once every eight years, a system-wide low. The ratio of maintenance to cosmetic surgery was nine to one. Most Lunarians who wanted a face change did it at home as a hobby.

Pluto was at the other end of the spectrum. Lilo thought it vulgar. It was a deep-seated distaste that was beyond her power to reason away. Plutonians were peacocks. They wore their social status on their skins.

Lilo and Vaffa moved through a maze of floating advertisements of ghostsmoke and holomist that followed the prospective customer and played breath-catching tricks with perspective, all the time broadcasting direct to the inner ear, thus evading the noise-pollution laws.

They managed to whirl out of the mainstream into a green eddy of parkland. The trunk of a tree provided sculptured seats growing from the bark. Lilo looked up, and decided it would take her five minutes just to walk around the tree.

It was like the eye of a hurricane. Holo ads approached them, but were stopped by an invisible wall.

VISIT THE CHARON FERRYBOAT.
BUY EROTICON. USE IT, EAT IT, WIPE IT ON, RUB IT OFF, COP IT.
GIVE TO THE PERSONALITY BANK.
TRADE IN YOUR FEET TODAY. BUY NEW ASTAIRES. PUT ON THE RITZ.

The park was deserted. Plutonians did not seem to need peace and quiet. Lilo and Vaffa sat and watched the people go by.

"Breasts seem popular this year," Vaffa observed after a while. "Nearly everybody has at least two. Hey, what do you call *that?*"

"Electric testicles. I read about them."

"Kind of pretty," Vaffa mused. "Like lanterns."

"It's supposed to be the quickest way to assure a copping partner that you're sterile. Look, do you have any idea where we're going? I need another bath, and a quiet place."

14

The gravity trains departed from the level just below Center. Lilo bought two tickets, nervously sticking her hand into the slot of the genoprinter before doing so. It had worked well enough on Mars.

Tweed's nixonian hand reached across five billion kilometers. She felt the scrape of the sampler across her palm, the machine whirred, and somewhere in the banks of the Pluto Central Computer an entry was made:

JOVIAN-342 (ID-L-502-KC-98) BOARDED FLORIDA—BARROW SHUTTLE 0349 HRS. 4/8/71.

The security check was automatic, and it came up green. The name Jovian-342 did not appear on any list of wanted persons, and that was the end of it. Had the Pluto computer felt the need to check further with Lunar records, it would have learned twelve hours later that Jovian-342 was a member of the Church of Cosmic Engineering, an upstanding citizen of Luna, and an enthusiastic traveler. What it would not have learned was the fact that Jovian-342 had emigrated ten years before and was now presumably paired in the Rings, cut off from the rest of human civilization and unable to protest the theft of her identity.

Lilo did not know how Tweed had done it. She did know that the people who ran the main computers were potentially above the law, so the safeguards against illegal tampering were stringent. But it had happened in the past, and would happen again.

The inside of the car was plush brown velvet and subdued lights on chrome. She sank into one of the couches and strapped in, with Vaffa taking the seat beside her. The car eased into a tunnel and glided slowly upward. Airlock doors got out of the way and closed behind the car as it picked up speed. Lilo counted twelve of them. Then stars appeared outside the window. She pulled her feet up under her and rubbed them. She was cold.

It was purely psychological, but the frozen gas outside seemed to claw at her. She hated the cold. There was nothing warm here, even in the daytime.

A large man came down the aisle and sat on the arm of Vaffa's chair. He gave her a big grin, then tried to sell her a membership in a sexcircle. Vaffa was annoyed, but when she tried to push him away her hand went through him. He was only the first. Soon they were surrounded.

Vaffa jumped when one of them touched her.

"Pardon me," the man said. "I see you're from Luna."

"Yes," Lilo said. "Is it that obvious?"

"Your nose," he said. "It's pointed." His own was as flat as a bad prizefighter's. He had eyelashes half a meter long. It made him blink in slow motion. "And other things. No offense, I hope. I just thought you might be interested in what I'm selling."

"You know, you could be replaced by an illusion," Vaffa said.

"What are you selling that couldn't be hawked by a holo?" Lilo asked.

"An antiholo generator," he said.

It was a small bracelet, stamped with a number to call for repairs. They were leased, not sold, like a computer terminal. They came in a range of prices and models. Some merely held the holos at arm's length. Most Plutonians thought this was enough. If you couldn't see the ads, how would you know what was fashionable?

The man showed no surprise when Lilo and Vaffa took the heavy-duty Annihilator model.

The train pulled into Barrow and the windows fogged. The outside of the car was coated with frost as they debarked. Melting slush dripped from the sides of the car into gutters in the carpeted platform.

"What can you tell me about this guy?" Lilo asked.

Vaffa was scanning the walls. She never seemed to relax.

"Ex-teacher. The guy's weird. Never really got over being kicked out of the Educational Association. But the Boss lets him work Pluto alone. His job isn't that important. Not until now, anyway."

"Did he have something to do with intercepting that transmission?"

"Yeah. That last message from the Boss filled me in on some of that. He has access to Hotline data. He sends it to the Boss, and we get it about the same time as the StarLine board of directors."

"Why? I mean, up to now, what good has it done you?"

Vaffa shrugged. "He likes to know things. We're fighting a war."

Lilo had to keep reminding herself of that. The Free Earth Party versus the Invaders. No shots had been fired as yet. Lilo had little hope for the outcome if Tweed ever managed to get the conflict heated up.

But it was the most important thing in Vaffa's life. She was always alert for enemies. Now she was edgy, and Lilo thought she knew why. Vaffa had traveled many times to Titan, but had never strayed far from the spaceport. Luna was the only environment she knew well. She was suffering from culture shock.

Lilo was familiar with the phenomenon. It is not true that one corridor is just like another. There are trifles a person does not consciously notice: the shape of the ceiling fixtures, the foreign arrangement of dials on the corner air sniffers, the unfamiliar designs of fountains, callboxes, sprinklers, door flanges, medical terminals, and crash locks. Even the air smelled wrong. Pluto air was scrubbed only seven times before reuse. It was heavy with humanity.

They reached their destination and rang the bell. The door flange popped and they stepped over the lip into chaos.

The room was large, but it seemed filled by seven or eight children. They never stopped moving and yelling. A foot-race was in progress, with furniture serving as obstacles. Lilo and Vaffa backed against a wall to be out of the way, and waited. Across the room, a man was talking to a pregnant woman. He looked up.

"Party's over!" he yelled. "Come back later. You, would you hold the door for them?" Vaffa held it open, and the man herded the children. They giggled, and lunged at him, but he held out an arm and they fell back, laughing. He seemed to have an almost magical power over them. Soon they were all in the corridor.

"You'll have to come back later," he was telling the woman. He took her hand and guided her to the door. Lilo looked at her bare belly. It couldn't be many more days.

When she was gone, the man looked at them and shrugged.

"She wants a bootleg teacher," he told them. "Some foul-up. She didn't get an ironclad contract with the teacher she picked out, I guess. I get them all the time."

"You'd think that with only one chance, people would be more careful," Lilo said.

"Ain't it the truth? She could have at least had someone explain the contract to her, even if she is illit. I . . ." He looked at her, and smiled. He held out his hand.

"I'm Cathay."

"Lilo." She took his hand. He glanced at Vaffa.

"I know you," he said, evenly.

"Nevertheless, we've never met," Vaffa said.

"Then it was your brother. Your clone. I *know* you." He seemed about to say more, but left it at that. "Well, have a seat, I guess. Whatever looks comfortable. Can I get you anything?" He was looking at Lilo.

"Something mildly intoxicating," she said. "I'm not choosy."

"Got just the thing." He disappeared into another room. Vaffa waited a moment, then got up and followed him. They came back one at a time, Vaffa with one drink, Cathay with two. Both seemed tense. He handed her a glass of green liquid.

The drink made her feel better. She relaxed into her chair and studied Cathay. He had a lot of curly brown hair, long legs, and a boyish face. He was handsome without overdoing it, and Lilo liked that. She felt a physical attraction without having touched or smelled him, and that was rare for her.

"To what do I owe the extreme pleasure of this visit?" Cathay asked. "Wait, let me guess. Tweed's pregnant, and he's looking for a bootleg teacher."

Vaffa, who had taken a seat facing the door, sat even straighter in her chair. Lilo felt herself tensing, and realized how attuned she was to the other woman's moods. On the trip from Luna to Mars she had become adept at staying out of Vaffa's way in the small ship.

"I will warn you once," Vaffa said. "I won't listen to jokes about the Boss." She glared from Cathay to Lilo, and back again. Lilo looked helplessly at Cathay, wanting to tell him what form the second warning would take. To her surprise, he seemed to understand. He gave her an almost imperceptible nod, and sat back in his chair.

"Okay. Go on. It's about the Hotline, isn't it? What else could it be? The Boss is scared, and I don't blame him."

"You are aware of the content of the message?" Vaffa asked, half rising from her seat. "I think I would have been told if you were authorized to read it."

"Well, I don't know if I was authorized or not," he said. "But it was already translated when I got it. Did the Boss tell you my source is in the translation department? I can't get the raw data."

Vaffa relaxed a little. "Yes, he did say that. But you shouldn't have read it. Your function is to pass it on to the Boss."

Cathay shrugged. "I had to encode it to send it to him, and I'm as curious as the next fellow. No one told me to forget what I'd read. But I'll bear it in mind. What I still can't understand is what you're here for. I don't know what the Boss thinks you can do that I can't do better. I have contacts out here. I know my way around. You . . . well, you're muscle, I know that. Does he plan to have you bully the Hotline into a deadline extension?"

Lilo shifted nervously in her chair, but apparently Vaffa was not insulted.

"No. Our mission will be simple. You said the Boss is scared. That isn't quite right, but it's fair to say he is concerned. The message seems to be quite important, and potentially dangerous."

Lilo couldn't help laughing. "I guess you might say that. It's got to make you wonder, if nothing else."

"The way I read it," Cathay said, seriously, "is that we've been presented with a phone bill."

"But we never subscribed," Vaffa pointed out.

"That's an evasion," Cathay said. "It's true we never asked for the service. But we *used* it. We've been using it for centuries, and as far as I know no one has ever tried to send anything back in return."

"The costs . . ."

"That's beside the point. I've been thinking about this ever since I saw the message. What amazes me now is that no one ever saw this possibility. We've treated the Hotline as a natural resource, like vacuum. We wondered what the Ophiuchites might be like, but when they didn't volunteer anything about themselves I guess we just wanted to believe it was a . . . a sort of interstellar welfare program."

"When it was really more like cultural exchange?" Lilo suggested.

"Maybe. If that's it, they must be insulted that we never sent them anything."

"But what do we have that they could want?" Lilo asked. "They're so far ahead of us."

"Who knows? Listen, they probably asked themselves the same question. And what they did, apparently, was to send *everything*. We've used the new inventions, the biological engineering techniques and so forth. But we still can't tell what ninety percent of it is. Maybe it's art, or philosophy. Or gossip. Or nine billion Ophiuchites advertising for sex partners. But I don't really think the Hotline is cultural exchange. I think it's just what the message implies; it's a commercial venture. We're expected to pay for what we get, value given for value received. I wish I knew what the 'extreme penalties' business is all about, though."

Vaffa's brow had wrinkled as she followed Cathay's reasoning. Now her face smoothed as she got back on more familiar ground.

"We've drifted away from the subject," she said. "We were talking about our mission, why Lilo and I were sent to join you. It's simple. In a matter as potentially serious as this, the Boss feels the need of further information. It's impossible to know how to meet this on the information we have so far. Since it is impossible to ask the Ophiuchites the questions he must find answers for, we must try our best to find them in the original message."

"That makes sense," Lilo said. Vaffa looked at her, and Lilo knew Vaffa was grateful to hear that. It had not made much sense to Vaffa. She had been accepting the Boss's judgment of the situation largely on faith.

"What I mean," Lilo went on, "is that it's hard to imagine they wouldn't have put everything we need to know into the message. Even if we could ask them questions, it would take thirty-four years for a reply."

"Exactly. You notice the message contains many words which are assigned a translation probability."

"That's normal in Hotline data," Cathay put in.

"So I understand. But all we have to go on is the translated message you obtained. What we need is the raw data. The Boss wishes to have it so he can analyze it independently."

Cathay frowned. "That's not going to be easy. In fact, it's not possible."

"Explain that, please."

"Well, I . . . all right. My source works in the translation department of StarLine. She . . . you know how they get their data?" He looked at the two women, nodded, and went on. "StarLine has a station out in the zone of maximum signal strength of the Hotline. There used to be several other stations out there. Now StarLine has a monopoly charter from the Pluto government. Luna's challenged it a couple times . . . but I guess the political situation isn't important to this. Practically, Pluto controls everything outside its orbit.

"The people on the station don't broadcast anything back to Pluto because the signal could be pirated. They record everything that comes over the Line, and send it in drone rockets, high-gee jobs, that are retrieved here under tight security.

"Back when there was competition, they had some *extremely* fast drones. The people at the station acted as filters. When they saw something in the preliminary computer translation that might be valuable, they put it in one of these rockets to try and edge out the competition in patents, marketing, so forth. That doesn't matter now, but they still had one of the special delivery rockets. When they got this message, they used it. My contact told me how it came in, and that she didn't think she could get this one to me. I applied all the pressure I could, and she managed it. But she says that's strictly it. Security's so tight on this thing that no printout exists of the original data. It's stored in StarLine's computer, and if you think you can break in there and rob the memory, good luck."

Vaffa frowned. "No, that's out. The Boss explored that avenue before he dispatched us to Pluto. He's still working on an information raid, but the defense programs are formidable."

"The best on Pluto," Cathay said. "I don't know what you have on Luna."

"What about having your contact do the raid for us, from the inside?"

Cathay considered it. "This is restricted to the top four or five people. Only about twenty even know of the existence of the message. She wouldn't be given the top-rated access codes, and would have no way to get them."

"What is your means of pressuring this woman?"

"I . . . uh, her child is one of my students. She got herself in a bind, like that woman who was just here. Pregnant, and no teacher lined up. She came to me, and I cleared it with the Boss. Also, and I guess this is pretty important, I had to give her a lot of Tweed's money this time, for this message. In *addition* to threatening . . . well, to telling her I'd walk out on her child." He looked away from them. Lilo was embarrassed for him. The only acceptable reason for abandoning a child in the middle of the educational process was the death of the teacher.

Vaffa seemed not to have noticed. "Why won't that work again?"

"She made enough money last time to hire a *licensed* teacher, under the table. It can be done, no matter what the EA tells you."

"Still, you'd better explore it with her."

"Okay."

Vaffa frowned again. "In the meantime, we'll have to assume your estimation is accurate, and look into the alternative."

Lilo glanced at Cathay; he looked as puzzled as she felt.

"What alternative?" she asked. "You said the only copy of the original message is in the StarLine computer. What other way is there to get it out?"

"None. Oh, the Boss made inquiries, but has found no one placed even as well as Cathay's source. And work will go on toward gaining access to the computer itself via its regular output channels. But none of that is likely to work. So we'll have to get it directly. We'll buy a ship and go to the Line."

Cathay had not taken it well, once it became clear that Vaffa meant for all three of them to go. He argued for hours, and finally reached a position he swore he would not abandon.

"It's just not possible. I can't leave for at least three years, even if I don't take on another child. The youngest one I have now will be needing me for that long."

"You were not authorized to enter into any educational contracts," Vaffa pointed out. "That you did is your own affair, but your first loyalty—your only *important* loyalty—is to the Boss."

"Crap. You can't ask me to abandon those children. It's a sacred trust. When you take on a contract, you *finish* it."

"You will not finish these." Lilo noticed Vaffa's carefully formal speech and the complete calm that had settled over her. *Look out,* she thought.

"I *will* finish them. Nothing you can do will—" Vaffa delivered a chopping blow to the side of his neck, and turned in a crouch to face Lilo, who was sitting very still. Vaffa gradually relaxed and sat down, brooding. She ignored the unconscious man on the floor. Lilo picked him up and staggered into his bedroom. She put him on the bed and sat down beside him in the darkness.

"Lilo, come in here." She got up and went back to the main room.

"I think I'll have to kill him," Vaffa said.

Lilo sat down slowly. "Why? He hasn't done anything, has he?"

"It's what he's likely to do that bothers me." She sighed and rubbed her neck. She looked as though she might be unhappy about what she was going to have to do, but she also looked determined to do it.

"It was a mistake to send just me out here," she said. "I can't trust either of you, and I can't watch both of you at the same time. One of you will have to go."

"Why can't he stay behind? He's been here alone all this time, hasn't he?"

"The Boss is worried about what he might do. He knows too much now about this Hotline message. Aside from the company people, he's the only one on Pluto except you and me who knows about it."

"But isn't he . . . I mean, like me? A condemned criminal?"

"No. He's nothing but a disbarred teacher. The Boss contacted him when he was on the skids, and promised that if he'd do some work for the party, he'd get a chance to teach again with a new identity. He's supposed to wait another couple years. We didn't know about this bootleg teaching. It looks like he's getting restless, and he shouldn't be doing that according to what we—" she stopped abruptly, looked helplessly at Lilo, and put her head in her hands.

Lilo suspected Vaffa had been getting into an area she wasn't supposed to talk about. But she clearly wanted to talk.

"I can't help you make a decision if you won't tell me all the details."

"Who said I was asking for your help?"

"Nobody. But you said you'd trust me. We made a deal."

"I know. I want to trust you. I'll *have* to trust you if I'm going to let him live."

"But you don't know if you can. And it's no good telling the Boss that you made a deal with me. You went beyond your orders on that, didn't you?"

"Yes." She looked miserable. Vaffa's life was based on following orders; it disturbed her deeply to do something on her own.

"You'd better check with the Boss first, anyway," Lilo suggested. "See what he thinks about Cathay. Maybe he still needs him. You don't have to tell him about the deal we made."

Vaffa thought about it a long time, then nodded. Lilo relaxed. There would be at least twelve hours before Vaffa could get an answer from Tweed.

Cathay was still out. Lilo got a basin of water and sat on the bed beside him. She sponged the mark on his forehead where he had hit as he fell. He moaned, opened his eyes for a moment, then closed them again. Lilo plugged him into the bedside medical monitor and was told that he was sleeping, and did not have a concussion.

She undressed and got into bed with him. She put her arms around him from behind and hugged him close.

For an hour she stayed perfectly still. She tried to drift off to sleep, but her mind kept coming back to Cathay and what she could do about him.

Eventually she decided to wake him. She moved her hands slowly down his chest, over his belly. It was flat and hard. He had an erection. She grasped it and ran her thumb lightly over the rubbery glans. He stirred.

"How's your head?"

He felt it carefully. "Not so bad, I guess. My cheek's tender."

"Keep it quiet," Lilo cautioned. "Do you know anything about fighting?"

He turned onto his back. "Well, I think I could do a little better than what you saw. She got me completely by surprise. But no, I'm not a fighter. She'd demolish me. What about you?"

"No. You're going to have to go with us, you know. She has a direct order not to leave you here. There's only one alternative."

"I know. I guess I knew it from the start, with *her*."

"So what are you going to do? Uh, would you like me to stop this?"

"No, please. It feels wonderful." He turned to face her and began stroking her body. "I don't want to talk about this, anyway. It's too painful."

"We have to talk a little more. I need to know what you're going to do. We have about a day."

He rolled onto his back again. She was still gently rubbing his penis; now he put his hand over her hand. They were both still for a long time.

"Why?" he said, at last.

"If you're staying, she's going to kill you. You'll want to do what you can think of to stop her. I . . . was thinking. Oh, hell. What I wondered was if I should . . . should take a chance with you and maybe together we—I'm not *proposing* this, mind you, I just thought we ought to discuss—"

"Would you trust me that far? You don't even know me. If I decided to stay, I don't have anything much to lose by plotting with you. Maybe I'd even have a chance to stay alive. But why should you get into it?"

"It may be the last chance I'll ever have. Do you know anything about me?"

He faced her again. "Nothing specific, and I don't want to. It doesn't matter to me what you did. I know you're one of his cloned criminals." He noted the surprise on her face. "Yeah, I've learned a few things about him. Enough to get him into big trouble. He's right to want to get rid of me." He sighed, and rolled onto his back again, away from her. He laced his fingers behind his head.

Lilo thought he was through talking, and found that she really didn't mind. They could talk afterward. Right now, she was getting aroused. He was a beautiful man. She liked his smell, and the feel of his hands on her. She scooted down the bed and raised herself up one elbow, then bent over him.

"He collects them," Cathay said, absently massaging her scalp with one hand. "He's got dozens of them on a secret base somewhere, poor bastards. They're plotting the overthrow of the Invaders." He laughed bitterly, and looked down at her. "But if you are a Free Earther you wouldn't be so afraid of that woman. I mean, you'd be afraid, but you'd be respectful, you know what I mean?"

She let her breath out slowly and rested her cheek on his belly. All right, he wanted to talk after all.

"I've seen what she can do. I also think I know some of her weaknesses. She's very confused right now. Tweed should never have sent her on this trip alone."

"He didn't," Cathay said. "He sent you, too."

"What do you mean by that? You think I'm a Free Earther?"

"No. But he sent you. He would have a reason."

She lifted her head to look at him. "My being here seems to be an accident. We were on the way to Titan when he got word of this message you sent—"

"No. It wasn't that way at all. I sent him that message three months ago. I don't care where he told you and Vaffa you were going; your destination was right here. Probably the pilot didn't even know it. The message would have gotten to you just in time to divert to Mars."

"It was a pretty close thing," she conceded.

"Not at all. That means he wanted you out here. He wanted Vaffa as his only loyal agent among us. If he thought Vaffa couldn't handle you, be sure he would have sent someone else to trail you from the spaceport."

"I don't get it. It sounds like a game. Does he want us to do anything for him out here, or just to tear each other apart?"

"It's never simple," Cathay sighed. He took her arm and gently coaxed her up alongside him. She pressed close to his side, enfolded in his arm. "I've dealt with him for fifteen years. Five more . . . well, he promised me a new identity. I've begun to doubt it, but you have to have *something* to live for."

Now he no longer wanted to talk about it. He hugged her closer, then moved down and began kissing her breasts. But now it was Lilo's turn to push him away and raise her head to study him.

"I still don't understand what you're saying."

"All right. Vaffa's a great soldier, but a lousy general. She has no initiative. That's what you're here for; to make the hard decisions that might come up, things that can't wait a day to be resolved by the Boss. *Not* the life-or-death ones, nor the ethical ones—Free Earther ethics. He can trust Vaffa to be right on those. He has you judged very well. I know something of what you've been though, and how well he *does* know you. You won't gang up on Vaffa. That's out of the question."

"How can you say that?" she demanded. She felt her cheeks heating up; it was part anger, part shame. She had just about decided that resistance at this point would be futile, that her best chance would be to wait until they returned to Pluto and she knew more about her opponent.

"For one reason, because your best chances of escape will be later. You can see that. Your cage is insubstantial. You won't learn the limits of it by rattling bars. You will win your freedom piece by piece, by slowly finding out what you can get away with and putting it together into a successful escape. If that's possible, which has not yet been proved, so far as I know. At this point, there's a very good chance that Vaffa is *not* alone. Tweed would not have to tell her that he has someone else watching you. He thinks you'll realize this, and not try to get away."

It *did* look like the sort of tantalizing chance her first clone, Lilo 2, must have taken, Lilo realized. She remembered her resolve to suspect the easy escape, to look for the unlikely one. But she was still angry.

"What if I say the hell with common sense? Damn him, anyway. Go for broke, throw in with you, and we knock her off. How can he tell that I won't make an irrational decision? Unless this is just another test and there's really no message from the Hotline."

"There is, but I'm glad you saw that possibility. You've trusted me entirely too quickly for your own good, you know." His tongue was at her nipples again, and this time she didn't protest. She stroked his back and let her eyes close slowly. The last of the muscle kinks from the high-gee trip were fading beneath an enveloping warmth, a tingling that went from her hot earlobes to her toes. But she opened her eyes again and looked down at him.

"You didn't answer my question."

"He *doesn't* know. Your best chance might actually be to make a try right now. He has no real defense against your doing something totally illogical. He can't predict that."

"Then how can he chance it?"

Cathay sighed. "Because he knows *me* pretty well, too. You can't join me if I'm not willing. And I'm not. I'm going. I'm choosing to live. I will abandon my students, abandon my self-respect, or what's left of it, one more time. Now that I've revealed that, bared my shame to you, will you please shut up and open your legs?"

He said it with lightness in his voice and a half-smile, but when he entered her he was fierce, determined to lose himself in an excess of passion. Lilo surrendered and let him set the tempo, at least for the first time. To her surprise, she was responding well. Part of that was her physical need; it had been a long time. Another part was feeling sorry for him. It was not pleasant to admit what one is willing to do to go on living. But part of it was something else again, maybe the beginnings of that sort of feeling that could one day transform a simple act of recreational copping into that thing which is so subtly and yet so hugely different—the act of love.

Career Counseling, a reader-response eventbook. Programmed by the E-Z Educational Peripherals Company.

READER: I can't read.

CAREER COUNSELOR: That's okay with me. I'll respond orally from now on. You just ignore those words on the screen, all right?

R: Uh, okay. How can I, I mean, what do I have to do to be a holehunter?

CC: A holehunter! That's one of the more popular career ambitions we encounter. It sure sounds romantic, doesn't it? You're your own boss, you have this ship all to yourself, and you can get rich. Is that what attracted you to holehunting?

R: Yeah. I guess so.

CC: We try to steer young people away from holehunting as a career. There's a lot of problems. For instance, what do you think one of those ships costs?

R: A lot, I guess.

CC: Whew! You said it! You've got to get money together for the initial investment in your ship. Outfitting
it for a trip costs a lot more. And it's dangerous. What
you do, in case you don't know much about it, is just
go flat out in your ship for as long as your engines are
good for. Then you sit back and watch the mass detec-
tor. You may have to wait fifteen years, and you may
never see anything. So you stop dead, and you start
back the way you came. Three trips out of four you
won't find a hole, so you'll be broke when you get
back. Your first trip will be your last. If you survive it.

R: What do you mean?

CC: It's dangerous! If you find one, you've got to slow
down long enough to figure out just where it is, and
where it's going. Sometimes, you'll plow right into it!
But if you do all that right, you've got to come back to
get it with an electromagnetic tug. There are folks who
sit around Pluto and watch for that. They'll follow you
back. You might be half a light-year from the sun. You
gonna call the cops? You'll have to fight for it.

R: Well, I can fight, good as anyone. What I wanna
know is, do I have to know how to read?

CC: I don't see why. What's your computer for, anyway?

*The verdict on Cathay was blunt and to the point. Vaffa showed it
to me after she'd decoded it. Trying to vindicate herself in my eyes? I
hoped so; if she cared that much about my opinion, whether she was
aware of it or not, it strengthened my position. The Boss did not need
Cathay, not if allowing him to live meant leaving him on Pluto,
knowing what he knew.*

*I think Vaffa made her plans in the first minute after reading the
message. Her mind was that linear. She had to shift gears painfully
when I told her Cathay was going with us.*

"But he wants something in return," Lilo said, on the spur of the
moment.

"It won't do him any good. What?"

"He realizes he has no bargaining power," she said, improvising.
"But he's been useful to Tweed in the past. He can continue to be

useful in the future, when we return, if you don't make him into a permanent enemy now."

"Go on."

"The three educational . . . contracts he holds." They weren't actually legal, of course. He was strictly bootleg, but to him, the contracts had the force of law because he had promised to stand behind them. "The mothers of those children will be in shit crater, you know. With the teacher shortage, how are they going to find someone to take over the education of their children? Cathay says the waiting list is ten years here. They'll be grown before substitutes can be found. Everyone's booked up, committed to teach kids who aren't even born yet."

"Not my problem."

"No. But Tweed's a rich man. Other bootleg teachers can be found, but they're expensive."

Vaffa considered it. "I'll ask the Boss."

The next day brought confirmation from Tweed. He would pay the money to the mothers of the children. It seemed to surprise Vaffa; she had asked the question mainly to satisfy Lilo, to whose judgment she had begun to defer in small ways.

It came as a big surprise to Cathay, who was elated and tried not to show it to Vaffa. Lilo saw it, and it made her feel good. It occurred to her that it was almost the only thing she had been able to do on her own initiative since her escape from prison. But even then she wondered if Tweed had foreseen it, else why the quick acceptance? Did money matter that little to him? Did he buy her argument that it would placate Cathay, make him useful to Tweed after his return? Or did he fear that without the money the mothers would become angry enough to denounce Cathay—leading to an investigation and possible trouble for Tweed—even though the mothers would get into trouble themselves? As usual, Tweed's motives were opaque to her.

But now they had to obtain a ship, and Vaffa didn't know the first thing about doing it. Lilo didn't, either, but she acted as if she did, and she did not doubt that she would be better at it than Vaffa.

Working from Cathay's phone, they quickly got the idea of what the market in second-hand ships was like. There were always ships for sale; they became available as holehunters went bankrupt and had to sell out. But the market was brisk, and prices were always high. Lilo checked with a dozen brokers, and relayed the results to Tweed through Vaffa. The most encouraging thing she could report was that by paying three times the already inflated market value, they might be able to obtain a ship in four to five months.

"Why so much?" Vaffa asked.

"It's complicated," Lilo said. "There's more buyers than sellers. You have to get on a waiting list. The courts award the assets of a bankrupt hunter to a broker, who collects a commission. As soon as a hunter who's gone bust comes in, the ship is sold. They can ask almost anything for it. The waiting list runs to three or four years. To move up on the list, you pay a bribe to the broker. To move *way* up, the bribe can be three times the price of the ship."

"Isn't that illegal?"

"No, strangely enough. They were very open about it. The broker makes the list. The courts have nothing to say about whom the ship is sold to. So the broker cleans up. It sounds like a nice racket."

"What about dealing directly with a holehunter?"

"Nope. The ones that are solvent aren't selling, at any price. The ones who're broke don't own a ship any more. They go into receivership, and the courts always give them to brokers. I told you it was a racket."

"And what about new ships?"

"An even longer waiting list, higher prices, and bigger bribes."

Vaffa looked sour. Business was not her field of expertise. "I'll relay it to the Boss."

"You might mention something else," Lilo said, thoughtfully. "We only need this ship for the one trip. It seems silly to buy it. Also, can you fly one?"

"I thought you let the computer do that."

"True. But holehunters go a long way out. A lot of them don't come back, because something goes wrong, maybe with the computer, and they don't know how to fix it. A lot of those people think hunting holes is as easy as getting from Luna to Mars, but they're wrong. Fifty percent don't return from their first trip. So you're going to need a pilot, because *I* don't know anything about fixing ships, and neither does Cathay. I can do computer work, as long as it's not too complicated. But I don't know anything about fusion engines. We'll need someone who does."

Vaffa sighed. "So what are you proposing?"

"I don't know if this is possible, but we could give it a try. Maybe we could charter a ship, one that belongs to a hunter. Even one tenth of the price of a ship would be attractive, I'd think. That is, unless money is no object. I don't know just how rich the Boss is."

* * *

*I don't think you can get rich enough that money is no object. If
you think that way you either don't get rich or you don't stay rich.
Tweed was fabulously wealthy, but he was interested in my idea. I
don't blame him; some of the prices we quoted him would have run a
fair-sized city for a year.*

*I didn't care one way or the other about Tweed's money. What
was important to me was that you could buy a ship over the phone.
To charter one, you had to go out and look for holehunters. There
were no agencies that handled charters; who ever rented a ship that
size, anyway?*

*Vaffa would not be able to handle it, certainly not alone. That
meant I would get to go outside, to stir around, to get my bearings. If
I saw a perfect chance, who knows . . . ?*

After two weeks they had got nowhere. Day after day they had returned to residential corridors lit by widely spaced pale blue nitelites,
and collapsed into bed.

Tweed was beginning to get impatient. Vaffa said he was talking
about a deadline; if they had not managed to charter a ship in another two weeks, he was going to have them buy one. By that time,
they would already have lost a month, and he was unwilling to let
any more time go by before getting his bid down.

Lilo was not happy about it. She didn't care about the lost time,
but thought that if they bought a ship they would still be faced with
the same problem: hiring a pilot. There were plenty of them around
but Lilo was sure it would be hard to hire one. And for the same
reasons they were having trouble chartering a ship. Vaffa scared the
hunters away.

Holehunters were as quirky a group of people as the human race
had ever produced. In many ways, they were almost as different as a
human paired with a symb. It takes a special temperament to seal
oneself into a single-seat ship for a trip that would last from twenty
to forty years. Most of the ships had about fifty cubic meters of living
space; some had less. The endpoint of a voyage could be as much as
half a light-year from the sun. The people who survived such loneliness for such a time tended to be different.

"Most of them didn't really like people much before they went
out," Cathay said. "When they come back, they haven't seen anyone
for at least twenty years. A lot of them decide they didn't miss all
that much."

They were back at Cathay's home after another day of haunting
the pleasure palaces around the spaceport. Tonight Cathay had done

as Lilo suggested, lowering the air temperature so it would be cozy to huddle around the fireplace which concealed the electric heater. They had all applied a mild hallucinodisiac cream onto their genitals, then inhaled a muscle-relaxant powder. They had coated their bodies with lucent oils: Lilo was lavender, Cathay was pearl, and Vaffa crimson. The result had been a stretched hour of slow-motion slithering, low-key and undemanding. Now they were lying face down, Lilo in the middle.

She felt good. It was like the peace that could be achieved when you had regained your breath after a ten-kilometer run, but without the pain and exhaustion that would have preceded it. She had wanted Vaffa in a good mood for what she was about to propose, and it looked as though she had succeeded. Vaffa was inclined to be per-functory about copping; Lilo assumed that the woman had never at-tracted anyone to love her and had decided, like so many, that sex was overrated. Tonight might well have been the first time she had experienced copping as a sensual delight, not merely the pursuit of orgasm.

"Well, *I* certainly can't understand them," Vaffa said.

"That's because you've never run into anyone who dislikes people as much as *you* do," Lilo said. She hoped it would go over well, not be taken as an insult. Vaffa had never pretended to like people.

"Maybe you're right," Vaffa said. She seemed about to smile, but her lips did not quite know how to manage it. Lilo sat up on one elbow and faced the faintly glowing apparition. Her head felt a little thick now that she'd raised it; there had been entirely too many things to drink and smoke and sniff during the course of the day. Tiny red tongues of flame were dancing over the hairless woman's back. Lilo pursued them with her fingertips, pressing firmly into yielding muscle. Vaffa arched herself sensuously, with a contented moan.

"They're very sensitive, holehunters," Lilo said. "Am I right?"

"Very," Cathay mumbled. He shook his head to wake up, and sparks flew from his hair. Lilo was delighted.

"I think they're reacting to you," Lilo said.

"In what way?" Vaffa lifted her head, managing to look very like her pet python.

"I'm not sure. But they get almost telepathic. They don't see peo-ple for twenty years. When they get back they're sensitive, very touchy."

"Very perceptive," Cathay said. "The hunters, not you."

"Thanks. But they seem to feel when someone's dangerous. And I think they're feeling that from you."

Vaffa considered it, then let her head fall back. "You could be right." Lilo used both hands on Vaffa's neck and shoulders.

"I think I am. You're a killer; we both know it, so there's no need to mince words."

"No need at all."

"I happen to think there's more to you than that. Maybe you never got a chance to express it. Anyway, the hunters may not know that you've killed, but they sense the menace."

"I think you're right."

"Which leaves us the question of what to do about it. How can we charter a ship, and save the Boss a lot of money?" Lilo could have gone on, but it sounded like the place to stop. It would be better if Vaffa came up with the idea herself.

Cathay smiled at Lilo, then carefully turned away before Vaffa could see. The room was quiet for half an hour. Finally Vaffa rolled onto her side and rested her head on her arm. Her voice was sleepy when she spoke.

"Then you'll just have to go out alone."

16

Saint Peter's Casino was on fire, just as it had been the last time Lilo visited. Flames licked upward from the bottom edges of hanging tapestries, crackled through blistered oak paneling. The row of pews in the nave was an inferno, a whirling fire storm that reached to the ceiling. Smashed furniture had been heaped around the *Pietà* and set to the torch; the white marble was now coated with soot. Lilo took a sandwich and a drink from the snack bar that had been set up on the altar. She had been standing around the crap table all night and her feet hurt. St. Pete's bored her. But it was almost closing time. Soon Jesus would be there.

She went back into the Sistine Pit and worked her way over to the tables as one of the walls of the building crumbled. The smoke that had been trapped in the upper reaches of the chapel cleared enough for her to see Michelangelo's ceiling, by now considerably the worse for wear. There were cracks where holes had been drilled to anchor the crystal chandeliers which hung over every table. Beyond the vanished wall an angry Vesuvius could be seen belching fire and brimstone. Someone had a better sense of the dramatic than of historical geography, Lilo thought.

"Twenty on fifteen," she said, taking a seat to the left of the man she had been watching all night. He had lost heavily on the dice, and had shifted to roulette in a desperate effort to change his luck. The croupier in her black-and-white habit spun the wheel and the ball clattered into number eight. Lilo watched her chips being raked away along with the man's.

"Pardon me," said someone at Lilo's left. "Are you available?" She glanced at him. His eyes were glassy and his breath was sweet with the smell of Zongo, a powerful aphrodisiac. It was obviously not all he had ingested, and Lilo wondered what he saw when he looked at her. But she laughed when she looked down at him. His genitals had been radically modified according to the dictates of some new fad.

"Get out of here," she scoffed. "What good would that thing be to me?"

"It's okay," he slurred, nearly falling against her. "I've got an adapter." He brandished something pink and soft that seemed to be breathing. Lilo pushed him, and he staggered into the arms of a bouncer.

"Hey! You brought me luck!" the man next to her cried. The croupier was pushing a tall stack of chips in his direction.

"What'd I do?"

"You hit my elbow. I was going for twenty-six, you hit me, and it went to twenty-eight. I left it there. I mean, what the hell? I couldn't do worse than I've been doing, huh?"

If the aggressive little man had still been in sight, Lilo would have kissed him. The holehunter had ignored every conversational advance Lilo had made all night as he sank deeper into a black mood.

"Are you going to quit while you're ahead?" she asked.

"Ahead? . . . I don't know. You're lucky; what do you think?"

"I don't think we have much choice. J.C.'s coming."

And indeed he was. Bloody, naked, thorn-crowned, the bearded figure was driving the moneychangers from the temple before starting the task of rebuilding it.

"Saint Peter's will be in limbo for one hour, my children," he called out. "No need to leave, but you'll have to clear out of the gaming areas while we clean up. Refreshments are being served in the Pope Agnes Library, upstairs. Y'all come back, now, and bring money." He pulled a wall switch, and everything changed. Half the patrons vanished, along with most of the cathedral. There was a low white ceiling set with bare lights. Cleaning robots began to whir down the aisles, beeping angrily when they encountered the feet of slow-moving patrons.

"What do you say?" Lilo asked. "Are you tired of being taken?"

He laughed. "Maybe I ought to get out, for a little while anyway. You brought me luck. I'm at your disposal."

"All right. I think a bath might do us both some good. How long have you been here, anyway?"

Lilo knew very well that he had been in the casino for thirty-seven hours. Vaffa and Cathay had spelled her, keeping an eye on him, though Vaffa had stayed strictly in the background. She also knew his name, which was Quince, but she didn't tell him that. He was a holehunter, and a slightly unusual one, which was the cause of her interest.

Lilo had been working hard for the six days since Vaffa had given her a degree of freedom. Vaffa had decided that Lilo would be the one to operate on her own, because, while she did not really trust either one of them, she trusted Cathay less. But it had been a tough decision, and one she was still sweating over.

The job had not been easy, even without Vaffa. Quince was the best bet so far. The problem seemed to be that those hunters who owned their own ships didn't display the slightest interest in chartering them. A holehunter hunts holes, as she had been told many times and with great disdain; taxi drivers sell rides. The few working hunters who were on Pluto were there waiting for ships to be overhauled before setting out again, and they damn well did not intend to stop off at the Hotline.

Quince was a little different. Vaffa's research had turned him up. He had made three trips, all about thirty years in duration. He had been lucky the first time out and returned a very rich man. That money had financed his second trip, and his third, and he had not found a hole either time. When a hunter returns empty it generally falls to a bankruptcy court to divide the spoils. But Quince still owned his ship. He had a little money left, but not enough to outfit himself for a fourth trip. He had had no luck in finding backers; speculators tend to superstition, and have little desire to back a two-time loser. So he had tried for a year to win enough at the tables to go back out once more.

Saint Peter's was on the eighteenth level of the entertainment complex beneath the spaceport. They took a lift to the concourse and soon found a public bath. They stripped, and plunged into the soaking pool. Lilo floated on her back and listened to him complain about what a terrible run of luck he had been having. She commented sympathetically now and then, and gradually began to talk more about herself. He was easier to get into conversation than most hunters she had met. She decided it was because he'd been on the ground so long.

They moved to the sauna and didn't say anything as the heat baked their bodies. Then it was a quick plunge in ice water, and a more leisurely session in the shallow pool as steam curled around them. Lilo was scrubbing his back when she first brought up the subject of a trip.

"To nowhere?" he said. "What's the point of that?" He had not failed to notice the stacks of hard Lunar currency she had thrown away while sitting at his elbow. Lilo was "a rich tourist from Luna."

"No point. It would be fun. I could tell all my friends how far out I'd been. *Every*one's been to Pluto."

"How far did you have in mind?"

"Oh, I don't know. I could think about that later." She sat on the side of the pool while he soaped her feet and legs. "But you don't really sound like you're interested."

He didn't say anything, and she didn't want to push. He seemed preoccupied as they moved through a small tropical garden where sprays and waterfalls rinsed the soap from them. They paused on a wooden footbridge, leaning on the rail. There was another couple shimmeringly visible behind the veil of a waterfall. She put her arm around his waist and stroked him as they watched, but he didn't respond. They moved through a corridor of hot-air blowers and a spray of powder. Lilo bought a brush from a machine and sat on a cushion combing the hair on her legs.

"What would you be willing to pay for a trip like that?"

"Oh, gee. I don't know. What do you think it would cost?" Another thoughtful silence threatened; she decided to prime him. "I guess—well, your expenses, of course. Whatever it actually costs you to get out there. Plus a fee."

They moved to the lamps and reclined on a long table with a

dozen other people like pink and brown strips of bacon lined up on a griddle. After ten minutes they turned over.

"You still didn't say where you want to go."

"How about the Hotline?" She could hear the gears turning in his head, estimating costs and times. She already knew to a nicety what his expenses would be, given the size and acceleration of his ship. "I'd really like to go out there and listen to it. Just think, thousands of light-years away, people talking to *me!*"

"Seventeen light-years," Quince said, absently. "And you can't really—" He seemed to change his mind. "You might enjoy it," he finished.

They rinsed again, were blown dry and powdered. They skipped the massage, dressed, and went back into the concourse. Quince still seemed to be pondering a decision, so Lilo left him alone. She steered him into a lounge and ordered drinks for both of them. They found a secluded booth with dim lighting. Lilo glanced nervously at the glowing numbers on the cuff of her shirt; she was late. She knew Vaffa had tailed her the first two days she had been allowed out alone. Now she was supposed to be punctual about meetings. It would not be long before Vaffa began searching for her, and Lilo didn't know what would happen when she was found. She began to fear Vaffa would burst in on them and ruin the deal, so she decided to give him one more push.

"Okay, so I'll pay your expenses, plus . . . oh . . ." she named a figure fifty percent over what he would need to outfit and fuel his ship for a hunting run. He seemed tempted. Reflexively, he named a higher sum. It was half what Lilo had been authorized to pay.

"It's a deal," she said, holding out her hand. He shook it, and she felt a great relief. Vaffa could hardly fault her for being late because she had to close the deal.

"I'll have the money to you in lagtime, as soon as it clears my bank on Luna. Then you can call me as soon as you're ready to go." She held her breath for a moment, then plunged on. It had to work, it just had to. "Oh, there's one other thing. So you can figure weights and masses or whatever it is. My husband and my wife will be coming along."

"Three of you?"

It wasn't a question, but a way of saying the deal was off.

"Where have you been?"

Vaffa was as much relieved as angry, but she hid it well. She had been waiting near the edge of Center Park for half an hour, trying to decide how much tardiness would indicate desertion. Now she nearly broke Lilo's wrist as she grabbed her and pulled her deeper into the park. They took a wicker cable car to the three-hundred-meter level of one of the huge trees. Lilo could have used another drink, but instead of going inside Vaffa led her out on one of the broad, flat limbs. Soon they were among concealing foliage and hanging vines.

"I don't like the look of this," Lilo said, glancing down.

"You shouldn't. You're going straight down unless you give me a very good reason why you were late. I told you I would tolerate no—"

"Stop it. *Stop it!* You can throw me down if you decide to, but I won't listen to any more threats from you. Damn it, I'm doing my best, and I want to be treated like a human being." She waited. Vaffa slowly released her hand. It seemed to take a great deal of effort.

"Thank you. Now we had a deal. I'm talking about the promise I made on the way here. You either trust me or you don't, and if you don't, what's the point of making deals?"

"I don't know how *far* to trust you. My instincts tell me not to."

Lilo shrugged. "Your instincts are right. But not right now. Our time will come later, I imagine. But I'm going with you to the Hotline, I've already decided that."

"Does that mean you—"

"Hold on. I'm not through yet." Lilo was breathing hard, and realized she was spoiling for a fight. She could not be a match for Vaffa physically, so it would have to be with words. She felt a bit lightheaded; she had talked back and got away with it.

"You're driving me crazy, you know that? We're not a good match, and yet we've been constantly in each other's company. When I made that promise to you, I frankly didn't know if I'd keep it. But now I see the value of it, *if you will honor it as I am doing.*"

Vaffa looked tortured. Lilo thought the blood ritual must mean a lot to her, and that Vaffa felt badly about not trusting someone who had gone through it with her.

"*How?* How can I trust you? If I was in your position, I don't think I'd ever think of *anything* but escaping."

"I didn't, at first. And it's never far from my mind. But I can give you two reasons why I won't be running now, and I hope they'll ease your mind, or else you might as well push me. First, I'm virtually certain you're not the only one of Tweed's loyalists here on Pluto. There's probably someone, maybe two or three, who follow us everywhere. Even if there's *not,* Tweed is operating on the assumption I'll assume there *is.* I think either one is just as likely, the first maybe a little more so. Anyway, that means if I ran I'd have no better than a fifty–fifty chance of getting away with it, not counting the things you'd do to get me back. When I run, it's going to be a *lot* better than that."

"And the second reason?"

"I don't know if you'll believe this one, so you'd better think hard about the first. But for the record, I'm worried. I don't like the sound of that Hotline message. I don't like it at *all*. I think someone had better look into it, and it might as well be me. So I want to go out and hear it for myself."

Vaffa lowered her eyes for a moment and rubbed her bare scalp. Then she nodded, and sat down cross-legged on the tree limb.

"All right. I'm . . . I'm sorry. I said I'd trust you, and I will from now on. On the same terms as before, though, don't forget that. If you betray me, I'll hunt you down and kill you, no matter how long it takes."

"That's all I'm asking for." Lilo sat beside her. She stretched out with her arms behind her head.

"So how did it go with the holehunter?" Vaffa asked.

"Washed out. He won't do it."

"*What?*"

"Put your shirt on. That's why I'm late. I had him *that* close. We were talking terms."

"Then what's the problem?"

"You. Oh, not you personally. You and Cathay. He flatly refuses to take more than one passenger. None of us can go alone, for obvious reasons, so the deal had to fall through."

"But why? I checked him out. His ship would handle four easily over that distance."

Lilo sighed. "I know. You have to try and understand what these people are like. They don't *like* people. It was *torture* for him to consider taking me alone. Three people scared him so badly he could barely talk."

"I guess I still don't understand."

Lilo tried again, because she didn't, either. "Put yourself in his place. He's spent most of his life alone on that ship. It's like part of his body. He's slowly going insane here on Pluto, and he knows it. To him, sharing his ship is as repulsive as . . ." she flailed her hands helplessly, ". . . I don't know. Sharing a toothbrush. Think of your own metaphor. He just won't do it, not for anything."

"Then we're back where we started."

Lilo pursed her lips, then turned her head and smiled.

"Nooo. As it happens, we're not. I hired him as an expert consultant. Gave him enough for a stake at the tables. Asked him the big question: Is there *anyone* who might do what we need, do it faster than we could do it ourselves by buying our own ship? Or was it hopeless? Would every hunter react as he did?"

"Go on. What did he say?"

"He gave me a name. No promises, you understand. But if anyone will do it, she will. She's crazy, even by holehunter standards. And I'm going up to see her in two hours, on the next shuttle."

"Why didn't you say so in the first . . . no, never mind. I suppose I can't go."

"That's right. No sense in spooking her with the three of us right off. This will take finesse."

"Then that's you, obviously."

Lilo turned her head, looking to see if the other woman had been trying to make a joke. That would be a first. But Vaffa's face was as stolid as ever.

"What's her name?"

"Javelin."

17

The singular personage named Javelin lived in her ship, the *Cavorite,* which was currently stationed at the Pluto spaceport—the real one, as opposed to the vast plain over Florida which was the landing facility for shuttles. It was a vast zone of space, but rather crowded, as the radar screen of Lilo's scooter showed. There were a thousand factories, power stations, mirrors, and farms; nearly all the heavy industry and a lot of the agriculture of Pluto. She was happy to leave the driving to the traffic-control computer.

The scooter mated with the lock of the *Cavorite.* Lilo was surprised at the size of the other ship as she climbed over the struts of the scooter toward the open door. It had looked strange coming in; most of it was engine and fuel tank, like any holehunter ship, but even that looked oversized. As for the lifesystem . . . could that be *brass?*

The lifesystem was streamlined, for no apparent reason. It jutted like a golden nipple at one end of the massive fuel-tank cylinder. It had none of the haphazard, strung-together look Lilo associated with deep-space vessels. It was a fat bullet, blunt at the nose and tapering slightly at the end. Four stubby fins were positioned equidistantly around the stern, where it sat on the fuel tank. The nose had a lot of glass in it, and round portholes were visible in a line down one side.

The lock seemed ordinary enough until she saw the big brass air-pressure dials with scrollwork needles spinning rapidly. She pulled open the inner door and cracked her helmet seal at the same time.

She was in a small room, about three times the size of the airlock. There was plush purple carpet on two facing walls, while the other four were paneled in mahogany. Bolted securely to each of the carpeted walls was a deep leather-covered chair with a carved ebony table beside it. On the tables were Tiffany lamps, crystal ashtrays, and an assortment of magazines. Lilo stared at the dates; the newest one she could see was two hundred years old.

There was no way out of the room except the door to the lock. In the wall opposite the lock was a circular hole large enough for Lilo to put her head through. Not that she was about to do that. She sat in one of the chairs, making that wall her temporary "floor," and looked up at the other chair on the "ceiling." She didn't care for the effect.

She had not recognized the square pane of glass in the wall opposite her chair for what it was: a scanning, electron-gun, flat black-and-white television screen. Javelin must have blown the tube herself; Lilo was sure none existed outside of museums. Now it lit up with the life-sized face of a woman. She was attractive, though more mature than was fashionable. Lilo seldom saw anyone who kept her apparent age above twenty-five. Javelin looked more like the middle thirties. The picture was head only, and Lilo felt vaguely disappointed.

"So you want to charter a spaceship," Javelin said. "It's a novel request, I'll grant you that. I'm probably the only holehunter who might be intrigued by it. But I'm not intrigued enough, at this moment, to do business with you. Let's hear it, and it's going to have to be awfully good."

Lilo had been prepared for a long, circuitous discussion. The hole-hunters she had met seemed to operate that way. Javelin caught her a little off balance.

"Uh, could I ask one question? I thought you wanted me to come here so you could see me face-to-face. But it looks like I can't even get into your ship."

"This *is* face-to-face," Javelin said. "I've never bothered to install video transmission equipment. For me to see you, you had to come to this room. Now, where were you planning to go? And I'll give you another hint. Lay it on the line. Don't back into it; tell me exactly what you want."

"All right. I . . . that is, me, my wife, and . . . let me start over." Lilo was sweating. She had the uneasy feeling Javelin knew something about her, and it was obvious she wanted the truth. Maybe Quince had called and told her something.

"Me and two other people need to get out to the Hotline."

"Where on the Hotline? Are you talking about the transmitter at . . . 70 Ophiuchi? That would be quite a trip. But I suspect you mean you want to get to a point on the line that marks the area of strongest signal strength as it passes the Solar System."

"Exactly. Could you get us there?"

"Certainly. Why do you want to go?"

"I can't tell you that. I'm sorry, I just can't."

"That's all right. You're entitled to your little secrets." She looked thoughtful, and Lilo was worried. She sensed she was up against a shrewd person, possibly a very old one. There was no way to tell for sure; but she always got a strange feeling when she was around someone who was over three hundred.

"Where are you from? And what are the names of the other two who would be going?"

"Luna. Vaffa and Cathay. How old are you?" She had not meant to ask it.

"If I don't mind your asking?" She made a small smile. "Old enough to be the missing link in your family chain, Lilo. I was born in 1979, Old Style. My name at that time was Mary Lisa Bailey. I was the first woman on Mars, if you're interested. It was my only footnote in the history books."

Lilo was not sure if she was being lied to. She had run into extravagant claims of age before, and generally discounted them. As far as she knew, there were no Earthborn people still alive. The Invasion had been five and a half centuries ago, after all, and biological science had been in its infancy. Still . . .

"That would make you—"

"The oldest living human. Don't spread it around. The last thing I need is to be discovered again as a human interest story on the news.

By the way, I've decided to take you and your friends. When can you be ready to go?"

"You've . . . uh, let me see. This is going a little too fast for me." She never thought she'd say that to a hunter.

"Well, get thinking, woman. You don't need any shots or passports where we're going. I'll allow each of you thirty kilos of luggage. When can you be packed?"

"How about tomorrow? Don't you have to—"

"We burn in eighty-four-thousand standard seconds, then. Have your boarding passes ready. You do your own cooking and cleaning. I'm signing off now. There's some structural changes I'll have to make if you people are going to move around inside the ship. Walls to knock out, that sort of thing. You bring the champagne, okay?"

The screen went dark.

"I don't know why she caved in so fast," Lilo said. "Will you quit bothering me about it? Maybe she'll tell us." The three were approaching the vast bulk of the *Cavorite* in a scooter, a larger model that allowed them to carry their helmets. Each had a suit and a small suitcase.

Lilo had been replaying her conversation with Javelin all day long. She had told Vaffa that she was not worried about anything, that Javelin was just eccentric and probably didn't *have* a reason for taking them other than her own amusement.

But privately, Lilo was disturbed by several things, all of them so ephemeral she could barely define them. Of course there was the large question of why Javelin had agreed in the first place. The more she thought about it, the more she was convinced the deciding factor had been the mention of being from Luna, and the name of Vaffa. Something had happened just behind Javelin's impassive face when Lilo had said that.

Then there was the talk about the Hotline itself. Had there been a reason for Javelin being so specific about the destination? It *had* to be just her peculiar sense of humor, suggesting they might be considering a trip to 70 Ophiuchi. The deepest penetration by a human into interstellar space was no more than half a light-year; 70 Ophiuchi was seventeen lights away. But she had paused—hadn't she?—before mentioning the star.

The reception room was changed from her earlier visit. The wall opposite the lock had been knocked out, and the chairs were no longer bolted to the walls. The room was crowded now with odds and ends of antique furniture, so much that they could not see how to get to the other end.

Javelin appeared on the other side of the jumble. It was the first time any of them had seen her, but their view was impeded.

"Hello there," she called, peering at them through the furniture. "You'll have to help me load this stuff into the scooter before you get settled in. I won't be able to boost it with the three of you along." Then, quicker than the eye could follow, she was beside them.

"Holy Mother Earth, don't *do* that!" Vaffa seemed genuinely shaken. Lilo was a little dizzy herself. It was uncanny, beyond belief, how Javelin had threaded herself through the seemingly impassable maze.

Lilo looked at Javelin and saw a two-meter cylinder, swelling gently from the extremities to a fatter part in the middle, with a hand at each end. The cylinder was flexible at four points, which were her knee, hip, shoulder, and elbow. Growing from her "shoulder" at a slight angle from the rest of the cylinder was her head, with brown hair cut efficiently short. She wore a simple blue tube of cloth that left her arm and leg bare.

That was Javelin, with her arm held straight up. When she put her arm at her side, she looked like a jackknife.

What she had done was not a simple matter of getting rid of her right arm and left leg. Dispensing with two limbs—usually the legs—was common among spacers. But Javelin had worked to an esthetic vision of slimness. Her rib cage, right shoulder, and left hip had been redesigned with plastic structures replacing the bones. She had got rid of her left kidney, right lung, and a lot of intestine. Her elbow and knee had been reengineered with ball and socket joints.

She was limber as a snake. What was left of her could wriggle through a hole twenty centimeters in diameter.

"Do what?" Javelin asked, innocently.

". . . *that*. What you did. I don't like people coming up on me that fast."

"I'll bear it in mind. Now will you lend a hand?"

They got the items moved into the scooter. It might have gone faster, but all three were fascinated by Javelin's movements. She would grab a handle at the side of the lock with one hand, reach out with her leg and use the hand on that end to snatch a piece of furniture, pull, and bend like an eel as she guided it through the hatch.

"This way," she said, when it was done. They followed her out the door, all of them moving awkwardly in zero-gee. There was a long hallway, two walls carpeted and two paneled in oak, with ornamental brass rails on each of the paneled walls.

"Life-support equipment back here," she said, indicating the walls. "Living quarters are forward." She started off, hand over hand, which in her case meant grabbing the rail and swinging her body in an arc until she could make contact with the other hand on the end of her ankle. Three swings like that and she was arrowing down the center of the corridor, leg first, looking back at them with a broad smile on her face. She hit the far end, soaked up momentum with her leg, and vanished around the corner.

"What will modern science think of next?" Cathay said.

"Don't knock it," Lilo said. "It seems to work pretty well. She makes me feel almost . . . outmoded, you know?"

"Yeah. But she'd be a real sight in a gravity field."

"I gather she never goes down. *Never.*"

Javelin was waiting for them at the end of the corridor, at the first of two locks. She ushered them through, with comments about the ship's air-integrity routines that she expected them to follow with no nonsense. Then they were into the living quarters.

"Sorry about the size," Javelin said, opening the doors to two small rooms. "This isn't the *Queen Mary*. As it was, I had to move out my stamp collection. So two of you will have to room together, unless one of you bunks on the couch in the solarium. Go ahead, stow your luggage. Now come this way."

Lilo was dazzled. She was not sure how much Javelin was underplaying, whether she actually regretted that there were only two "guest rooms" on a ship that by all economic laws should have had none at all. The rooms were small, but lavishly furnished, paneled, and carpeted, like everything else she had seen. They passed two more facing doors, one leading to a workshop and another to a medical laboratory. Lilo got only a glimpse of each.

The solarium was the biggest part of the living area. Javelin led them in, and kept going forward.

"I'll be right back," she said. "Make yourselves at home. Coffee bulbs over there, drinks in the bottles against that wall." She darted through a small hole in the forward bulkhead.

"This place is crazy," Cathay said. "Absolutely crazy."

Lilo agreed with him. She had been in all types of ships, and had seen nothing like the *Cavorite*.

"What do you call this?" she asked. "Early Victorian? Late Captain Nemo?" But Cathay had no answer, and Javelin was gone.

The solarium was about ten meters in length, and four meters across. Unlike the rest of the ship, it had a definite floor, which made no sense at all to Lilo. Things can be done so much more economically in free-fall. Not only that, but the floor was parallel to the axis of thrust. Under boost, the room would stand on end. At *no* time would down be in the direction of the floor. Vaffa pointed this out.

"Well, when you think of it, she spends such a tiny part of her trip boosting . . ." But it still didn't make sense.

The ceiling was curved, following the cylindrical shape of the outer hull. Twelve great panes of glass, six on each side of the room, curved overhead to meet at an ornate wooden beam that ran the length of the room. It was obvious why she called it the solarium.

The room was festooned with plants, vines, and flowers. It featured a two-keyboard pipe organ at one end, and a slowly spinning toroidal aquarium at the other; tiny angelfish gaped at Lilo when she put her face close to their revolving world. In between, the motif was plush velvet-upholstered chairs and sofas, carved wood, and lots of brass trim. Lilo felt swamped with detail; everything was infested with curlicues.

Lilo stuck her head through the hole where Javelin had gone, and she got a surprise. As she had suspected, the room beyond was the control center for the ship—though again, it was very different, with its brass-ringed instruments, its lack of digital readouts, and several things that looked like manual controls. Beside the narrow pilot's chair there was one long lever, capped with a crystal knob, that was plainly marked STOP and GO. But the real surprise was that the room was empty. Since it was at the nose of the ship with nothing beyond it but space, Lilo thought it odd.

She backed out in time to see Javelin enter the solarium from the aft corridor. So she had her own ways of getting around.

"This is an astounding ship," Cathay said to her.

"Do you think so? Thank you. I like it. I should—it's been home for nearly three hundred years. I lifted the basic design—the outside, that is—from an old magazine cover. Pre-Invasion. Pre-space, for that matter."

"That's crazy," Vaffa said, flatly.

"Do you think so? I don't. Obviously the artist who thought up the design knew nothing about spaceships. He was trying to sell magazines, so he made it sexy instead of logical. I liked that."

"But the weight penalties," Lilo said, feeling baffled. "If form doesn't follow function, don't you lose efficiency?"

"It's funny you should say that. It's true, mostly, but don't you have any poetry in your soul? I've been battling hard-assed engineers since the first moon colony. We've become a race of engineers. What we never seem to understand is that after it's time to railroad, there's time to build a *beautiful* railroad. The state of the art has advanced enough; we can afford to pay a small penalty in efficiency. But deep-space ships still look like a hat rack fucking a Christmas tree."

"Pardon me?"

"Copping. Sorry, it was an archaic word. Come to think of it, all the concepts in that metaphor were archaic. But *Cavorite* is less inefficient than you'd think. Once I'd made the one extravagant decision—to go out alone in a ship five times bigger than what I need for the bare necessities—the rest of it was virtually free. A little thin metal for the false shell outside. Some furniture that looks massive but really isn't; the wood is a thin veneer over standard structural foam. The organ doubles as input to the ship's computer and library, which is out of sight. The aquarium is part of the recycling system, and if the fish are okay, so am I. You'll see. It works."

Lilo still had her doubts. But Quince had spoken of her with awe. She was said to be the most successful hunter of all time.

"If you're about ready to go, I should start on the final countdown. Still some things to do. I searched your luggage, and studied the X rays I took of you as—"

"You *what?*" It was Vaffa. Her face was quickly turning red.

Javelin looked her up and down. "Yes, I'm not surprised at your reaction," she said, dryly. "You had several crystals and several other components in your things. With a little spit and bubble gum, you might have turned them into a pair of hand lasers. I ditched them, in the interest of a safe, calm voyage."

Vaffa had planted her feet against the aft bulkhead. She launched herself across the room, toward Javelin. Her arms were extended, her mouth open in a snarl. Lilo didn't want to watch. Javelin was so tiny, so fragile-looking. Vaffa started to twist in the air, coming around for a blow at Javelin's midsection.

It was over almost before it began. Javelin twisted, bent at impossible places, planted one hand against the floor. She shoved, turned as Vaffa sailed past her, and chopped across the larger woman's neck. Vaffa hit the pipes above the organ, loosely, and floated.

Javelin glanced at her once, then turned her attention to Lilo.

"I have to know the nature of the device implanted in your abdomen," she said. "Also the thing attached to the left side of your pelvic bone."

"I don't know what they are," Lilo said. "I've suspected there might be something in me, though."

Javelin nodded. "Like that, huh? All right. One of them looks like a simple homing device. I thought the other was a bomb, but decided it wasn't. More likely it's a narcotic drug ampule. That would go along with the homer, wouldn't it?"

"I guess so." Lilo's cheeks were burning.

"Fine." Javelin seemed to want to get off the subject, too. "You'll want to remove them. Feel free to use the surgery. I can put them overboard, or you might think of something else to do with them." She let her eyes move slowly to Vaffa, still dangling loosely in midair, then smiled at Lilo.

"Boost in six hundred seconds. You'd better get to your cabins."

18

Cathay and I moved Vaffa to one of the cabins, and we decided to share the other. As we belted her into her bunk, the ship was undergoing changes. Vaffa's bunk moved from the floor and positioned itself against the aft bulkhead. In the solarium, the fish tank was draining.

Boost was one gee, about what I'd got used to on Pluto. Now we were living on the wall. But the washbasin and refresher facilities had done a flip-flop, and the lighting shifted as we moved so it was never in our eyes.

Outside, the corridor was now a vertical shaft. I could live with it for the twenty-four hours we'd be boosting.

They spent most of their time in their cabins, and they didn't see Javelin. Lilo went to the solarium once, but to do it she had to climb eight meters on a ladder which had extruded itself from the corridor wall. And now the solarium was not a pleasant place to be. The organ was now on the ceiling, hanging ten meters over her head. There was another ladder, and she climbed it to poke her head into the control room, but Javelin wasn't there. She realized that they were not likely to see her until the ship stopped boosting. Javelin would get around by means of her system of narrow pipes, where the rest of them could not follow.

Cathay and Lilo could see Vaffa across the hall. She made no move to visit them, spending her time pacing. Lilo was nervous about it, wondering how much of the blame for the situation she was going to have to take. Vaffa was going to suspect a deal between Lilo and Javelin, and would be hard to live with.

There was not much to do but sleep. They went through one night period, with the ship's lights dimmed. It was not until they had been boosting for twenty hours that Javelin contacted them. Again, it was by a flat television screen, this time set into their ceiling.

"You're gonna hate me," she said, "but it's decision time, kids. Time for the laying of cards upon tables, for the revelation of hidden motives. Possibly you've wondered why I was willing to take you on this little jaunt."

"We have, some. Are you going to tell us?" Lilo glanced across the hall. Vaffa was at her door, leaning out over the drop-off, listening intently.

"Yeah. Well, insofar as I know myself. As to why I *took* you, I guess a lot of that was simple perversity. It's not what I might normally do, so I did it. You've got to watch yourself when you get as old as I am. You have to try new things, sometimes for no better reason than that they're new. Otherwise you rust."

"How do you know?" Cathay asked.

"I don't. But it's worked so far. I'd be a fool to change my tactics now. As to why I was willing to *go,* in the sense of with or without you, to the Hotline . . . I've become very interested in the Hotline in the last few months."

Lilo saw Vaffa step quickly onto the ladder, then into the room with them. She stood beside them, looking up at the screen.

"Why are you interested?" Vaffa asked.

"The same reason you are. Anyone would be, don't you think?"

"How would you know about that? It's restricted information, limited to a few . . ."

Javelin raised one eyebrow. "I might ask how *you* know about it. But I've got my own theories on that. How *I* know is the same way I know anything about the Line. At any given time there's always a couple holehunters in the path of the Hotline signal. There's not much else to do; they listen in. And we talk to each other. It may take a few years to finish a conversation, but we've got plenty of time; we're not in a hurry. The hunter community knew about the message before the StarLine board of directors did. We've been talking about it for months now. It's been a cause of some concern to us. So I'm going to check it out."

"You want to see if it really translates the way it seems to?"

"No, no," Javelin laughed. "It does. There's no doubt about that. It's a threat, all right. Listen, you're going out there to get the message in its original form; that's your only possible motive for wanting to go out there at all. Well, I've got it, in my computer. We've checked it six ways from Sunday. Now we're interested in finding out what the 'severe penalties' are all about. I've been . . . well, sort of elected, though that's a pretty formal way of describing it—to go out and see. If they've got the muscle to back up their threat, we hunters might need to look for some new customers."

The statement shocked Lilo, but it scandalized Vaffa.

"Just like that? You want to find out which way the wind is blowing?"

"More or less."

"Whom do you plan on selling to?" Vaffa snorted. "The Ophiuchites? The Invaders?"

"Either one if the price is right."

"Then I spit on you and all your kind. You're talking of treason to your race."

"Piss on your race, Free Earther."

Lilo quickly stepped in. "Are you expecting some kind of second message? Spelling out penalties, perhaps?"

"It's possible. But that's not why I'm going."

"Then I don't understand. What good is this trip to you?"

Javelin smiled again. "Here we come to the decision I spoke of. Our bargain said I'd deliver you to some point along the line of transmission of the Hotline. But it's a long line. You probably had in mind the closest point, but you didn't specify it, did you? What I propose to do is take all of us to a point half a light-year from the sun, and on that line. I have reason to believe it could be very interesting."

"Why?"

"For the purpose of meeting the Ophiuchites face to face."

Vaffa seemed puzzled by the idea. Cathay grinned, as if at some private joke, but when Lilo looked at him he shrugged. Lilo's neck was hurting from looking up. She followed Cathay's example by stretching out on the floor and folding her arms under her head. They waited.

"You're probably curious as to why I think they're out there." Javelin looked a little disappointed in their reaction.

"That's a fair statement," Cathay said. He seemed to be enjoying himself.

"Okay. Hunters have a different perspective on the Hotline than the StarLine company does. They sit in a station spang in the middle of the area of greatest signal strength. And why shouldn't they? The messages are garbled enough even there. But it limits their viewpoint. Essentially, they listen from one motionless point in space.

"Hunters criss-cross the Line in all directions, at various distances from the sun, and both closer and farther away from 70 Ophiuchi than the StarLine station. When we cross it, we listen in. Our computers note when we first receive the signals and when we finally lose them.

"About a hundred years ago, we began to notice a few things. It was only after many years that we were able to be sure of them. It's hard to get reliable time-checks at the speeds we operate at, and it takes a long time to cross-check all the data. But now we're sure.

"A laser signal is a cone. It's a very narrow one, but it does have an apex at the end of the laser, and it spreads very slowly the farther it goes. We began to notice a parallax shift. At one edge of the cone, the signal seemed to come from one side of 70 Ophiuchi, then when you got to the other side, it had shifted. We began to plot the lines that define the outer surface of the cone. Other evidence backed us up: the cross-section size of the cone at various points, and the rate of drop-off of signal strength. It all indicated one thing: The Hotline doesn't originate at 70 Ophiuchi at all, but from some place about one-half light-year from the sun, in the *direction* of 70 Ophiuchi. And that's not likely to be an accident. They wanted us to think they were that far away. Which brings up all sorts of interesting possibilities."

"I need to make a radio call," Vaffa said. She sounded subdued.

"I thought you might. Let's see if I have Boss Tweed's phone number here in my files. . . ."

Vaffa looked down at Lilo and Cathay. Lilo was about to protest, but Javelin interrupted her.

"They didn't tell me anything. I checked your phone records before you came aboard, and you've made a lot of calls to Luna. I was sure you were a Free Earther, and you proved it a few minutes ago. Now you're slavering to have someone tell you what to do, so you don't have to think. Who else would you be calling but Boss Tweed?"

"That's none of your business," Vaffa yelled. "Now you put me through. We chartered this ship, and—"

"And has it occurred to you that you shouldn't talk to your captain that way? In case you hadn't noticed, I am in *complete* control of this ship. You can't even enter the bridge; your pointy head would make it, but not your shoulders. This ship goes where I want it to go, and you will watch your mouth if you want the oxygen ratio in your room to stay the same."

Lilo was on her feet now, and she dug Vaffa hard in the ribs. She got away with it, which was a measure of how much the other woman had learned in the last month.

"We really do have to check back, though," Cathay said, reasonably. "You're talking about vastly increased expenses, and none of us has the money for that. Tweed would have to authorize it."

"You're right, and you're wrong," Javelin said, calmly. "Understand that your situation has changed completely. I know why *she* is along." She made a face. "She's loyal to Tweed. You two don't seem to be, if my instincts are worth anything. I assume he has some hold over you. Well, that's over. I don't condone slavery, and I won't take orders from a man six billion kilometers away. You will call Tweed, but you won't ask him for anything. You will *tell* him this. Pay attention now; I don't want to repeat.

" 'The *Cavorite* is headed for the Hotline sending station.' Here you can insert the explanation I just gave you. He's bright; he should understand. 'Expenses for this trip will be about four hundred times the figure originally discussed. A drone tanker is now departing the catapult head on Pluto, and will soon start to accelerate at nine gees. As you know, these ships are not recoverable; hence the drastic increase in expenses. It will rendezvous with us in about twenty million seconds. Without it, of course, we would have fuel to reach the station, but not to return.

" 'If you, Tweed, wish to be represented on this expedition, you will cause to be deposited in my account in the Bank of Lowell a sum which my bankers have already communicated to you. Should you not desire to pay, your interest in this expedition will be considered terminated. The ship will go on as planned, underwritten by the Holehunters Trade Association of Lowell, a fact which you are free to check. And your agent, Vaffa, will be put out the lock and invited to walk back. Signed, your obedient, humble former slaves, et cetera, et cetera.' "

"You can't do that!" The veins were standing out on Vaffa's neck. Her clenched fists were bleeding. Cathay seemed delighted, and Lilo wanted to allow herself the euphoria she felt, but knew she wasn't home free yet. Carefully, gently, she stroked Vaffa's shoulder. If the woman exploded now, it could be fatal.

"Listen to me, Vaffa," she whispered. "You've got to do what's best for the Boss, don't you? Don't do that! *Let go of me!*" The grip on her arm loosened for a moment. Cathay had come over and put his head close to theirs.

"She's right," he said. "Don't lose your temper. Think it out. Sure, she's got the Boss over a barrel, but she's offering him a good deal. She'll *kill* you if you can't learn to live with this, and then the Boss is *never* going to get out to the Ophiuchites and find out what he wants to—"

"She couldn't kill me! That freakish, puny little—"

"Think about what you're saying, Vaffa. This is her ship. You can't even get into her *room*. You don't have a weapon, and there's no telling what she might have. She even beat you bare-handed. You're going to have to swallow your pride and admit it. You've got to do this for Tweed, remember, for the Boss."

Slowly, painfully, Vaffa released her grip on Lilo's arm. Her shoulders slumped, and she sank slowly to the deck with her head in her hands. Lilo glanced up at the screen and the impassive face. She went out into the corridor, up the ladder, and into the solarium. A screen came to life, close to her feet. She looked down at Javelin's face.

"I want to thank you," she said, and felt tears coming to her eyes. She didn't bother wiping them away.

"It's okay. The situation had to be resolved."

"It isn't, not yet. That's what I wanted to talk to you about. I . . . it occurs to me that you could space all of us. After you've got the money."

Javelin shrugged. "I won't. It's a chance you'll have to take. I'm not above pulling a fast one to save myself some money—no hole-hunter ever is. Stinginess is second nature to us. But I won't break a bargain. I contracted to take you there, and that's what I'm going to do."

"Why?"

Javelin looked a little embarrassed. "Well, we're going to meet some aliens, maybe. I guess I do have a little loyalty to the human race. It didn't seem right to go alone; I thought I ought to take a cross-section of the race, if I could."

Lilo laughed. "A holehunter, a killer, a disbarred teacher, and a condemned criminal."

"Is that what you are? You'll have to tell me all about it one of these days. We'll have plenty of time."

Lilo choked up. She *did* want to talk about it. She hadn't been able to bring it up with Cathay; maybe Javelin would be the person.

"What about Vaffa?" she asked.

"I don't know. I'll take her along if she behaves. But I won't feel I've broken the contract with Tweed if I have to destroy her like a mad dog, as a menace to the safety of the ship."

"That's it. I'm worried about her. She's not good with abstractions. I can explain to her that being good, not causing trouble, is what the Boss would want her to do. Otherwise, you kill her and Tweed loses out. Damn! Why should I be trying to save her life? She's threatened to kill me many times. She's killed two of my clones."

"All you'd have to do to kill her," Javelin observed, "is to leave things alone. She'd clash with me, and that would be it, right?"

"I think so." Lilo sighed. "I don't know if it's that I hate to see anyone killed, or if I'm afraid I might get killed before you got rid of her. Anyway, it's an explosive situation. Here's what I want. I don't think Vaffa's capable of disobeying a direct order from Tweed. I want to add a demand to your list. He must order her not to harm you, or me, or Cathay. She's to be relieved of her duties guarding us. He must impress on her that she is his only representative on the ship, that it's all in her hands. She's got to live to report back to him, and to do that she must live peacefully with us."

"Done. Will that work?"

"I'm sure of it. It will settle her mind, make her accept it. And Tweed will go along. He won't be happy, but he doesn't have much choice, does he?"

"That's how I saw it," Javelin said smugly.

Lilo smiled, and finally dared to let herself believe she was free. She was cooped up on this ship, but she was *free*.

"How long will we be gone, by the way?" she asked.

"The trip will take about three hundred million seconds, going out."

"Would you mind putting that into standard Earth months?"

"About one hundred and twenty. Twenty years, round trip."

19

We could have made the trip to Poseidon much faster than we did. Even hauling my entire Ring base, that tug Cathay stole had plenty of power; it was built to shove quantum black holes around with a minimum of fuss.

But the whole stunt depended on arriving at Poseidon at exactly the right time, coming from just the right angle. We were constrained by the relative positions of Jupiter and Saturn at the time of departure, the orbital speed of Poseidon, and its rotation rate.

I had never bothered to give my rock hideaway a name. As we neared Poseidon and cut in the tug's engines again to get the rock up to speed, Cathay named it Vengeance.

They were hanging motionless relative to Poseidon, about fifty kilometers away. Without magnification it appeared as a small, irregular patch of gray, but on Lilo's screen it could be seen in more detail. It was dark and jagged, and coming around the horizon was a small cup with a fierce blue light in it.

Lilo thought back to the last time she had seen Parameter/Solstice. She had wanted them to come along, but it was obviously out of the question. If she and Cathay were successful with what they were about to do, there would be no time for dropping Parameter off anywhere; they would have to leave the system quickly. But Lilo wished they could have been with her to see their plan work.

If it worked, she reminded herself, swallowing nervously.

"Ten seconds," Lilo called out. She was wired into the computer, monitoring its performance through the cameras on *Vengeance*. She could feel the tiny bursts from the steering rockets as the guidance program made fine adjustments to the course. Now the target was coming up at blinding speed, made accessible to Lilo's senses only through the computer link. She got a glimpse of silver, then the impact destroyed the camera.

"A hit," she said quietly. She pulled the computer cord from the socket in her head.

Vengeance had gone into the nullfield bowl that contained the black hole. In a fraction of a second the mass of rock was churned into a mixture of lava, hot gas, and plasma. It splashed.

Immediately, the hole began to devour it. The gravity gradient quickly collapsed the matter close to the hole and began to pull it down the bottomless pit, releasing energy as it was compressed. As matter was destroyed, more moved in, but was pushed away by the pressure of the reactions happening just outside the event horizon. There was a huge explosion, and ninety percent of the mass of *Vengeance* was blown free of the combined gravity of Poseidon and the hole. What was left began to collapse again.

None of this made any difference to the hemisphere of the nullfield. It was proof against anything the human race had yet been able to produce. The impact of *Vengeance* had no effect on it.

But Lilo watched very closely to see how the electromagnetic field generators were withstanding the strain. The one wild card in Parameter's equation was the generators. They were already supporting the mass of the hole. What could not be known for sure was whether they would hold up under the sudden acceleration caused by the impact. If they failed, the hole would start to drift downward, quickly destroying the nullfield generator beneath it. With the field off, the hole would drift through Poseidon as if it were empty space, and they would have to try to recover it on the other side.

"I don't see any movement, do you?" Lilo asked.

"No. It seems to be holding."

There were more explosions, coming only a few seconds apart, until the molten remains of the rock had rid itself of enough mass to reach stability. Now it was a tightly packed white-hot star, brighter than the surface of the sun, and only about a meter in diameter.

"Let the astronomers wonder about *that* for a while," Lilo said, and turned on the radio. "Can you hear me down there? Vaffa, Vaffa, are you listening?"

There was no answer for a while, and Lilo kept repeating herself until a male voice came over the radio.

"Who is calling?"

"This is Lilo, returned from the dead. And Cathay is with me. We brought back your ship, along with a present. You felt it coming in a few minutes ago. Is anyone hurt?"

"I don't know," Vaffa said, impatiently.

Lilo understood that he really didn't care, either. She shivered. It was her first contact with Vaffa.

"Just what did you hope to accomplish, anyway? You must have known you couldn't kill us with whatever you did. The best you could hope for was to entomb a few of us—which you did—but our suits will protect us until we can dig out. Which we are doing." The voice was imperious, used to being obeyed, but there was a note of uncertainty.

"He's damn sure you're not that dumb," Cathay said, with satisfaction. "Sometimes it doesn't help your nerves to know a lot about someone."

"I hope so," Lilo whispered. Then, into the mike: "What we accomplished is to push Poseidon out of its orbit. That's done, and it's too late to do anything about it. It was spectacular, let me tell you. In a few minutes people all over the system will be wondering what's going on out here. Does that suggest anything to you?"

There was silence from the other end.

"Before you run off to consult with the Boss, there's some things he needs to know. The way we figure it is simple. Everyone's going to wonder what's going on out here, but they'll figure it's Invaders up to something. This is Jupiter, after all. They won't dare send anyone to investigate. You can see if Tweed agrees with that."

There was no reply, so Lilo went on.

"We would like to point out that we are in possession of a powerful radio. I'm sure Tweed's been worried about that for some time now, wondering where Cathay is and what he's going to do. He's probably ready to get out, quick, if something should start to break. Okay, that's fine. But it's bound to take him some time. What we want you to ask him is this. How much time is he willing to buy?"

"Explain that, please."

"I was going to. First, an answer from you. How long would it take you, not counting ninety-six minutes of lagtime, to get Tweed on the radio, talk to him and get his answer? Don't hesitate; tell me right now." Cathay had emphasized the importance of that. According to him, Vaffa was not very bright, and was not a good liar. He should not be given time to think. They would be helped by the fact that his impulse would be to ask Tweed for orders as soon as possible.

"Well, I . . ."

"Now! Tweed's life depends on this. Don't make us doubt what you're saying."

"I speak to him in code, through a laser that is relayed to Luna by a satellite, so the signal will not be traced. The lagtime will be ninety-seven minutes today, because of that. He carries a prompter; it has never taken me longer than three minutes to get to him."

"Very well. It's bargaining time. Cathay and I are interested in the fate of the people under your guard. We realize that you are capable, if ordered to do it, of killing them. Tweed might order you to do that, we decided." Lilo found it hard to believe, but admitted that Cathay knew more about Tweed and Vaffa than she did.

"We want you to tell the Boss that would be a very stupid thing to do.

"We're going to broadcast the facts about the Poseidon installation all over the system. If they catch him, they'll kill him.

"The important thing to him is *when* we do this broadcasting. Now listen carefully. If he does as we tell him, we will hold off for a period of one standard month. Obviously, it's not in our interest to publicize this place. We don't want it known what's going on out here because we're all illegals in one way or another, including you. If an Eight Worlds ship lands on Poseidon, we'll all be executed.

"What we have to do is work toward our common interests. We need time, and so does Tweed. But we also need assurances that the people down there will not be massacred." She took a deep breath.

"Here's the deal. Tweed is to issue orders to you, and all your clone brothers and sisters, to leave the station and congregate in the open one kilometer from the nearest entrance. Unarmed. Before you leave, you are to deactivate the barrier leading to your private quarters and allow Niobe and Vejay to enter and see for themselves that no one is still inside. After that—"

"I've just learned that Vejay is unaccounted for," the man said. "Apparently he is buried. Niobe is here."

"All right. After Niobe has entered your quarters and seen you depart from the station, she will tell us so. We will then land and take you prisoner. Tweed is to further order you, in the hearing of Niobe and anyone else she wants with her, that you are not to harm anyone, now or in the future.

"In return for this, you and your clones will be allowed to live, as long as you stick to your orders. Tweed will be given one month to get away from Luna, to do whatever he planned to do to get underground if he was discovered."

"How do we know you'll keep your word about not killing us?"

Vaffa said. For the first time, he sounded worried, and Cathay slapped Lilo on the shoulder. Lilo grinned back at him.

"Obviously you can't be sure. You'll have to take my word for it. But your alternative is certain death, if an Eight Worlds ship is brought here in response to what we have to say, or if you harm the prisoners. Understand, we *will* broadcast if we have to. If Tweed won't accept our terms, it means all the people down there will be killed by you, anyway, so there's nothing for us to lose. This way you have a chance to live, too.

"Tweed's alternative is simple, too. He has exactly one hundred and fifteen minutes from right now to comply with our demands. If we don't hear from Niobe in that time, we start talking."

"We're calling him," Vaffa said. "I have only one more question. How do I know you're telling the truth about knocking Poseidon out of its orbit? How could I tell that?"

"Uh . . . I guess I can't prove it's not a bluff. But it doesn't change anything. The broadcast goes out in one hundred and fourteen minutes."

"Very well." There was a pause. "I suspect you're telling the truth about that. It was quite a jolt."

Lilo sat back again. She was sweating. She looked at Cathay, found herself hoping for his approval.

"How'd I do?"

"I thought it was pretty good," he said. It was sinking in on him now that they were really committed. His son was down there, out of his reach, dependent on Tweed's decision. "What if he does something else? I almost wish we hadn't done it. It's . . . it's such a responsibility."

Lilo reached over and touched him, gently. She knew she didn't have as much at stake as he did, and yet it was very important to her that the trick work. Her initial dislike of Cathay had faded as she came around to his way of thinking, as his interests began to coincide more easily with hers. On the trip from Saturn, they had grown close. She was anxious to meet his son, who was supposed to have been her clone's best friend. She hoped she would get the chance.

"What can he do?" she said. "We've gone over it a million times."

"I know. I just get scared he's got some trick."

"Look. When Tweed gets the message from Vaffa, he's got two hours. A couple minutes to make up his mind, forty-eight minutes for his answer to get to us, then another forty-eight before our broadcast could reach Luna. He's a *public figure*. The police computers know where he is, because he's an assassination target. If he drops out of sight quickly, with no notice, the whole machinery will be looking for him in sixty seconds."

"But he must have prepared something. He knew I'm out here, with a radio, and could blow the whistle on him any time."

"But he knew you wouldn't. He felt safe enough about that, because if you did, it would kill your son."

Cathay was shaking now, and Lilo stroked his shoulder. The control cabin of the tug was too cramped for them to even turn to face each other, but she managed to kiss his cheek.

"Tweed doesn't have a choice," Lilo said. "If he doesn't do what we told him to, he'll have only two hours to get so far underground that the kind of massive search we could stir up won't be able to find him. I just don't think he can do that."

"But could we really broadcast?" Cathay was in increasing agony now. It was going to be a long two hours.

Lilo said nothing. The choices were really out of their control now; had been since *Vengeance* smashed in. If they didn't get confirmation from Niobe in two hours it would mean that things too ghastly to think about were happening on Poseidon.

And then they damn well would broadcast.

Tweed was a familiar figure in the public ways of King City, and he had always loved it. The sight of him lumbering down Clarke Boulevard was beloved by most of his former constituents. Some days he would waddle aimlessly and amiably, pressing the flesh, with a smile and a pat on the back for all.

But the love of the people sometimes had to be kept at arm's length. One had to hobnob to keep winning mandates at the polls. On the other hand, there were times when it was necessary to move freely without being mobbed. His hat was the signal. If it was in his hand, they could feel free to talk to him. When he was wearing it, it was understood that he was busy on the people's business.

Hat firmly on his head, Boss Tweed pounded down the center of the corridor, implacable as a rhinoceros, spouting blue clouds of smoke from his cigar.

He turned corners with the ponderous grace of a tugboat, gradually working his way into less frequented parts of the city. There was an anonymous door at the end of a deserted stretch of corridor. It opened to his palmprint; he stepped into a small room and sealed the door behind him. At the press of a button, the room began a slow descent.

Off came the black and gray coat, the baggy pants, the shoes of hardened leather, the white spats. Soon he stood naked in front of a pile of clothes. Without his shoes he was nine centimeters shorter, but he was still a big man.

He did something to his face and the sagging jowls sagged even further, dropped, and fell into his hands. They were warm to the touch, made from a plastic that sat on the borderline between living and dead material. He dropped the two quivering masses onto the pile of clothes, onto the stovepipe hat he had worn every day for fifty years. The hat collapsed on itself.

For a moment he stood staring down at the pile of clothes, and he began to shake.

"No," he said. "No, this isn't the end. It's just a setback." He leaned against the wall behind him and waited for the fit of weakness to pass. With his face buried in his hands, more scraps of plastiflesh peeled away. When he finally looked up, his sense of purpose restored, he was a different person. He had shed thirty years of apparent age, along with the subtle gestalt of lines and protrusions that had marked his face as that of a male human being. He was androgynous now; his huge paunch could not conceal the fact that he had no genital organs. Two swellings on his chest could have belonged to a woman or a very fat man.

He heaved himself erect. With a wet slithering sound, twenty-five kilos of rubbery plastiflesh fell from his belly, his arms and legs, and his buttocks. The breasts remained, jutting out over a flat stomach he had not seen in fifty years.

Tweed was now outwardly a female, but a close examination of the labial folds hidden under the triangle of pubic hair would have revealed no vaginal opening. No hormones raged through Tweed's body, nothing that could divert him from his purpose. He had decided on neutrality long ago, and had never regretted it. Now, it was going to help save his life. The first step in adopting a new identity was radical cosmetic surgery, usually involving a sex change. That alone would never be enough to turn the trick, but it was an essential first step. He had just accomplished it in record time, as he had planned long ago if it ever came to this.

"Came to this . . ." he muttered. Again he felt weak. He staggered, and nearly fell on the slippery floor. The plastiflesh had dissolved, and so had the clothes. The water and gray sludge left behind by the disintegration was sucked into a drain in the floor.

He thought back over the years since the first glimmerings of the vision, the future of a liberated Earth. He knew there were those who thought him an opportunist, who felt he was just cashing in on a vein of opinion which had been growing in Luna for a century. But he was sincere.

Tweed had been sincere enough to take his only son and carefully raise him to be a killer, a follower of orders no matter what those orders might be. He had pored over ancient books for a year before trying it, but he had raised a soldier. The methods of the U.S. Marines and the Red Army had worked admirably, combined with drug therapy and behavioral psychology. Vaffa had never disappointed him, except for a lingering sadness that he and his clone brothers and sisters had been such dull company.

It would be a scandal, all right. Even with the month's grace period, things would begin to come out as soon as it was clear that Tweed had actually disappeared. People would be looking for him, computer search programs narrowing down on him, at first with concern for his safety. Later, when questions started to be asked, things would start to come to light. Vaffa would be the first of those things, but there would be more. There were two Vaffas still on Luna, and no chance to do anything about them.

Now he faced the nearly impossible struggle to re-establish himself as a data-banked citizen with a right of life. He could no longer be Boss Tweed. He had to fit himself into the cracks between the integrated circuits, the very task he had set for a dozen condemned criminals as their only alternative to working for him. It could be done—party members were in key positions in many of the most powerful computers—but it would take time.

"It's just a setback," Tweed said again.

But did it have to be? His/her new face frowned deeply as once more the facts were reviewed. There was still time to countermand the orders to Vaffa, but it was running out. The face contorted, and she/he slammed a fist into the wall. Lilo!

Tweed had always known, down deep, that with the kind of chances he/she was taking it was inevitable that one day someone would make it to freedom. Then, a few months ago, that call from Pluto. Lilo, dictating through Vaffa, telling Tweed what he had to do. It had galled him, but he really had no choice. Now this final blow, and again it came from Lilo. But which one? The teacher, Cathay, had dropped the pilot of the tug close to Poseidon after he took possession of the ship. The man had said Cathay was alone in the ship, that Lilo had fallen into the hole, or into Jupiter. How had she come back to do this?

Tweed remembered now that Lilo had a base in the Ring. It had to be that one. The other one was dead. She took a vicious satisfaction in the thought. The communicator was in her hand, ready to link with the relay station and tell Vaffa to kill them all. She stopped with her thumb on the button.

Two hours. That's how long there would be if the order was given. In two hours Lilo would be telling everything, and all the police in the system would be after Tweed. Could it be done? She had tricks Lilo had never heard of; the sex change alone would leave a false trail that might confuse the authorities for as long as three or four hours.

But that assumed no one was looking for her yet. If she gave the order to Vaffa now, the pursuit would start in two hours. And it would be literally snapping at her heels. She ran her thumbnail around the transmit button.

No. She needed a few days to get far ahead of them. In four days—in two, with luck—she would be someone else, with a personal history going back seventy years and all properly logged in the data banks. Boss Tweed was dead, and the new woman he had become yearned to avenge him. But it would be too costly. She must always think of the long term. In two or three years she would be back. She would be someone else this time, but it would not be like starting from scratch. The Free Earth Party would go on, and she would lead it.

The communicator fell to the floor and the elevator door opened. The nude woman stepped out and hurried down the corridor. There was much to do.

The cafeteria was filled to capacity and a little beyond the safe limits, though Lilo found it hard to believe. The place didn't look crowded.

There was no large meeting area in Poseidon. Vaffa had discouraged groups of more than ten people at a time. There were large areas in the dead spaces but there had not yet been time to reclaim them. One meeting had been tried in an abandoned room, but no one liked it with everyone's suit turned on. It was impossible to read faces.

So the cafeteria had been chosen, but it was almost as disconcerting. People had to be evenly spaced around the rotating cylinder, and they had to sit all around its inner circumference, with the result that the speaker could be standing directly overhead. It made for a lot of sore necks.

"But I was promised two weeks," Vejay was saying. "I've done the best I can. If you can just give me another four days, even *three* days, I—"

"We all understand your desire to give us the best possible drive, Vejay," Cathay said. "But you just told us that what you have *will* function—"

"But I can only guarantee a couple months, at best, then I'll have to—"

"—if you'll just listen to me—"

"I still have the floor, don't I?"

Lilo slumped further down into her chair. Meetings bored her. Why couldn't Cathay just tell him to pipe down and set a time for the burn? But then, she conceded, that's why he was a better president than she would have been. She recognized it; when her name was put into nomination she had quickly withdrawn it. And Cathay had handled it well. So far he had been able to do just what his advisors had said must be done if they were to have a chance, and had made it seem as if it was fair to everyone. If that wasn't the definition of a good leader, Lilo did not know what was.

But she had never expected that getting a group of eighty people to agree on anything would be tougher than beating Tweed in the first place.

The drive was ready, no matter what Vejay said. He was a lover of fine machinery, and the thing he had cobbled together on the other side of Poseidon offended his sense of beauty. But it would work. It would work long enough to get them beyond any possible pursuit. And that was the critical thing, as Cathay was pointing out once more.

"Tweed must have known that if we gave him a month, we'd give him two months, and forever for that matter. We have no advantage to gain by exposing him. I know there's a minority who want to do just that, but I'll remind you again that we're not out of the woods. You people who hate him that much should be the very ones to know that if there's a way he can get to us by treachery, out of sheer spite, he'll do it. That's why we planned to move in ten days from the very beginning. I know it's been hard . . ." There was a chorus of loud comment greeting the statement. ". . . but we've just about arrived. We're within hours of being able to boost, and once we get started, our chances improve by an order of magnitude."

Lilo let her attention wander again. She scanned the crowd restlessly. She had not had time to get to know many of the people present, though a lot of them had a maddening habit of assuming friendship based on their acquaintance with her dead clone. She smiled when she spotted Cass sixty degrees around the curve of the floor. So far, he had been one of the few not to presume on his previous friendship with her clone. He seemed willing to start from scratch. In this case, she approved of her sister's judgment.

Sitting in front of her, in a tight group, were the Vaffas. There were eight of them; not as many as had been feared, but more than anyone was comfortable with. There had been nine. The death of one of them at the hands of what had to be called a lynch mob was the first crisis the community had faced. The other Vaffas, already fearful, had occupied a room and vowed to fight to the death. It had taken careful work by Cathay to get them out again. They had stuck to their end of the bargain, not raising a hand against anyone. It remained to be seen how they would fare in the long run. There were many long-standing grudges to settle. Already they were regarded as second-class citizens, which they did not seem to mind as long as people left them alone. But they were going to be a problem.

"Now we'll hear from the ecology committee," Cathay said. "Krista, will you report?"

Krista was one of the few people Lilo knew well. With work going on around the clock to get Poseidon ready to move, Lilo had been with her for marathon sessions devoted to repairing damage to the hydroponic gardens caused by the crash. Krista was a hard worker, one of the kidnapped scientists Tweed had put on the station when he couldn't find what he wanted in prison. Lilo liked her, except for the tendency she displayed to be interested in what Lilo had done to land in jail.

"I wish I could offer more solid guarantees," Krista said. "Tweed deliberately tried to keep us dependent on the monthly shipments. He knew what he was doing, I guess. We're short on some trace elements that are being lost in the secondary recyclers. Lilo and I are working on a tertiary system to recover what we have, but unless we can find larger amounts by mining the rocks, we could be in trouble in a few years."

"But what's the outlook on the new system?" Cathay asked.

"Well, I'd hate to say for sure, but—"

"We can do it," Lilo shouted. "We have to do it, so we will. Sit down, Krista."

The rest of the reports said much the same thing. Damage was not completely repaired in several areas, but the work was progressing.

Everyone wanted more time, but finally agreed there was nothing preventing a fast takeoff.

Cathay heard them all to the end, then banged his gavel.

"You people elected me; you gave me the power to assign a time for the starting of the drive. I'm going to exercise that power now. We move in eighteen hours."

How can I summarize a trip that lasted ten years? To say that it was dull and that nothing much happened would be at the same time a terrible understatement and untrue.

I'm sure Javelin began to regret it within the first month. She had taken us on as a lark, as something to break the routine she had lived under for such a long time. But she would not have lived that way for so long if it wasn't, in reality, a very good routine for her. We saw little of her after the first month. Her quarters were accessible only to her. When we entered the solarium she would go to her own parts of the ship.

Vaffa opted out early. She had no great desire to sleep the trip away, being frightened of suspended animation, but in her own words, "If I don't do something soon I'm gonna kill something."

Cathay and I grew close. Several times. In between, we scarcely spoke to each other. I recall one blistering row over whose turn it was to feed the fish. It wasn't his fault, and it wasn't mine. In a different situation we might have evolved something lasting, but there was no one else, for loving or for hating, or for petty anger. Part of it was sheer stubbornness on my part, I admit it. I didn't wish to love him simply because there was no one else; I needed more reasons than that. He saw this as insane, and he was probably right. But there was no help for it.

We kept coming back together mainly because of my sexual needs. I've always found my hand an unsatisfactory sex partner. I've never

been able to stay angry at a lover for too long; I begin to need him,
Javelin was no alternative. I copped with her once—which was a great
surprise to me, since I had thought she was actually neuter. Her solu-
tion to the problem of female genitals without a crotch to put them in
was ingenious, functional, and fascinating, but ultimately disap-
pointing. She was an indifferent lover, too self-centered to be con-
cerned with satisfying me.

I ended up holding out two weeks longer than Cathay. Javelin
looked relieved when she administered the injection that put me
under for eight years of sleep.

They had been decelerating for three weeks.

Javelin had been right; there was something out there. It showed
up on the radar screen as an object the size of a large asteroid. It was
impossible as yet to look at it directly because the light of the ship's
drive interfered with the telescope. Javelin had carefully aimed for a
point a hundred kilometers away from the object, so that her drive
would not be seen as a weapon.

But no one had yet seen Javelin. Cathay, Lilo, and Vaffa had been
awake four weeks, exercising every day to get back in shape from the
long sleep, but Javelin had stayed in her room. They could talk to
her, but only over the audio circuits. Lilo assumed the woman was by
now even more acutely aware of their presence on her ship, and even
more unhappy about it.

When she did make an appearance, it was after first cutting a door
from the inside of her room. She now had two arms and legs, and
could no longer fit through the tiny entrance she had used. It was not
the sort of surgery she could have accomplished by herself; Lilo assumed she had mechanical aids in her room.

Javelin seemed self-conscious about it. Lilo was going to make a
comment, but when she saw how awkwardly Javelin moved in the
one-gee acceleration—tending to forget about her left leg and right
arm—she said nothing. There had been some neural rewiring done,
Lilo felt sure. It was as if Javelin had suddenly donned glasses that
inverted everything she saw; it would take a while for her brain to accept the change.

At first Lilo wondered why Javelin had done it. In the past she had
accepted the brief periods of immobility enforced by the boost of the
ship; they never lasted more than a month, and were a small price to
pay for ten years of easy movement in free-fall.

But now every day brought them closer to the Ophiuchite outpost,
and Javelin's reason became obvious. There was no way of knowing

what they would find. It could be anything from weightlessness to many gravities, and Javelin had thought it best to be prepared.

The Hotline station was a torus, a thick, dark doughnut with an outer diameter of seventy kilometers, spinning slowly.

"It looks like a tire," Cathay said, staring over Javelin's tiny shoulder at the telescope screen. "See how it's flattened?"

"That would give them more flat surface on the inside," Javelin pointed out. "Flat on the bottom, and an arched roof overhead." She hit a few switches on her console. "They're pulling three quarters of a gravity on the inside. You know, it's pretty big for that kind of rotation. And the density fooled us. It's about twice as dense as water, which isn't much. There's not much metal in it."

"What do you think it's made of?" Vaffa asked. Nobody answered.

There was a tower growing from the inner edge of the wheel. It was massive at the base, but tapered quickly into a needle as it rose toward the center. There was a nodule at the hub of rotation. Javelin did some more computations.

"There must be something heavy inside, just opposite the base of the tower," she announced. "Otherwise the mass of the tower would throw the rotation off balance."

"And that's where we have to go, right?" Cathay asked. "To the top of the tower?"

"I don't know where else we could go," Javelin said. "Everything else is moving too fast. You'd better all strap in. I'm going to have to do some maneuvering."

"Shouldn't we try to contact them first?" Lilo asked. "They must know what frequencies we use. I imagine they've been listening to us for centuries."

"You're right. But what should we say?" Javelin looked uncertain for the first time since Lilo had known her. They all looked at each other, and no one seemed anxious to make the first contact. Javelin turned the dials on her screen and made the scope zoom in on the docking module in the center of the wheel. They had all noticed a faint light on one side of it; now Javelin brought it into focus.

No one said anything for a while. The light was actually several lights, and looked like nothing so much as tubes of ionized neon gas. They spelled out a word: WELCOME.

"We've been waiting," said a voice over the radio. "If you'll come in to about five hundred meters, we'll throw you a line. See you in about twenty minutes?"

21

How can I summarize our life on Poseidon?

The news programs we monitored during the first days called us "The Runaway Moon." There was great consternation from Mercury to Pluto. The departure of Poseidon was seen as the precursor of some disastrous turn of events in connection with the Invaders. There were calls for armament of all human peoples in the system to prepare for the coming fight.

It didn't come, of course, and gradually all the fuss died away. Much later we heard someone suggest that Poseidon could have been moved by technologies known to humans, and that indeed it might have been human outlaws who had done it. The idea did not seem to go over well, and in any case we were by then too far away and moving too fast for anything to be done about it.

We worked frantically for a year. The impact of Vengeance *had caused a lot of damage to the tunnels and rooms. A power overload had caused failures in the heating system which powered the hydroponic farms; all the plants died. For a while we lived on stored food, in the darkness. There was not enough air to pressurize the corridors —many of which would have leaked badly if we did—so we lived in our suits and observed strict oxygen rationing.*

There had been no way for me and Cathay to know if the impact of Vengeance *would cause irreparable damage to a vital installation on Poseidon, one that we would need to survive after taking control. Cathay said Vejay was certain everything was already there to make the planetoid self-sufficient. In the end, we had to gamble with the lives of everyone on Poseidon.*

In the first flush of victory, everyone was glad we did. Cathay was swept into office as our first president. Even I was admired. It didn't last. In six months Cathay was out of office and we were both avoiding the faces of people we met in the dark, airless corridors.

But it worked. For many years Tweed had been sending equipment to make the base less dependent on supplies brought in by ship. The most hazardous part of his operation had always been sending ships to Jupiter, and the fewer he sent, the better he felt about it. One by one, the needs of Poseidon were taken over by small, mostly hand-operated, fabricating machines. The energy was there, more than the machines could ever use. Raw materials could be mined or transmuted by the limitless power. There were machines for making light tubes, integrated circuits, and pumps. The machines which had built the base were still there, and could be used to clear rubble or dig new tunnels. There was equipment to make new parts for things that wore out.

In three years we were a stable ecology, if not yet much of a community. The days of oxygen rationing were just a memory, and the inhabited base was actually larger than it had been in fifteen years. The population had grown by twenty children, and four more were on the way. I could hold up my head and be a respected member of society now that I was Chief Hydroponicist and Grand Panjandrum of Mutagenic Foodstuffs. Every time I developed a new plant that was better than the things we had been eating for three years, my prestige rose a little higher.

By the time five years had passed, things were settled down. We had an old-style school with the students outnumbering the teachers. It turned out to be not so bad, after all.

We were all surprised at how much time and effort it took to keep things running. Our world would not have allowed us survival if we hadn't maintained it constantly. That's true of all human societies since the Invasion, but it's usually behind the scenes, unnoticed. Only three percent of the population of Luna, for instance, is directly involved in an environmental industry. On Poseidon, we all were, and we often held two or even three jobs. Most of us were farmers in addition to our other functions. We worked ten-hour days.

The catch was that while we were a technological society, we lacked a lot of the base that should support it. We employed computers to map the gene changes on the plants we mutated to grow in the changed conditions, and then we cultivated those plants with shovels and hoes. The automated cybernetic and judgmental machines so common in Lunar society—the devices that do so much of the actual physical work—were in short supply. We didn't have the sophisticated industry needed to build such machines, or to provide replacement parts for our best computers when they broke down. We were reduced to the IC chip, the incandescent light bulb, helium-chilled superconductors, and other of the more basic, long-established technologies. It wasn't exactly the Neolithic Age, but sometimes it felt like it.

And after nine years, we were moving at half the speed of light.

First contact.

Lilo had considered everything, or thought she had, from beings of pure energy to the standard monstrous life-forms that were a fixture of cheap adventure fiction. She had considered the possibility that the Ophiuchites might be humanlike, bipedal, bilaterally symmetrical. It was an efficient design for some purposes. It had occurred to her that they might be literally beyond her understanding, more related to Invaders than to humans.

What she found was a stretch of corridor that might have been the one she had played in as a child. At the end was a conference room with a carpet and a long, wooden table with a dozen chairs.

"Would you say it's about one gee?" Javelin said, as they entered the room. Lilo was startled to hear her voice; the room absorbed all echoes.

"Yes, about that." She glanced at Javelin. She had never seemed smaller than she did now, standing on two feet in a gravity field. She barely reached to Lilo's waist.

"Why do you think that is?" Javelin went on. "This place rotates for artificial gravity, wouldn't you think? Yet we're at the hub. It should be weightless."

"It follows that they have gravity control," Vaffa said.

"Yes, but then why do they need the rotation? If they can give us one gee here, why can't they do it at the rim?"

"Maybe it's expensive," Cathay said. "Maybe it's a gesture of friendship."

"Let's don't draw too many conclusions," Lilo said. "We've got to be on guard against that."

"Keep an open mind," Vaffa said.

Lilo knew they were all whistling in the dark. They were standing at one end of the room, hesitant to go any further unless invited. The voice, after its startling intrusion on *Cavorite*'s radio, had told them where to enter the Hotline base, and to go to the end of the corridor. After that, there had been nothing.

Now the door at the other end of the room opened and people started coming in. They seemed to be quite ordinary men and women, dressed in a style that was perhaps two centuries out of date. They were attractive people, the sort Lilo might have run into in any public corridor in Luna.

"Please, please, have seats," said one man. "Pull up a chair. We're not formal around here."

None of the four could think of any reply, so they all sat down. When the Ophiuchites were seated, every chair was filled. The man who had spoken was at one end of the table, and now he got to his feet. He put both hands on the table and looked at them. His brow furrowed slightly.

"We knew you'd be nervous," he said. "I don't know what we can do about that. We've tried to keep the surroundings familiar, but it will probably be a while before you feel comfortable."

He looked at each of them in turn, and favored each with a smile.

There was something odd about that smile. It seemed warm enough, but Lilo got the feeling there was nothing beneath it. It tried to be an expression of friendship, as the earlier frown had tried to show concern. She glanced at Cathay and Javelin to see if she was the only one who saw that.

"It *is* awkward," the man went on. "Your species has only limited experience with this situation. Mine has been through it thousands of times. We know much about your species-type, and about your race specifically. You're apprehensive about this meeting, you have many questions, and this all seems very strange to you."

He paused again, and looked this time at the double line of his companions seated at the table. They were all nodding, and now a few uttered polite assents. They sought eye contact with the four humans, a familiarity Lilo did not feel ready for. She felt disoriented. For all she could tell, these people might be the board of directors of some large company, gathered to discuss business.

"First we should introduce ourselves. I'm the spokesman for the contact team, and my name is William." Each of them stood and gave a name, and none of them convinced Lilo. All the names were archaic, common names from Old Earth. When they were finished, Javelin stood and introduced herself and the others did the same.

With the formalities over, William sat down and all the Ophiuchites visibly relaxed. There was a murmur of conversation. It almost escaped Lilo's attention because it was so commonplace, but when she strained to hear individual remarks she realized there were none. It was a literal murmur; as artificial as canned laughter. A show was being put on for their benefit. They were participating in some kind of living theater.

"You can consider yourselves our guests for as long as you want to stay. Would you like anything to eat? No? Very well, but don't be shy about asking, as we have a long presentation. I hope you don't mind. We've found that if we begin with a question-and-answer session it takes a long time just to get to the point where you can ask meaningful questions. And I'm sure you don't want to sit through a dry lecture. So we've put together this little piece of film that should fill you in on the background that led up to this historic contact. Alicia, would you get the lights, please?"

Somone was setting up what looked like a film projector. A screen lowered from the ceiling, and as the lights went down, the machine began to clatter. Titles appeared on the screen, accompanied by swelling background music.

Hierarchies
Produced by the Hotline First Contact Committee

The film opened with a shot of scattered stars and galaxies. The voice of the narrator was the perfect choice, Lilo thought. It was the Standard Computer Voice, the SCV that all humans heard every day of their lives. The controlled, soothing modulations had a good effect on all of them. They were able to relax a little for the first time.

"Greeting to the people of the Sol system, formerly the Race of Earth, from your nearest neighbors among the peoples of the galaxy. For many hundreds of years our two races have been in contact through the communication device you call the Ophiuchi Hotline. Now the time is drawing near when great decisions must be made, great steps taken, when things must be told to you which before now you had only guessed at.

"The universe is a far stranger place than you have heretofore imagined. This will come as no surprise to those who have considered the questions of philosophy which have been posed since your race came down from the trees. We would not have you think we are about to answer those questions; we are much alike in many ways, and for us, as for you, many things seem destined to remain mysteries. But there are things we have learned which you should know, as you are approaching a turning point that will determine your survival or failure as a race.

"We have called this broadcast *Hierarchies*. As you have already been shown in the most convincing terms possible, your race is not destined to be a dominant one in the galaxy. Your planet has been taken from you by beings greater than yourselves. They had no trouble doing so; it was as inevitable as the law of gravity that they should have none. You live now in the airless places, the too-hot and too-cold deserts of your planetary system. Some among you pray for liberation. Others are beginning to try and do something about it.

"You will not be liberated. We would return your planet to you if we could, but it is beyond our power. Your struggles to reclaim the Earth on your own will come to nothing.

"Having made these statements, we must now tell you why this is so. A good place to start would be for us to tell you something about ourselves."

The film lasted about an hour. Lilo let her eyelids droop, slouched in the comfortable chair, allowing information to wash over her just as it was meant to. The production values of the film were very good, very much like a commercial spot with quick cuts and finicky attention to detail.

They were told about the Ophiuchites in outline form, with animated sequences that never showed a living being. It failed to surprise Javelin, as she later told Lilo, since in the four hundred years of operation of the Line there had never been a scrap of information about the people who were sending it.

According to them, they were a race without a home planet. They were not natives of 70 Ophiuchi, or any other star they could name.

Javelin leaned over and whispered in Lilo's ear, "I wonder. I think they're covering up."

"Could be."

They claimed to have been around a very long time—their exact origins, as they expressed it in the film, "lost in the mists of history." They had records going back seven million years, and in that time there had been no changes in their society.

The film recapped what humans had speculated about Invaders, confirming most of it.

"The beings you know as Invaders are members of what can be called a stratum of intelligence. There are many races in the galaxy similar to them, including a race native to the solar planet Jupiter. These races evolve only on the gas giant planets. They are not tool-using, as we understand the term, but rather are able to manipulate the world around them through methods which are beyond our powers of comprehension. It might be helpful to think of them as telekinetic; they are not, but many of the things they do are similar to what we might do if such a power existed.

"To the Invaders, time is a dimension of substance. How this affects their perception of life we can only guess, and it does us little good to do so. But this fact puts them as far beyond our reach as we would be above the inhabitants of a hypothetical two-dimensional world."

The film went on to confirm what Lilo had been told about dolphins many years ago, that they were the second level of intelligence. Vaffa snorted, and Lilo glanced at her, wondering how she was taking all this. It was believed by the Free Earthers that aquatic mammals were merely animals, that the tales of Invaders coming to Earth to free them were nothing more than folklore.

"Tool-using species, those which evolve on land and in an atmosphere which permits combustion, are the third level of intelligence. We share this level with you, but it should be pointed out that there can be levels within levels. You are not our equals, and may never be. We can talk to you about certain matters, but there are things which you are not ready to understand, and things which we are not ready to reveal. Because now we come to the point of the message, to an explanation of what we are doing here and why we have been communicating with you these many years."

For the first time, a face appeared on the screen. It was a standardized face, handsome but unmemorable, and it took a second for Lilo to realize it was "William." He performed another smile, as unconvincing as the ones Lilo had seen in person.

"As we said earlier, we are a race that has lost contact with its roots. It might be hard for you to understand how that could happen. We can only surmise as to the exact details."

The screen showed an Earth-like planet over William's shoulder. "We must have evolved on a planet much like your own. In the natural course of things, we were pushed off the planet, as you have been. We have watched this process happen thousands of times, and it

changes very little from race to race." On the screen, thousands of
ships fled the planet and traveled to various moons and asteroids in
the system.

"In time, races like ours and yours begin to wonder if they can recapture their home world. They begin to take steps in that direction.
Before too long the gas giant beings put a stop to these experiments.
As before, they have no trouble doing so." Lilo watched as indefinite
shapes swam up from the blue planet to swarm over the others. It
was clear what was happening, with no need for narration.

"This is what happened to us. Already evicted from our home
world, we were attacked in our places of refuge. As in the original invasion, only a few of us survived by escaping to the nearer stars. This
is a fate you face in a short time.

"You are all aware of the increased importance of a group calling
itself the Free Earth Party. Your race has quietly accepted its exile
for many centuries now. The time has come for dissenting voices to
be raised. It is unlikely that anything could be done to suppress them.
We can point out to you—and we formally do so now—that the leader
of the Free Earthers, Tweed, has been engaged in experiments at
Jupiter and in close-Earth orbit which by now have certainly drawn
the attention of the Invaders to the humans living in the Eight
Worlds. These experiments were misguided, but Tweed is not a monster. We can sympathize with his desire to reassert human domina-
tion of the home world. We can only observe that the attempts are
futile.

"If it were not Tweed, it would have been someone else. If you
succeed in stopping Tweed, there will be others to take his place. We
know from experience that when the time for an idea has arrived,
there is no use trying to suppress it. Some among you will refuse to
believe our warnings and you will go your own way. You will continue to test yourselves against the Invaders. In time, you will be
ready to try an invasion of your own. It will fail, and those of you
who remain in the Eight Worlds will be annihilated.

"Some of you will escape. Interstellar travel is already in your
reach; there just has never been sufficient economic pressure to force
you to obtain it. But some of you will believe us, and get away in
time. I wish I could tell you that the story ends happily at that point."

Again the picture changed. And changed again. Star after star
flicked onto the screen in stylized representation. Many had gas giant
planets, and were removed from consideration. Others contained ox-
ygen-breathing races living on airless worlds, as humans were doing

now. Only a few had livable worlds with no second-level forms in the oceans, and almost all of those were already inhabited.

"The galaxy is a crowded place," William went on. "Our race discovered this quickly. The search for a place to live is a long and hard one. Some species never manage to find a niche. They become extinct. Others fragment, never able to maintain contact among their far-flung branches. Gradually, they mutate. New races are born in interstellar space. There is a process of evolution going on between the stars more fierce than that which gave birth to your race on your hospitable world, and all the competing species are intelligent. Where interests conflict, no quarter is given. War is too simple a term to describe it. Species can change, combine, absorb one another.

"We call ourselves the Traders. In one sense, we have no single home planet, though there must have been an original race which first evolved our life-style. As we exist now, we are an amalgam of many races which have achieved an equilibrium enabling us to survive."

The Hotline station appeared, turning slowly. A red beam of light emerged from it, and passed near a yellow star.

"The Traders are an organization set up to provide ousted races with the knowledge they will need to survive. We broadcast information, as we have done to you. Over the centuries we have taught you how to manipulate your own genetic structure. For your own reasons, you have not seen fit to change yourselves. You have ignored the bulk of the information we have sent you, information largely concerned with alternatives you face in the alteration of your human DNA. This is an unusual situation; few races we have encountered hesitate to change themselves when the need arises. For some reason, your race has adopted an attitude so powerfully biased against racial change that you cannot even understand the information we send you concerning yourselves.

"You can no longer afford that quirk. You will have to cease defining your race by something as arbitrary as a genetic code, and make the great leap to establishing a racial awareness that will hold together in spite of the physical differences you will be introducing among yourselves. And you *must* define your race more successfully than you have done so far. Today, you could not tell us what it is that makes one a human being.

"What you see before you," William spread his hands and looked down at his body, "would qualify as a human by the standards you now employ. This body is genetically human. But I am only a temporary resident in it, in the same way that many individuals among you

now live in cloned bodies, and will live in other bodies in your life-times."

The scene shifted again. Lilo felt a sense of expectancy and was not sure why. She saw the Grand Concourse in King City, Luna, a place she had visited many times. People walked in front of the cam-era, going about their business.

"Here comes the stinger," Javelin whispered. "Hold onto your credit meter and your gold fillings." Her nostrils dilated and her eyes were bright. She smelled a deal coming up, and it was all she needed to make her happy.

"We call ourselves the Traders. You know what it is we give; you have been getting it for centuries. No one thought to ask us if we wanted anything in return. We do, and what it is is both very simple and rather difficult to explain.

"What we want is your culture."

How could I tell of my ten years on what used to be the Eastern seaboard of the United States of America?

What made me so sure I was on the American continent was for a long time a source of considerable bewilderment. For several days after the death of Makel I wandered in a more or less dazed condi-tion. It seems as though it took nearly a month before I dared to ask any of the questions that would continue to puzzle me for ten years. They can be summed up as What happened?

One moment I had been falling through Jupiter's atmosphere, and the next, I was in the surf of the Atlantic Ocean. And I knew it was the Atlantic.

But that wasn't quite right. One event didn't follow the other; rather, they merged into each other. I'm sure I recall sitting under the bushes, shivering, before I was in the water. I recall crawling out of the water before I remembered being in it.

The whole experience was so subjective that I doubted from the first I would ever get any good answers by thinking about it. But it didn't stop me thinking. The conclusions I came to were so tenuous they might be worthless, and yet I felt good about them in the same way that I had no doubts about where I was.

I had fallen into an Invader—or a Jovian, if it makes any difference. For reasons of its own, the Invader had moved me. Perhaps I was told something in those scrambled seconds, minutes, hours, or centuries during which the transition took place. Or perhaps some level of my mind had been able to see how and to where I was moved.

Why? Why should the Invader care enough about me to do whatever was done? Was it accidental? I didn't know, but I had the persistent feeling that I had been displaced in space and time for some reason, and that it would become clear to me later. In the meantime, I had the hard task of survival facing me.

There were adventures by the hundreds. In a sense, every day was an adventure. But I found that it is much more pleasurable to read adventures than to live them. I never knew in the morning if I would live to see the sun set.

And yet with all the troubles, all the close calls, the story is mostly one of wandering, of slogging day after day down the woods and marshes and beaches of the Atlantic.

I always moved south. My knowledge of geography was not as good as it might have been, but I did know that it had to get warmer the farther south I went. After my first winter I had an abiding interest in staying warm.

My method was to pick an encampment when the leaves were starting to change colors. I would either build a hut from mud and sticks—Tweed, your training paid off!—or find an indigenous group of people and live with them while the snow fell.

I learned many skills: how to build a rude boat for crossing rivers, how to make and shoot a bow and arrows, how to set traps and track game. On a good day I might cover three kilometers, or I might settle down for weeks or months with some friendly group.

My size was a great help in everything I did. The people I met were in religious awe of me because of it. I never met anyone who was as tall as my shoulders.

It was tricky at first, learning to get along with them, finding the best way to enter a camp and set myself up as a sort of traveling goddess. But while they spoke a thousand dialects, they were all based on English. I could communicate with them. Tales of Diana, the great silver huntress with the legs of a horse, spread before me. Villages turned out to welcome me, and to see me turn into an apparition for a few seconds by switching on my nullfield. They eagerly and fearfully touched the metal flower above my breast. I became the warrior princess of legend, the metal-bodied Bride of Frankenstein, the Cyborg Diana.

I was subservient in their eyes to one thing only, and that was the Dolphin. Every holy place in every village had a wooden statue of a great fish with horizontal flukes and a blowhole.

She had been going north for some weeks now. She had gone northward before on her long journey, but it was always to go far enough up a river to find a suitable crossing. Once over, she had resumed her route south.

This time it looked as though it might be different. She had not been able to see any land to the west of her, and the ocean seemed to be a different color, more green than blue. The land was marshy, and she did most of her traveling with a canoe and a long pole. Huge reptiles lazed in the mud or swam slowly by her, but she did not fear them.

She had not seen snow for two years. The winters were mild, if this land could be said to have winters at all. She had kept moving from force of habit, and from the inability to decide what to do with her life. No call had come from the Invaders, no sign to tell her why she was there. But to stop moving would have been to face becoming part of a tribe. Even as a goddess, she did not think she could stand it.

She had done what she could, imparting to the people she met what knowledge she had that might be of use to them. There was no way to know if they heeded what she said after she was gone. And, truthfully, she did not know if it would do them any good. Possibly the solutions they had evolved to deal with their environment were the best for them, but they were not for her. Their lives were short, full of pain and suffering. The only thing they had that was good was the sense of community, the security of being surrounded by comrades, and she knew she could never participate in that. She was different, and could not be assimilated into a tribe except as a woman apart from the others.

Lilo was not the woman she had been. Her skin was brown and weathered now, her hair bleached by sun and salt water. She had no mirror, but knew there were unfashionable lines on her forehead, around her eyes and mouth. Ten years had aged her from a clone of

the standard decanting age of nineteen apparent years to a woman of forty. There was a white, puckered scar from her right temple to her jaw, and another on her left thigh. The palms of her hands and the soles of her feet were thick with callus, and the hair on her calves was not as smooth and luxuriant as it used to be.

At the end of the fourth week of northward travel, Lilo decided she had come to the end of the long peninsula at the southeast of the continent. The natives called it *Florda*.

Now she stopped her journey. There was no reason why she should not continue up the gulf coast, around the curve to Mexico and finally South America. But she had no heart for it. She turned her boat around and started poling through the placid waterways, back to the Atlantic.

When the water was blue again she picked a spot near the ancient ruins of Miami and built a hut. For the first time she began to cultivate a patch of ground with seeds given to her by the natives, to experiment with pottery, and to raise wild chickens and rabbits.

The local tribes respected her privacy except for certain holy days when they came and asked for religious rites which were obscure to her but seemed mainly aimed at procuring good hunting. She was willing to pray for them, as long as they left her alone during the rest of the year.

There was plenty to do to keep busy. When she needed relaxation she went out in her boat and fished. She liked that; she could just sit and watch the water and not think about anything. She no longer felt bitterness for what had happened to her. When she thought of anything, it was of Makel.

Lilo had stayed aloof from everyone since the day he died. Nothing in her life had moved her as deeply as the boy's death. It had been such a pointless, such an ignominious way for a human being to die. Since then she had seen the deaths of many people, and it was always with the same feeling. *We were not made for this. The human race deserves better.*

Lilo was not used to such strong illogical feelings. She had wrestled with herself for years, on the one hand telling herself that a human was just another animal and could die like any other animal. But it never satisfied her. Logic wasn't enough. It could not encompass the issues. She began to feel that the land she walked on should belong to the human race. It had, once. Maybe the people who lived before the Invasion had done a sorry job of taking care of it, but they had been trying, even then. Now all the humans on Earth had been thrown back into savagery. It hurt her to see it.

Going to Earth had made Lilo a Free Earther.

One day a huge dark shape appeared from under the water, not three meters from her boat. There was a tremendous, hooting rush of air, and a column of spray dispersed around her.

She stood and stared at it. It was at least twenty meters long, and blunt at the front end. The Sperm Whale.

Lilo hurled her reed basket of fish at the shape, and it bounced into the water. The hide gleamed, unhurt. She threw her paddle, a rough clay bowl she used to hold bait, and anything else she could find in the bottom of the boat.

Slowly, the leviathan rolled. Huge flukes appeared and waved for a moment in the air, then sliced soundlessly into the water.

Lilo shook for an hour.

The next day, silent yellow shapes appeared at the horizon. She stood on the beach and watched them, though it hurt her eyes to do so. They were at the limits of visibility, but that was not the problem. They were *shapes*. They were all shapes at once; they would not hold still.

She had seen them before, below her, as she fell through the Jovian atmosphere, just before her senses fragmented and she found herself on the beach—found that she *had been* on the beach for some time, as she was still falling through Jupiter. She had blanked the experience from her mind; now it came back: the incredible, stop-action, living lap dissolve that had left her on Earth.

Again she could not control her shaking, but this time it was much more from anger than fear.

She cut down a suitable tree and spent her days sitting on the sand looking out over the water, working the wood. She made it three meters long, and tipped it with steel painstakingly beaten from scraps she had collected. Then she waited.

The spouts appeared early one morning. Lilo watched them, taking deep breaths of the sea air until her fingertips tingled. Every nerve in her body was singing as she stripped away her leather jerkin and loincloth and raced across the sand to her boat. She was no longer afraid to die. The day was right for it, and the whales waited to taste her harpoon.

Did they know she was there, intent on killing them? She did not know or care. She rowed strongly out to the mass of rolling black bodies.

Overhead, the Invaders darted. They did not accelerate or slow down; they simply moved. They entered and left the water without sound or splash, occupying one volume of space as easily as any other. Lilo stood and shook the harpoon at them, then checked herself. Even in the mania of her anger, the blood-red depths of her rage at them and what they had done to her people, she knew that certain things were beyond her. She would take her revenge on flesh and blood, then die because there was nothing left to do, no sense in walking endlessly down bare beaches or in sitting placidly beside a mud hut.

It was there in the water beside her, a broad dappled black hide just below the surface. She reached to the metal flower on her collarbone and was transformed into a creature of bright blue distortion, hot as the broken sun that blazed from her face.

She heard a scream. Her arm came up, straightened, jerked, and the wooden shaft shivered in her hand as it sank into the mountain of blubber.

The Silver Huntress, Diana, stood on the whale's back, shouting. She held the harpoon in both hands as the monster's tail came up and smashed down on the boat.

The whale dived.

24

The film reached its end, and for a moment it flapped noisily around the reel until one of the men reached over to turn the projector off. The lights came up, and Lilo, Javelin, Vaffa, and Cathay were confronted with eight faces, all looking at them expectantly. The atmosphere in the room was tense; the Traders were waiting for something.

For some reason, Lilo was convinced they were about to break into a song-and-dance routine. The situation was divorced from reality in almost the same way as a musical comedy, where characters pause in the midst of action to sing. If they do, I'll go crazy, Lilo thought.

"Well," William said. "Well. What do you think?"

Lilo looked from William to Alicia to Thomas to . . . whatever her name was.

"Effective," Cathay ventured.

"Solid. To the point," said one of the Traders.

Javelin cleared her throat.

"Uh . . . yes. It's a nice piece of work. But did we really come here to discuss the artistic merits of your propagandists?"

"We *would* like to know what you think," William said. His voice oozed sincerity. "Of course we realize you have no powers of your own to either accept or reject what we've offered. You're not envoys for your race."

"What are you going to do with it? I assume you didn't put it together just for us."

"We'll broadcast it. Not over the Hotline; this time it goes directly to every inhabited planet of your system. It's customary for us to work this way. You must have realized that we have never used our transmitter at full strength. Our laser is not big enough to broadcast across seventeen light-years, but we can send a stronger signal than any you have yet received. We deliberately garble and distort the signal at this end, simulating what you would expect to happen to it if it had come from 70 Ophiuchi. We wanted you to think of us as being very far away.

"When we know that being discovered is only a matter of time, we send the first message that you received. Someone usually shows up. If no one does, we wonder if we're wasting our time. You did very well."

Javelin shifted in her chair, a sour look on her face.

"Yes, but what do you expect anyone to make of it?"

"Please?" William looked down his nose at her.

"What I'm saying is, you want something in trade for the free information you've been sending us. Okay, anyone can understand that. But what you want is our culture. I'm afraid I didn't follow just how you intended to get it."

"I thought the film made that clear."

"Not to me," Cathay put in. "I didn't understand that, or just what the alternatives are to the human race if we don't cooperate."

"Ah." William pursed his lips. "Perhaps we need to make some changes in the final sections before we release it. You see how valuable this can be to us? I'll turn you over to our Minister for Assimilation. Alicia?"

If William seemed stilted and slightly unreal in his mannerisms, Alicia was little more than a manikin. Lilo could imagine strings leading to her arms and legs. She wondered just what kind of beings these Traders were. Alicia soon answered her.

"As I hope you understood from the film," she said, "what you see before you is not the result of Trader culture or Trader genes. This room and our bodies were tailored for this meeting. We had been studying you for nearly eight hundred years, listening to your radio and television broadcasts. We have been here much longer than that; our first visit to Earth was twenty thousand years ago. Since then we have waited for you to come to us.

"We have been learning how to be humans."

She spread her hands. "It is an impossible task to do at a distance, but this station is an experimental laboratory for the assimilation of human cultures. There are two hundred environmental cells below us, duplicating the conditions of various human societies of the present and past. In addition, we are prepared to conduct cross-breeding experiments, merging cultures already in our possession with what we learn of human culture. As you can see, we have at this time only an imperfect grasp of the essential outlooks and mind-sets that make a human a human."

"Yes, I understand that," Lilo said. "Or I think I do, anyway. You're saying that you have no culture of your own, that you lost it, or it was assimilated into others so thoroughly that you can't separate it out any more."

"True," Alicia said, "so far as it goes. But this was not accidental. We had observed in the other races around us that the vitality tends to be sapped from a people when they are forced to live a million years of a transitory and nomadic existence. That spark that each race possesses—each one of them different—is extinguished, and they vanish. This had happened to many races. So we have made the deliberate effort to change ourselves at every opportunity. Individuals persist—I myself am over two million years old as a group consciousness. I think it would be futile to try and explain to you what that means."

"Yes, you said that in the film," Javelin said, impatiently. "What you still haven't told me is what you want to do. With us. The human race."

"It's very simple. We wish to coexist with some of you for a time. The only way to learn a culture is from the inside out. There are techniques—very like the memory recording that you developed independently, and which we helped you refine—for the superposition of one mind over another. We wish to hitchhike in your minds for a few years. After that time, we will be as human as you are, not the imperfect constructs that you see."

"Do you think this idea will be accepted?" William asked.

"You mean do I think people will buy it?" Javelin asked. She sighed. "I can think of easier things to sell. What will it be like? Like a symb?"

"No, no, nothing so drastic as that. We will be unnoticed observers. After a few years we will leave you to your own devices. But you don't have very long. The Invaders will not give you more than a century before they exterminate you from all your Eight Worlds."

"And how many . . . ah, how many hosts would you need?"

"A few thousand. To get a representative sample. After that, we can learn humanity from each other." He paused. "We know this is a strange request. The fact is, it is the only thing your race has to offer us. It is the only reason we have bothered to send you the things we have discovered and collected over seven million years. We don't need your gold or silver, your paper money, or anything you would see as wealth. We know all your technology. We don't need you as slaves, as a source of food, or as another link in our chain of empire. And we're not interstellar philanthropists. In point of fact, we are invaders. Your race has experienced a second invasion, and this time you welcomed it."

"What do you mean?" It was Vaffa, always alert to danger.

"This has been a long-distance invasion. We now come to the core of the matter, the penalties for nonpayment we mentioned in the first message. Have you ever heard of the Trojan Horse?"

Lilo looked at her friends. Only Javelin was nodding.

"If you were not of a mind to give value for value received you should have been slower to accept us when we came bearing gifts. But we saw no reluctance. We seldom do. It is a nearly universal trait among races to accept what looks to be free.

"The symbs. They were never a great success, but they've been in the Rings for a long time now, and they breed prolifically. There are now upward of one hundred and ninety million symb-human pairs in Saturn's Rings. Each one is a time bomb. If we were to send the proper signal each pair would be fused into a single being, and it would belong to us, not you. They would be ready to carry out the missions they were programmed for many years ago. They can travel from planet to planet, in hibernation, and when they reach human worlds . . . well, I leave it to your imagination." He sat back, and so did all the others.

Lilo had no trouble imagining it.

Humans lived underground everywhere but Venus and Mars. Those two places would probably be safe, since they had an atmosphere, but everywhere else the symbs could wreak havoc with the surface life-support facilities.

The possibilities multiplied in her mind. It was easy to forget in the day-to-day existence in secure warrens beneath the surface, but the space environment was constantly at war with air-breathing animals. The one advantage had always been that, though the environment was hostile, it was not malevolent. It did not seek with a will to destroy humans. With proper precautions it could be held at bay.

But with millions of saboteurs, soldiers perfectly adapted to the space environment . . .

She felt sick when she thought of Parameter. She knew a little of the complexities built into a symb which allowed a pair to survive in space. Solstice could change her body at will to meet the needs of almost any situation. It was not hard to believe that she could dissolve the thin dividing line between her own body and that of Parameter, fusing the two of them into one supremely efficient organism. But what would be left of Parameter as a human being? Parameter had told Lilo that though a pair was very close and could almost be thought of as one being, there always remained some part of each that maintained a separate identity. That would be gone now, if the Traders carried out their threat. There would be only Solstice, and on some level Lilo had never completely trusted the symb.

Was that distrust justified? The Traders had not really said so. Was Solstice as much a puppet to the Traders as Parameter, an unwitting potential ally?

Lilo was about to try to find out, but a loud noise interrupted her. It was a siren of some sort, and all the Traders looked up in consternation. Or at least they made the attempt to look worried, though Lilo shivered again to see just how alien they could look while looking just like human beings.

"Just a minute," said William. "Just a minute. There seems to be a problem. I'll . . ." He stopped, briefly, and suddenly did not look very human at all. His eyes closed, and all his muscles relaxed. Javelin was on her feet, looking anxiously at the walls around them. Vaffa had knocked over her chair and stepped back from the table. Lilo found herself on her feet, too.

When William spoke again, his voice had changed.

"There's been detection of Invader activity," he said, and then his words trailed off into a babble that was meaningless to Lilo, but seemed to worry the Traders. The group stirred uncertainly.

Lilo-Diana hung on to the harpoon while the animal headed for the deep ocean. It reached the bottom and leveled out, still swimming strongly.

The adrenalin slowly began to wear away, and Lilo was left with the bitter dregs of defeat. She had not killed the beast, and was not likely to. She was not sure if she had even hurt it.

Eventually she let go and the whale vanished in the blue water in front of her. She floated, neither rising or sinking.

Where did she go from here? Her hand touched the intake valve on her chest. She could turn off the suit and drown quickly. Or she could rise to the surface and strike out for shore. She would probably make it with the suit lung feeding her air, but did she want to?

There was something above her.

Without knowing why, she kicked upward to meet it.

It grew rapidly—(*below me now, still falling*)—and made no attempt to get away from her. The shape hurt her eyes. Yellow? No, many colors—(*a deeper yellow than the billowing clouds that now came into view around me, below me, another of the things like the one I had fallen into so many years before*)—all colors and all shapes, contained in one shape.

Her stomach lurched, and she was falling.

I don't know how long I fell, but the question probably has no meaning. I was falling through space and time, and through my own life.

It became no longer possible to know who or where I was. Every second of my life existed simultaneously. I was

standing on a rocky plain beneath a bright light, and knew I was on the world that used to be called Poseidon, but was now two light-years from the sun.

crying, hopelessly, with a depth of feeling never to be equaled in my life, holding the head of a dead man in my lap.

falling through the Jovian atmosphere.

facing the man called Vaffa, watching his weapon rise in slow-motion, hearing an explosion.

holding a knife in my hand, thinking about suicide.

looking at fish in a spinning, circular tank.

running through trees beneath a burning blue sun, laughing.

talking with a man named Quince in the public bath on Pluto.

sitting in a conference room at the hub of a seventy-kilometer wheel, watching a presentation from an alien race.

feeling an erect penis enter my body, with lights flashing around the walls of my room.

facing Vaffa, his gun coming up to kill me.

coming to life in a pool of yellow fluid.

five years old, holding my mother's hand as we followed the transporter carrying our possessions to a new home.

sitting in the green glow of my computer terminal, studying an interesting interpretation of Hotline data.

docking with a huge colony ship orbiting 82 Eridani. The planet was inhabited, and we would have to move on.

fording a stream in America, white water rushing around my knees.

giving birth to Alicia, my second child, on the way to the core.

holding Alicia's hand as she gave birth to my grandson.

facing Vaffa.

dying. Dying again. And again.

I recoiled from it helplessly. All moments had been now. They all vanished, leaving me confused images and almost no memory. The things I remembered were as often in my future as in my past.

It returned, that vertiginous feeling of inhabiting all my past, present, and future at one time. Again I recoiled, and this time rebounded along the four-dimensional length of that long pink worm with a million legs that was my life, from my birth to my many deaths. I was one entity, one viewpoint, one now. I traveled the whole length of my existence, backward and forward, into the future and the past.

I fell back again, disoriented, confused. I had been shown something my mind could not contain, and I felt the memories of it fading already. I existed in too many ways at the same time for me to comprehend it. My eyes would not function, or they presented me with images that my brain could not assimilate.

I don't know how long I rested in that quiet, black place I had come to. There was no time, but all my sisters were there with me. We began to see, a little. Something swam into my detached consciousness, a strange thing that I perceived without actually seeing it. Strange as it was, it was closer to familiarity than anything else around me. Suddenly I knew it was a valuable thing. It was something I had to have. (Someone was telling me I had to have it?) It belonged to them, to the Invaders, and I had to possess it.

I reached—

She remembered Cathay leaning over her, shaking her shoulders. Her head bobbed back and forth, loosely. Her eyes focused.

". . . all right? What happened?"

"Did they do something to you?" It was Vaffa's voice, and Lilo smiled when she saw the genuine concern in her face. Vaffa, Vaffa, there's hope for you yet.

"Who *is* that?"

"That's me," Lilo said, and sat up. It was Javelin who had asked the question, and Lilo had known what she was talking about. She had seen this moment during the kaleidoscope that had overcome her while the Trader siren wailed. She looked at the new occupant of the room—a tall, brown woman, dripping wet—and they nodded at each other. There was no need for any words between them. They had both been here before.

She was holding something in her hand, a silvery cube five centimeters on a side.

"Who are you?" Vaffa asked.

The woman looked curiously at Vaffa.

"I guess you can call me Diana, to avoid confusion. It's what everyone else called me."

The word sparked a fresh cascade of memories in Lilo's mind. She tried to hold them, but they were fading like a dream. A long trip, a fantastic trip, ten years of walking . . . hardships met and conquered . . . tall trees, huge trees that reached to the ceiling—no, that was from her own lifeline. She tried again to remember. There was another Lilo out there, on the runaway moon. She had been forced forward in time to her own death, three deaths, and backward to many more . . . hadn't she? She was no longer sure. But something was guiding her steps still, some knowledge of how things would be, of how they *had been*.

"Let's get out of here," Lilo said.

"What?" Javelin couldn't believe what she heard. "I've got a lot of things I want to—"

"No. It's no use. Just one question," she said, looking at William. "What's that thing in my . . . in her hand?"

William looked sad.

"That," he said, "is a singularity. Things are going faster than we expected."

"And what is a singularity?"

He shrugged. "I wish we knew. If we did, we would be the equals of Invaders. We call it that because it violates basic laws of the universe. We think it might not exist in our universe, at least not in the normal way. What you see is just a nullfield that covers the thing itself. You'll never see any more than that."

"And what does it do?" Lilo felt dizzy. She had known the answers to the questions she was asking.

"It seems to remove the inertia from a body. Don't ask me how. We've studied them for millions of years and we don't know how it works. We think it might convert inertia to some other property of matter and store it in a theoretical hyperspace, or fifth dimension."

"Without all the double-talk, you're saying it's a space drive," Javelin said.

"The basis for a space drive. When you learn to use it, which will be very soon, you will be able to reach high speeds very quickly, and with very little fuel. The stars will be in your reach."

"I stole it," Diana said, proudly.

"Hmmm?" William glanced at her. He seemed distracted. "Indeed? You stole it, you say? Wonderful. You seem to have put one over on the Invaders."

Diana looked proud for a moment, then uncertain. Lilo felt sorry for her. She already had some notion of what had actually happened.

"I didn't, did I?" Diana said.

"No. It's part of the pattern which will culminate in the extermination of what remains of your species in the Solar System, other than the remnants on your home planet. The singularity will reproduce itself. It may even be a living creature. I won't pretend that we know much about it, but we use them, like everyone else."

"But why did they give it to us?"

"I don't know their motives. But they don't seem to wish to kill entire species. They didn't kill anyone on Earth, you remember, not directly. Nor did they hunt down the survivors on Luna. They let you live until you started bothering them. Now they are giving you another chance to spread yourselves to the stars; I don't think they care if you take it, but the chance is always offered."

"Then they do care about humans."

William frowned. "Who knows what they care about? They've not seemed unduly concerned about the hardships of my race. That singularity may seem miraculous to you, and to me. To them, it is probably the same level of technology as the chipped-stone cutting tool."

Cathay was still looking back and forth between the two Lilos.

"Will someone tell me what the hell's going on?" he said. "Who is she, and where did she come from?"

"You don't recognize me?" Diana asked. "Can I have changed that much? The last time you saw me, I was falling into Jupiter."

"But where have you *been* . . . I mean, how did—"

"She was returned by the Invaders," William said. "They simply bent her lifeline back on itself. From the strength of our preliminary indications, she went several thousand years into the future, spent ten years on Earth, and was returned here. It was as easy for them as connecting two dots with a line would be for you."

Lilo was getting impatient.

"Can we go now? I can answer most of your questions when we get back to the ship."

"Yes, yes," William said. "If you want to leave, then go. We'll have to rearrange some of our plans, of course. We expected something like this, but not so soon. And not in our own backyard. It's very disturbing. Think about what we told you. It still stands, but you don't have as much time as we thought you did."

"We never even got to see the inside of their big ring," Cathay grumbled. "All we saw was an artificial construction."

"A stage set," Vaffa suggested.

"Whatever. Something they whipped up to make us feel at home."

Javelin was looking out *Cavorite*'s glass dome at the wheel. "I think they didn't want us to see inside."

Vaffa looked up. She had been brooding since they returned to the ship over an hour ago. She had listened silently as Diana told her story, and as Lilo tried her best to fill them in on the things she had learned, and how she had learned them. Halfway through her story, Lilo realized she was not getting it across to them. Javelin and Cathay were looking frankly skeptical, though it became plain that neither of them had any better explanation for the events they had observed. Javelin had advanced the theory—as diplomatically as possible—that Diana was an imposter, someone made by the Traders for reasons known only to themselves.

Lilo and Diana had not bothered to refute the accusation, and it soon died of its own weight. No one could think of a reason why the Traders would need to infiltrate humans so obviously. The question that continued to trouble them was, why did the Traders need to *ask* for human culture? Weren't they strong enough to take it?

The tentative conclusion was reached that they should wait and see. They knew nothing about the process the Traders intended using to obtain human culture. They knew little about Trader capabilities of any kind.

"What are we going to do?" Vaffa asked. "I'll admit it. I've never been as confused as I am right now."

"What do you mean?" Javelin asked. "Do about what?"

"About . . . everything! All those things they told us. Do you all believe them?"

Javelin looked helplessly at Lilo and Diana, genuinely puzzled. "What's got her so upset? Do you know what she's talking about?"

"Ah . . . probably she's concerned about . . . you know, the trouble that's going to be coming up."

"*Trouble?*" Vaffa squeaked. Her voice was getting dangerously shrill. "Trouble? You call the end of the Eight Worlds 'trouble'? That *is* what's going to happen, isn't it? Didn't I hear it right?"

"Yes," Lilo said. "That's what they said."

"Well . . ." She froze for a moment, mouth open, her hands suspended in a desperate grasping pose before she slapped them down to her knees. "Am I the only one who cares about it?" She looked around the group, finally settling on Javelin.

"Why pick on me?" Javelin said, slightly uncomfortable. "Sure, I don't like the idea of so many people dying. But they'll have a chance to get away, the Traders said that, too. All they have to do is take it. As for the 'Eight Worlds' . . ." She made a rude noise. "Why should I care? I'm not a citizen."

Vaffa looked to Cathay. He shrugged. "Do something, you said, right? Listen, I'll go right home and polish up my sword. Then it's you and me—I can count on you, can't I?—back to back and shoulder to shoulder against the Invaders—"

"Oh, shut up," Vaffa said. She looked at Lilo, and so did everyone else.

"It's going to happen," Lilo said, quietly, and Diana was nodding her agreement. "I'm sorry to admit this . . . but I don't really care. I don't love the government any more than Javelin or Cathay. Or you, Vaffa. You're dedicated to throwing it out and putting the Boss back in. But it doesn't matter. It's going to happen, that's one thing I'm sure of. I guess you people don't believe us, but we really did see into the future, at least as far as our own lives go. Many people are going to die. The Invaders will wipe out anyone who remains in the solar system."

"That doesn't bother you?" Vaffa asked.

"I . . ." Lilo was a little concerned about that, herself. But the answer was clear. "No. It's like . . . like it's already happened. I've already seen it. We can go back and add our story to what the Traders are already broadcasting, do our best to convince people to get out. But many won't. And that's the most we can do. It's inevitable."

But Vaffa could not accept that. Lilo looked at her, closed her eyes and tried to remember her. There was a change coming, she was sure of it. Vaffa was about to overcome her limitations—was she Tweed's child? Lilo seemed to recall that Vaffa would eventually tell her that. But she was no longer sure of much about the future. There were bits and pieces that usually did not fit together. She knew Vaffa was now wondering if she had done her job well for the Boss. But at the same time doubt had crept into her mind. Diana's story had impressed Vaffa more than anyone. For the first time, she saw the Invaders as real things, not as cardboard enemies.

But for the time being, her loyalty was still to the Boss. It wouldn't do to tell her that he had been forced to flee Luna as a direct result of the actions of another Lilo and Cathay.

The conversation went on, but Lilo ignored it. She was watching her other self, her clone, and the clone was watching her.

"I remember Makel," Lilo said, softly.

"And I remember Javelin when she was a much thinner person." Diana smiled, and Lilo returned it. "I also remember the impact of *Vengeance,* and being killed by Vaffa."

"Come back to my room," Lilo said.

Once settled in the bunks, facing each other, they didn't say anything for a long time. The voices from the solarium were like the buzzing of a fly. They were discussing the events of the last few hours, while Lilo felt very much above it. She still retained parts of her transcendental experience, her glimpse of the way things had been, were, and would always be. She knew she had a long life ahead, but the details were blurred and fading.

"It's going, isn't it?" said Diana.

"Yes. I just remember the high points of your past, and the other . . . this gets confusing, doesn't it. To talk about."

Diana smiled.

"I can't remember too much of the future," she said.

"Just an impression that it's going on for quite a while. For each of us."

"Yes."

They were quiet again. Lilo had the sense that something had not been said, but knew it would be. She looked at the silver cube in Diana's hand. It looked ordinary enough.

"Can I see that?"

Diana looked at it, as if she had forgotten it was in her hand. She tossed it to Lilo.

It traveled a meter from her hand, slowing down all the way, and stopped halfway between them. Lilo could not think of any force that could have slowed it down; in weightlessness it should have moved in a straight line until it hit something. Nevertheless, there it floated.

She reached out and took it. It resisted her slightly. It seemed to prefer being motionless, though not with any great tenacity.

"What does it do, I wonder?" Lilo asked.

"You think we should fool with it?"

Lilo was holding it close to her face, studying it carefully. She had thought there was a slight discoloration on one side and was picking at it with her thumbnail. "I won't, I just want to—"

It unfolded.

It was not an easy thing to watch; it was not a matter of sides detaching themselves or opening up in any way. It was larger cubes evolving themselves from smaller ones until she had what she thought was an unsteady stack of eight, but which turned out to be just one hypercube. Lilo drew her hands back in dismay, and the thing floated.

"Uh . . . what should I do now?"

Diana moved around it, craning her neck to get a closer look without touching it.

"You think we can put it back like it was?"

Lilo reached out. Evidently the arrangement was unstable. The singularity moved again as soon as she touched it, and it became a simple cube again, but with sides of ten centimeters. It now had eight times its former volume.

"I thought I almost saw how it was done," Diana said. She took the cube, but before she could try anything it had started folding again. This time it was inward, but when it was done she ended with two five-centimeter cubes.

"Maybe we ought to leave this to the mathematicians," Diana said, and set them carefully on the bunk beside her.

"If we learned how to use it, it would save Javelin a lot of fuel on the trip back."

"Hm. Well, I think we'd better ask her first."

Diana looked at Lilo, then looked away again. But her eyes were drawn back.

"I . . . the details are getting fuzzier. About what's going to happen to us, I mean."

"Yes?"

"But I have . . . well, do *you* have the same memory that I do? You and I were . . . together a great deal. I remember that you seemed to be involved in most everything I do from now on."

"Yes." Lilo relaxed even more. She couldn't have been wrong about it, but it was nice to hear that Diana remembered the same thing. There was now very little left of her memories of the future: dream glimpses dissolving as she examined them, impressions rather than memories. What was left was vivid and real, but like flashframes on a film or odd pieces of a jigsaw puzzle.

She could see the forest under the blue sun. It was at least a hundred years in her future, but Diana was there with her.

"I wonder what sun it is?" Diana asked, and they both laughed. "Won't it be fun to find out?"

26

The sun was hard to find in the sky now, and in any case, Lilo was on the wrong side of Poseidon. They had accomplished turnover a few weeks ago, and were now decelerating. Alpha Centauri was directly under them.

It had taken Lilo a while to get used to her sunflower garden. To tend it, she had to move along catwalks hanging upside down from the ground. It was like moving beneath some vast overhang of rock. Through the grid of the catwalk she could see stars beneath her feet.

The garden was three concentric rings of plants centered around the huge silver bowl of the nullfield which contained the hole. She could see it in the distance, supported on three invisible pillars evidenced only by the massive installations which generated them. A white radiance exploded downward from the open end of the bowl, pointing toward Alpha; silently, constantly putting out its one-twentieth-gee deceleration.

She moved along the catwalk, her safety line securely tethered to a cable that ran just above her head. The gravity was very small, but if she fell, that first step down was two light-years.

The sunflower was not a new invention; the germ of the idea went back to pre-Invasion times. They were three-meter parabolic dishes, each with a white-hot nodule at the center. The dish focused energy on the nodule. Photosynthesis took place, and the roots of the sunflower plants produced tubers with tough skins. Inside, they were sweet and soft like pineapples.

Each sunflower spent its life hanging down, its roots embedded in the ground overhead, its flower suspended by a thick stalk. To harvest the crop, Lilo hung a big metal pan from hooks on the catwalk and dug in the ground. Rock, newly converted soil, and tubers fell down into the pan. It was exactly the opposite of stoop labor, she reflected. It got you in your arms and shoulders, not your back.

She sat down to take a rest, and while she was dangling her legs over infinity a strange thing happened to her. Her life flashed before her eyes, and it was an intricate and various thing, not a simple journey from birth to death, but tortuous, full of pain and many deaths. And yet . . .

"Are you all right, Lilo?"

"What?" She looked up. "How long have you been here?"

"A few minutes," Cass said. He was a young adult now, looking like his parent in many ways. "You didn't answer when I said hello. Are you okay?"

"Yes. I'm fine." It was fading already. She tried to hold it, to contain that fantastic tapestry as she had grasped it for one glorious instant. But it was too much for her mind. She felt her two living sisters drop away from her, but knew it would not be forever.

Cass was sitting beside her now. He looked down between his feet.

"What do you think we'll find when we get out there?" he asked.
"What?" It was gone now. She was only herself. Had it actually happened? But she remembered, she *had* seen the future.

"What will we find when we get out there? To Alpha?"

"People," Lilo said. "Some people we know."